The
GERMAN
GIRL

BOOKS BY LILY GRAHAM

Lily Graham

The
GERMAN
GIRL

bookouture

Published by Bookouture in 2021

An imprint of Storyfire Ltd.
Carmelite House
50 Victoria Embankment
London EC4Y 0DZ

www.bookouture.com

ISBN: 978-1-83888-934-0
eBook ISBN: 978-1-83888-933-3

This book is a work of fiction. Names, characters, businesses,
organizations, places and events other than those clearly in the
public domain, are either the product of the author's imagination
or are used fictitiously. Any resemblance to actual persons, living or
dead, events or locales is entirely coincidental.

For Lydia, for being the best editor in the world.

CHAPTER ONE

Northern Sweden, 1995

The snow came early that year, settling around the forest like an old bear ready for its cave.

As Ingrid made her way through the silent wood, the sky above performed its northern waltz, a dance of light in shades of pink and green.

She whistled and Narfi came leapfrogging towards her, his large body sinking almost completely into the powdery snow dusting his black-and-bronze coat.

'Stay away from that fox,' she warned.

She hadn't missed the Arctic creature in the distance, its fur almost indistinct from the wintry landscape, its eerie blue gaze pinned on them. 'She's looking after her kits and doesn't know you just want to play.'

He whined, gambolling from her and as close to the fox as he dared again.

She shook her head, cheeks pink from the cold. Her eyelashes were spiked with ice. 'You want another scar?' she asked, pointing at his snout with a mittened hand, where he'd had a run-in with a wolf cub as a pup.

He paused, cocking his head, as if weighing her words before coming to a stop at her side.

'Good choice,' she said. Then sighed. 'Besides, you've got a task ahead of you,' she reminded him. 'I'm going to need you to work your magic today.'

Narfi frowned, making a grumbling, reluctant noise. His liquid brown eyes darted hesitantly from her to the lonely red cabin with its faded, peeling paint edging the frozen lake. It was almost hidden by the tall, snow-capped birches.

The walk was already laborious, her thighs aching from lifting her feet into the waist-high snow, but it seemed even more arduous at the prospect of what lay ahead of them.

At the door, Ingrid paused, resting her head against the wood.

'It could be one of his better days,' she told the dog with more hope than conviction.

There was a huffing, impatient sound. Even Narfi didn't seem convinced.

He'd let the fire die out.

The air blew out of Ingrid's mouth in a cloud as she walked inside the freezing cold cabin. Somehow, with the dark interior, it felt even colder in here than out and she swore softly. She looked around with a frown, eyeing all the clutter. Newspapers, old books, magazines, paintings and sketches, wooden carvings, fishing tackle, rifles, tins of food with missing labels. She itched to sort through it all, to create order from the chaos, and reveal the clean lines and good bones beneath the passage of time. To restore the pictures to the walls, sort through the paintings and sketches, but she knew she'd have to take it slowly, or the consequences would be dire. She found the lump of him, asleep on the padded kitchen bench, beneath several old coats.

He seemed to have some aversion to his bed that she didn't quite understand. But then, there wasn't a whole lot to Jürgen Anderson that she did. At least, not anymore.

He awoke at the sound of footsteps, going from half-asleep to wide awake and fully belligerent within seconds. And true to current form, he greeted the morning, and her, with a curse.

His salt-coloured hair was shaggy around his thin, weather-beaten face, which hadn't seen a razor in some weeks. He was still wearing the clothes she had seen him in last, clothes she suspected he'd been wearing for some time, judging from the sour smell coming off him. It was uncharacteristic. He took daily ice baths every winter, partly for health, partly to prove something. Perhaps those goals were long gone now. If she thought about that, the tears would threaten, and she didn't need that, not now.

He was enough work without the tears, as his commitment to being difficult from the moment he opened his eyes to the moment he closed them was a full-time occupation of late. On some level this commitment might have impressed her, but it couldn't while somewhere deep within the cranky old bear remained the man she used to know and love.

His voice became a jagged razor, as his rheumy blue eyes opened, and he saw her inside his kitchen.

'*För fan i helvete, din jävla idiot!* Do we have to go over this again, Marta? I told you last time – and I made it very clear, didn't I? I do not need you,' he spat. 'Are you brain dead or something?'

Ingrid closed her eyes for a moment, mentally gathering up the bits of herself that resembled her mettle, then put the basket she'd been carrying on the table with a bit more of a thud than was strictly necessary.

She took a deep breath and reminded him, 'I am not Marta.'

Marta was Ingrid's cousin. She was also the old man's last helper. It was fair to say that it hadn't gone well.

It had ended with Marta refusing to ever darken Jürgen Anderson's door, even if he died, and someone needed help moving his mouldering body... 'Even then – find somebody else,' was the way Marta emphasised the end of the 'arrangement' when she'd gone to her home a few days before. Then she'd laughed hysterically at the prospect of Ingrid taking over. 'Oh, he's going to eat you alive!'

When Ingrid had given her a hard stare, Marta snorted. 'Oh, that's almost cute – you think you'll be tougher than me. I haven't spent my life in the city with electric heating, child; go on, knock yourself out. But don't say your old cousin didn't warn you when you come here in tears in a day or two, your tail between your legs...'

So Ingrid had left, vowing that whatever happened with the old man, she would not go to Marta.

She turned to Jürgen now, who grunted. 'Pah! Same blonde hair, same interfering family.'

'Marta has brown hair,' Ingrid pointed out.

'I've never seen her wash it – for all I know it is actually blonde.'

Ingrid snorted. He was insufferable. 'I don't think it's Marta's hygiene you should be concerned about.'

'Just her cooking?'

It was the source of the trouble, to be fair. Apparently, after Marta had made him a meal – plain chicken with broccoli – things had gone from bad to worse. Marta had asked how it was and he'd casually taken the plate, walked outside and tipped it onto the snow, calling for someone named Obehang. 'Obehang, here boy.' At Marta's shocked look, he'd said, 'He's a rat, such a nuisance, a bit like you. Though, unlike you, he is someone

I'm allowed to kill.' He'd pointed at her dinner. 'Thank you, this might just do the trick.'

Which was when Marta had quit.

Despite herself, Ingrid's lips twitched, just like they had when her cousin had told her the story, although it was her cousin who began laughing herself stupid when Ingrid said she'd volunteered to take over.

'Will I be alive the day you admit you are wrong?' she asked Jürgen now.

'Probably not,' he conceded, and something almost like a smile ghosted across his lips too.

Yesterday, when she'd first come to check up on him, she'd lasted the grand sum of thirty minutes. It had felt like a lifetime. She'd managed to clean one cup, sweep part of the floor, melt some snow for water, and hang his coat on the hook at the back of the door, while being henpecked and harangued to within an inch of her life, before he'd thrown one of his heavy boots at her and told her to get the hell out of his house. A small bruise still smarted on her thigh.

The names he'd called her had stung more than the bruise. They still did. She'd spent the previous evening trying to convince herself that she should just give up her dream of moving back to the small hamlet she'd grown up in, in wild northern Sweden. Stjärna, in the Västernorrland region, had a population of just fifty. She'd sat up wondering if she were being a fool, if she shouldn't just return to the little grey apartment she'd called home in Malmö for the past ten years. Where life had been safe, and she'd had a good job as an accounts clerk. It had been a comfortable life, but also dull.

Out here, life happened more slowly, because it had to – there was no convenient supermarket nearby, everything required time and preparation, but somehow life seemed richer for it too.

Returning to that safe life wouldn't help either of them. Whether he liked it to not, he needed her. For the most part he was still lucid, but the cracks were starting to show – and if he didn't let her in he might be taken somewhere to be looked after full-time. She was his last chance and unlike the other helpers he'd scared off over the months, she had more to lose by giving in. She needed to make this work. She'd dreamt of moving back to this barely touched part of the world since she was a child. This was her chance. He didn't need to be happy she was here and checking up on him, and they didn't need to get on. All she had to do was ensure that he was alive, fed and hadn't burnt his cabin down in the night. Despite Marta's opinion on the matter, she was capable of that, even if he called her every vile name he could think of in the process.

She set her jaw and pulled the mittens off her icy hands. Her woollen hat would have to stay; it was far too cold to take it off.

'I'm going to make breakfast for us and then—' She couldn't help herself; she flicked her eyes around the room, wishing, not for the first time, that the old man hadn't chosen to live so simply, with no running water or electricity, and said, 'I'm going to get more snow to melt for your bath.'

His next words were choice.

Ingrid's ears turned red; she wasn't used to being spoken to like this – everything in her itched to give him as good as he gave. Instead, she shot him a pointed look, crossed her arms and scolded, 'You let the fire die out.'

Here, in the frozen winters of northern Sweden, where temperatures could reach minus forty, a mistake like that could cost you your life.

Her words caused him to deflate like an old balloon. Shrinking, as he folded in on himself. He rubbed his eyes, then sighed. 'I was trying to make the wood stretch a bit. I was going to go to the shed for more first thing this morning, but I must have fallen asleep,' he said, looking at the empty wood pile with a frown.

Ingrid didn't point out that morning wouldn't have helped – it wasn't as if there was more light then, not at this time of year. She itched to tell him that this was exactly the reason she'd come by the day before – to help with things like that. So that the old man didn't have to trudge to the shed in the middle of the night, and return laden down with a pallet of wood on a sled. She pursed her lips, keeping in the lecture she would have loved to have given him, while Jürgen examined the floor.

Narfi chose his moment wisely. Sensing the brief impasse, he made his way slowly towards the old man, whose eyes brightened slightly, as he petted him with a heavy hand.

The dog bore it with dignity, though his eyes warned Ingrid that some form of recompense might be required in the not-too-distant future.

Ingrid wasn't sure if it was a trick of the light or not, but the old man's anger seemed to have withered. So, she offered a truce. 'Coffee?'

'One sugar,' he agreed. '*Tack.*'

She nodded and was about to head towards the dresser, when he stood up, with a creak of old bones and joints, and shook his head. '*Nej,* Inge, I'll make it. Yours is probably not even fit for the dog. The swill they pass for coffee in the city,' he mumbled, slipping his feet into a pair of old worn slippers as he shuffled towards the gas cooker, 'it's an absolute joke.'

Ingrid hid a smile, thinking that it was good that he remembered that she used to live in Malmö. After their coffee and breakfast, she'd take the sled and stock up on the wood from his barn outside. She knew he didn't like to admit it but the activity was getting harder for him now, which was likely why he put it off. That and the worrying fact that he forgot.

Like an old gramophone that needed to be wound before it would play, Jürgen slowly turned more into the man she used to know. It helped that today he seemed to remember who she was.

As if reading her thoughts, he asked, 'Why are you wearing Marta's hat?'

'This?' she said, touching the lime green hat with earflaps. 'Oh, well, she gave me a few things – some "more practical" stuff now that I'm living here. You know how she is.'

He grunted, and there was a wealth of meaning behind that grunt. Then he shrugged and added, 'Well, she's not wrong.' He looked at it again, his lip curling in distaste. 'You know a person can be too practical.' Which for a man who owned exactly three shirts was saying something. She shrugged. Who was going to mind out here – the reindeer? Even they were too busy trying to keep warm.

Jürgen unhooked a pair of brown ceramic mugs from the dresser, pausing to fill the kettle from the canister that sat on the counter. It was filled with the water Ingrid had melted from the snow the day before.

So that's why he'd confused Marta and her, she thought – the hat. Though she knew it wasn't just that, was it? Whatever he said. She'd been here for enough time for him to register who she was… but still, it made sense now in some ways.

'Here you go – some proper coffee,' he said, handing her a mug of thick black liquid.

The 'proper' coffee was a cheap supermarket blend. So strong Ingrid wouldn't have been surprised if it melted the spoon.

'*Tack*,' she said, blowing on it, before taking a sip. It wasn't half bad, to be fair.

'Maybe later I can give your hair a trim?' she suggested, her eye falling on his long grey hair.

His blue eyes danced. 'Not unless you want to be put over my knee. I always thought you needed more hidings when you were little, Inge, or you'd grow up with ideas.'

She hid a smile. 'I seem to remember you telling Far that only thugs hit little girls.'

'Pah,' he said, taking a loud slurp of his coffee, and smacking his lips in pleasure. 'I've always believed in a firm hand. I would have told your father to triple your hidings,' he promised, with a wink, raising the flat of his hand, ninja-like. 'It must have been your other grandfather who said such silly things.'

Her lips twitched in amusement. They both knew she'd only ever had the one – and he was more than enough. 'It must have been.'

As the wood-burner billowed smoke into the snowy forest, and the grey sky turned a cloudy blue as the morning passed, the tough outer shell he'd assembled slipped away, and she saw a glimpse of the person she'd most adored as a child – like that first precious peek of sun after a long grey winter. He helped her clean the kitchen, sweep the floor and hang up the coats, and they enjoyed a simple breakfast of rye bread, gherkins and cottage cheese in companionable silence.

Afterwards, she made the trip to the barn, stocking heavy-duty shopping bags full of the chopped wood he'd dried out the previous summer. She was relieved to see the barn was full of seasoned logs and there would be enough to last the rest of the cold season. It was one of the reasons the family worried so much – out here survival was tough. Harder still, if you were like Jürgen Anderson, choosing to live so simply – there was no alternative to heating his home. No electricity at the turn of a switch or a central heating system. If he ran out of wood it could be fatal.

It was tough and sweaty work, despite the freezing cold air, but when she got back inside the cabin, unpacked the wood and started the fire, it wasn't long before she was at last able to take off her outer layers.

Her next task was to collect several more buckets of snow to melt for water, so that she could refill the water butt, as well as draw a bath for him. Then they watched the world outside from within the cosy cabin, as the light grew ever darker, and the deer made their way through the forest in this rare hour of light, so precious and over so fast.

Things changed when she insisted upon his bath. She got as far as pulling his shirt off him, before the lights in his eyes began to dim, like the setting sun outside, and he began swearing again, slapping at her hands, and arms, and making them sting. She bit her lip, tears pricking at her eyes; she hadn't been prepared for how painful it would be when he forgot. Not that anyone had sugar-coated his condition. Their once-gentle hermit was now often sour and mean. It was a bitter pill to swallow.

'Please calm down, Morfar. You need a bath. You're starting to smell.'

'I do not smell!' he cried, outraged.

She sighed, then picked up his shirt and pressed it to his nose.

He shook his head like a dog, ripping the shirt out of her hands, and throwing it on the floor. 'Stop it, Marta! I don't want you here, I don't need anyone, do you hear me? Get the hell out!'

Narfi started to bark, and Jürgen suddenly looked dazed. 'Bjørn?' he said, reaching out a hand towards the dog, his ire momentarily forgotten.

'Narfi,' she reminded him. 'And if you want me to leave, it's simple – just get in this bath, and soap yourself,' she said, handing him a bar of home-made lemon verbena soap from the small farm shop half an hour away. 'I'll turn my back.'

Which is why she didn't see it when he kicked the steel tub she'd spent the past twenty minutes filling with steaming water, until it cascaded onto the floor, slamming into the back of her legs.

She whirled around, screaming blue murder. He stood, half-naked in the corner, laughing. His voice suddenly high, little a little boy's.

'You should see your face, *Küken*. Better than that day we stole ol' Polga's boat!' She crossed her arms and he giggled. 'Come on, Asta, since when can't you take a joke?'

'It's Ingrid,' she snapped. 'And it's not funny – I spent ages filling that.' She knew he couldn't help muddling names. But right then she didn't feel much sympathy. He still smelled and it had taken such a long time to get that bath ready. She sighed, then got the towels and mop and cleaned up the mess.

Afterwards, she walked up the stairs and fetched a clean shirt and a pair of tracksuit bottoms, which she thrust into his arms. 'Put these on,' she demanded, in no mood for an argument. She was too cross to be surprised when he complied. Then she gathered up his old, dirty clothes, which she'd take back to her own cabin to run through the washing machine. 'You can smell for all I care,' she said between clenched teeth, realising with annoyance that she was behaving just as Marta had, but unable to help herself.

She slipped out of her soaking snow trousers. 'I'm going to borrow a pair of yours for the walk home.' She flashed him a hard look; she was different to her cousin – who was all fire and blather – in one respect. Ingrid was like a mountain goat, small and seemingly mild, but inside she was stubborn to the core and not afraid to use her horns if pressed. 'I will bring them back when I see you in the morning, so I suggest you try and get over it.' Then she felt a pang of shame, mixed with annoyance – it wasn't like he could help getting muddled – and she softened. 'You'll be all right? You've got enough food?'

He rolled his eyes. 'I'm fine. You don't have to look after me – I have underpants older than you.'

She gave him a hard stare. 'Don't forget to keep the fire burning.'

She ducked as he flung one of his slippers at her. Then she whistled, and Narfi followed her outside.

It was only much later, after her mile-long trudge back through the woods, struggling through waist-high snow, when she was inside her own tiny cabin – one of just eleven in their hamlet, dotted around the vast lake and forest – that she realised he hadn't been speaking Swedish at all.

He'd been speaking *German*.

CHAPTER TWO

He'd called her *Küken* – little bird. The word turned over in her mind, like a sharp stone lodged inside a shoe, its uncomfortable pricking making her unable to think of anything else.

Ingrid hadn't even realised the moment he'd switched languages. For her, after nearly ten years of speaking it at home, it was as natural as slipping off her shoes as soon as she entered her apartment after a long day at the office: her boyfriend, Ben, had been German. Ex-boyfriend, she reminded herself, with a pang.

Speaking German had become natural for her over the years, but it was not natural for Morfar. Not even close. It was a language he'd once got so angry at her for learning he'd almost turned violent.

The memory was old, but the emotions were still as sharp as a blade's edge. The kind of memory that every so often, when you recall it, leaves behind a fresh little wound. She'd been a child, and living in Stjärna – before her parents moved to the city when her father got a new job. Morfar had come into their cabin one day, and heard her practising German phrases. She was nine and wanted to surprise her new friend, Suzie, whose family had moved to their village. Suzie didn't know Swedish yet and she was having a tough time because the other children kept teasing her, and Ingrid wanted to help. She was excited and pleased when her mother had come home with some second-hand Swedish to German language books and tapes that she'd picked up from the bookstore after her work at a dairy farm, forty minutes away. Ingrid had begun practising every chance she could get. She enjoyed playing with the wooden animals Morfar had carved for her over the years, and having conversations while she sat in front of the fire.

'*Guten Morgen, mein name ist Ingrid. Wie geht's?*'

Suddenly, there was a wild, strangled sound, and she'd looked up in a fright, to see her beloved grandfather, her Morfar, turn grey, like dirty dishwater, like all the blood inside him had run down some invisible drain. Then, all at once, he flew at her, his eyes blazing, his hands curled into claws. The small wooden animals in her hands fell with a clatter to the floor and she yelped.

He was barely recognisable and Ingrid's bowels clenched in fear.

He pulled her up roughly by the arm, his face a hair's breadth away from hers as he screeched at her through bloodless lips, 'STOP! Stop it right this minute! Do you hear me? I FORBID IT!'

She gasped for air, hot tears spilling over her cheeks in streams that pooled inside the hollow of her neck. She shivered with shock. He'd never reacted to her like this before. His arms had only ever offered a welcoming embrace, his scratchy face had only ever been ready for a smile. His clever hands were always pointing things out, helping her put on an extra jumper or carving a wooden animal for her amusement – never this. They'd never been used to hurt her before.

She gulped for air, as her brain whirred, looking for an explanation. It came up empty – she didn't understand – what had she done wrong?

There was the sound of booted feet hitting the wooden floor in haste as her father came charging into the room, alerted by the sound of Jürgen's screams and Ingrid's loud sobbing. 'What's going on here? Why are you holding her like that!'

Jürgen had turned to him, his eyes wild, as he found a new source for his anger, letting Ingrid's arm go at last. There were white marks, surrounded by red, from his fingers. 'I found her – speaking – speaking…' He broke off, not saying the word.

Ingrid's father looked incredulous, and his anger was quick to spark. '*Speaking?*' He shook his head then looked at Jürgen with confusion. 'She's a child, Jürgen, they say things… perhaps things that they shouldn't. What happened?' he asked Ingrid, who was rubbing her arm, and struggling to catch a breath between her sobs.

'I – I don't know. I just said the words from the tapes. I was just trying to learn…'

Her father frowned. 'Tapes – what tapes? Learn what?'

'G-German,' she said, breathing heavily, gasping for air. 'I – I wanted to learn for my friend, Suzie – she can't speak Swedish, and I want to understand her better. What did I do wrong, Far?'

Ingrid's father's eyes widened. 'Nothing. You did nothing wrong, do you hear me?' Then he turned to Jürgen, his face hard. 'What the hell, Jürgen?'

Jürgen did not back down. 'I will not have her speaking that language in this house!' he'd raged.

Her father's eyes widened once more, his face twisted in sudden fury. 'This is my house, Jürgen,' he reminded him, his voice low, like a hiss. His fists balled at his sides. Truth be told he was more than a little shocked. Ingrid was a firm favourite of the old hermit, and he and Jonna often joked that if it weren't for their daughter they'd never see him.

'This prejudice of yours – it's not welcome here. I see no reason why she cannot learn another language – it wasn't the Nazis that created the language, and they do not represent an entire population, Jürgen. We haven't challenged you on this before, because our generation did not live through the war but I will not allow you to poison Inge with such rubbish. Get a handle on yourself – she's just a little girl trying to learn her new friend's language.'

Jürgen seemed to deflate, as her father's words penetrated. The red mist that had consumed him evaporated, and he looked utterly ashamed. 'Is your arm all right?' he asked Ingrid.

Ingrid sniffled, but nodded.

'I—' He cleared his throat. '*Inge*, I – I'm sorry,' he said, seeming to fold into himself, the look on his face heartbreaking. 'There's – it's just—' He broke off, pressing his lips together. He took a deep breath. 'I don't know what happened to me, please forgive me,' he said, looking from her to her father, who remained impassive, and back again.

'I think it's time you left, Jürgen.'

He nodded. To Ingrid it looked as if he'd suddenly become old, something she'd never really thought of him being before.

It was weeks before they saw him again. Ingrid couldn't remember if her father had said anything more to her about the subject or if her mother had; all she remembered was missing him. She would stare out their cabin window, as the autumn wind chased away the last of the red-gold leaves and the first frost arrived, turning the berries outside to crystallised jewels, keeping one eye towards their drive for any sign of his familiar straw hat, and long-legged, ambling walk, wondering if he'd ever come again.

When he finally did, snow had settled on the ground, and winter had dealt its last riposte, its victory ensuring they'd be bound inside by the cold for months. He brought her a new wooden toy, a small wooden bear that he'd carved just for her, like all her others. It was a snow bear, and its eyes were solemn and sad. Ingrid had understood, perhaps in some instinctual way, what he was trying to say, even if her parents didn't. Morfar was the bear, and her speaking German had roused him somehow.

There was a small exhalation at the end of the line. 'What did he say?'

Ingrid thought back to while she was filling the bath. His voice had changed. 'He sounded young, and he was saying something about a boat, he called me *Küken* – a little bird. Was it maybe an endearment of some kind he used on you?'

'No, never,' breathed her mother.

Ingrid frowned. 'Maybe he had to learn it against his will or something – at school, or later during the war? I know that Sweden was neutral but there was the fear that they might be invaded like Norway or Denmark, wasn't there?'

'Oh yes. A lot of the men were put on standby to train as soldiers in case that ever happened. Being neutral didn't mean Sweden just carried on as if nothing was happening, it was still a time full of fear – watching planes pass overhead wondering if one of those bombs was going to be for you, listening to the news about the world going mad, mass persecutions, concentration camps, starvation… I remember a teacher telling me that it was like hiding away in an attic when there were burglars inside, but the burglars knew you were there, and you were waiting to hear them climb the stairs…'

Ingrid blew out her cheeks. It must have been scary. Of course, Sweden had had to compromise a lot – it wasn't squeaky clean in its neutrality as they'd had to concede a great deal to Germany for the privilege of that neutrality, and so, for the ordinary citizens, it stood to reason that they might have been afraid that their agreement with the Nazis was as 'solid' as the one the Nazis had with Poland, before they crumbled the country in two like a cookie they shared with the Soviets.

'When I was growing up, he hated it whenever anything was in German – even the news. He would walk out the room if the television was on and they were speaking it. I always wondered

The incident changed things slightly, especially for her father, who was never completely comfortable with leaving Ingrid alone with him after that, even though over the months and years there never was another outburst from him.

She continued to learn German, though, encouraged in some way by her father, who hadn't appreciated being told what to do in his own home. But Ingrid never did speak it around her grandfather again. She'd seen the naked pain in his eyes, behind the rage, and she hadn't wanted to hurt him any more than he did her.

She frowned, as she played with the cord of the telephone now, as she thought of it. It was late, but knowing her night-owl mother, she'd probably still be up, reading. Besides, Ingrid was sure that she'd want to know how it had gone. It killed her that they were living in Malmö, so far away from him.

Jonna picked up on the second ring. 'It's me,' said Ingrid, after hearing her voice.

'How did it go?'

'Morfar remembered me today.'

'Oh, Ingrid,' said her mother, softly. 'Are you all right?'

Ingrid blew out her cheeks. She would not cry about this. She'd promised herself after she and Ben had broken up and she'd decided to take over Jürgen's care that she wouldn't fall apart. It was going to be a good thing, a fresh start. 'Yes. I can handle him.'

'Well, I think you're probably one of the few that could,' she agreed. 'But if it is too much and he's getting worse, well, then we need to rethink things…'

'It's fine – honestly. You know Morfar – it's partly the early dementia but also a lot to do with his pride and the fact that he doesn't like to admit that he needs help sometimes,' she said, thinking of his firewood. She knew he suffered from arthritis, which was particularly painful in the colder months, and was no doubt one of the main reasons he'd delayed on filling up his log pile.

'Well, yes, he's always been a bear when he thought people were sticking their noses in his business.'

Ingrid nodded. 'Always,' she agreed.

'You've spoken to his doctor?'

'Yes, he told me what he told you – he says that he's still there really, he just needs some help for now.' She didn't say the rest, she didn't need to – her mother knew it all already, and it kept her awake most nights consumed with worry; the least Ingrid could do was give her some relief on that front. Unlike Marta she wasn't going to give up, just because he was difficult. She thought of his crack about his underpants and shook her head, a small smile on her lips.

The doctor had told her that it was his short-term memory that was the biggest concern if he continued to live out here. For the most part he was still roughly cognisant, and his long-term memory was fine but if he started to forget to eat, that's when they might need to think about sending him to a care home. The trouble was, Ingrid knew Morfar: if that happened, he wouldn't last long – he was too stubborn, too independent, and far too ornery. At least with her there he'd have some level of freedom, if only she could make him see that…

She sighed. She'd worry about that later; for now, the one thing that was bothering her was his sudden switch into a language he claimed to despise. 'That's not the only reason I'm calling, though,' she said.

'Oh?'

'He spoke German.'

There was a sharp intake of breath. 'German?'

'Yes.'

There was a snort as if Ingrid was teasing her; Jonna's voice was quickly dismissive. 'Can't be, love.'

Ingrid sighed. 'Trust me – he was speaking German – I mean, almost like a native.'

'What! Are you sure?'

'Positive. I'd got so used to speaking it with Ben over the years that I didn't even realise we'd switched languages.'

They'd been together for nearly ten years; it had ended when they'd realised they both wanted very different things. Monogamy for her, for one… it was one of the reasons she'd taken a long, hard look at her life and finally taken the plunge to move back to northern Sweden – if she didn't do it now, when would she? When she'd found someone else? Got married? Settled down? Those things would make it much harder. There was never a good time to change your life – but there were times when it felt like the earth turned on its axis in such a way that all you had to do was take a leap. Like when she heard about Morfar's deteriorati? condition – something her mother had been keeping from h? knowing how stressed she was about the end of her relationsh? When she had finally told her the truth, the decision to move her parents' summer cabin and care for him had been insta? neous – and fortuitous, as Marta hadn't hung up the towel, s? burnt it and trodden on its embers.

Jonna continued. 'I – I always thought Morfar hated the? guage – I mean, it never made sense, really. But there was that? when you were – I don't know, maybe eight or nine? When? friend Suzie moved to Stjärna, I don't know if you rememb?

'Oh, I remember,' said Ingrid. 'Believe me.'

Her mother sighed. 'Well. Yes. I suppose it must have? impression. Your father said he'd never seen him like that? So angry… so wild. I never dreamt he could actually sp? language – considering how he reacted anytime someone s?

'Me neither. But he seemed to know it very well.'

if something specific happened during the war – something to him, you know, to make him react that strongly, but of course he never spoke of it.'

'Yes.' Even Ingrid had encountered that wall more than a few times in her childhood. She could count on one hand the personal details he'd told her over the years.

There was a pause, and then Jonna said, 'You know he was an orphan?'

Ingrid's eyes widened. 'What?' She hadn't known that. 'But that can't be true – he told me about his parents! I'm sure he told me about his mother. She was Danish, right?'

'You're thinking of Trine. She was his aunt.'

Ingrid blinked. 'His aunt?'

'I'm not sure of the full story but at some point, he went to live with her – I have memories of her myself, when I was little. She was kind. A great sense of humour, and a bit stern. But before that – before I was born – it's as if all those years before never existed. You couldn't get him to speak about it for love or money. I know I tried.' She didn't mention the years she'd pressed for more. The way she used to beg him. How she'd once screamed at him, 'It's not fair – everyone I know has a history – what's ours? How can I know so little about my own father?' It was only later that she'd worked out... maybe there wasn't a history there to tell – or maybe it was just too painful – too lonely? But even so – couldn't he have told her that? The only person he ever told her about was her mother... but that was hard too, as he'd lost her so soon after Jonna was born.

Ingrid bit her lip. 'That's so tough, Mum, I'm sorry. Why didn't you tell me about this before, though?'

There was a deep sigh. 'I don't know, I should have... it just felt like he'd given me this life full of so many questions without answers. I didn't want to do that to you too.'

Ingrid swallowed. Her mother had been trying to spare her. 'He loves you, though,' she told her mother.

'I know, and he was a good father too – I think he tried very hard to make my life happy, especially as for so many years he was the only person in it. I know that when you came along he mellowed a bit more; he just adored you from the start.'

Ingrid wiped away a tear. It had been mutual; it still was.

'Still, there's so much we just don't know. I mean… German?'

'I know,' breathed her mother. 'Well, I always wondered… if he wasn't involved in the war in some way.'

'What do you mean?'

'Like, perhaps he volunteered to fight.'

'You mean, join the British or something?'

'I honestly don't know. I've just always thought that there was more to it somehow – there was something deeper driving his hatred towards them – it didn't – doesn't feel like the result of something passive, if you know what I mean?'

Ingrid frowned. Thinking back to the look in his eyes when he'd shaken her as a child. It was blind panic. 'I do.'

It was a pigeon-coloured sky, dusted with pale stars, when Ingrid made her way to his cabin by the lake the next morning. He was sitting on the kitchen bench, his hair wild and unruly, a ceramic mug warming his hands.

He sighed when he saw her.

'So, this is what I'm in for, Inge?' he said, as Narfi sidled up to him, waiting patiently for the old man's heavy-handed petting, which came soon enough. 'You're checking up on me every minute of the day, is that right?'

Ingrid put a knitted bag full of supplies on the kitchen table – including his favourite cake. He was more lucid this morning

The incident changed things slightly, especially for her father, who was never completely comfortable with leaving Ingrid alone with him after that, even though over the months and years there never was another outburst from him.

She continued to learn German, though, encouraged in some way by her father, who hadn't appreciated being told what to do in his own home. But Ingrid never did speak it around her grandfather again. She'd seen the naked pain in his eyes, behind the rage, and she hadn't wanted to hurt him any more than he did her.

She frowned, as she played with the cord of the telephone now, as she thought of it. It was late, but knowing her night-owl mother, she'd probably still be up, reading. Besides, Ingrid was sure that she'd want to know how it had gone. It killed her that they were living in Malmö, so far away from him.

Jonna picked up on the second ring. 'It's me,' said Ingrid, after hearing her voice.

'How did it go?'

'Morfar remembered me today.'

'Oh, Ingrid,' said her mother, softly. 'Are you all right?'

Ingrid blew out her cheeks. She would not cry about this. She'd promised herself after she and Ben had broken up and she'd decided to take over Jürgen's care that she wouldn't fall apart. It was going to be a good thing, a fresh start. 'Yes. I can handle him.'

'Well, I think you're probably one of the few that could,' she agreed. 'But if it is too much and he's getting worse, well, then we need to rethink things…'

'It's fine – honestly. You know Morfar – it's partly the early dementia but also a lot to do with his pride and the fact that he doesn't like to admit that he needs help sometimes,' she said, thinking of his firewood. She knew he suffered from arthritis, which was particularly painful in the colder months, and was no doubt one of the main reasons he'd delayed on filling up his log pile.

'Well, yes, he's always been a bear when he thought people were sticking their noses in his business.'

Ingrid nodded. 'Always,' she agreed.

'You've spoken to his doctor?'

'Yes, he told me what he told you – he says that he's still there really, he just needs some help for now.' She didn't say the rest, she didn't need to – her mother knew it all already, and it kept her awake most nights consumed with worry; the least Ingrid could do was give her some relief on that front. Unlike Marta she wasn't going to give up, just because he was difficult. She thought of his crack about his underpants and shook her head, a small smile on her lips.

The doctor had told her that it was his short-term memory that was the biggest concern if he continued to live out here. For the most part he was still roughly cognisant, and his long-term memory was fine but if he started to forget to eat, that's when they might need to think about sending him to a care home. The trouble was, Ingrid knew Morfar: if that happened, he wouldn't last long – he was too stubborn, too independent, and far too ornery. At least with her he'd have some level of freedom, if only she could make him see that…

She sighed. She'd worry about that later; for now, the one thing that was bothering her was his sudden switch into a language he claimed to despise. 'That's not the only reason I'm calling, though,' she said.

'Oh?'

'He spoke German.'

There was a sharp intake of breath. 'German?'

'Yes.'

There was a snort as if Ingrid was teasing her; Jonna's voice was quickly dismissive. 'Can't be, love.'

Ingrid sighed. 'Trust me – he was speaking German – I mean, almost like a native.'

'What! Are you sure?'

'Positive. I'd got so used to speaking it with Ben over the years that I didn't even realise we'd switched languages.'

They'd been together for nearly ten years; it had ended when they'd realised they both wanted very different things. Monogamy for her, for one… it was one of the reasons she'd taken a long, hard look at her life and finally taken the plunge to move back to northern Sweden – if she didn't do it now, when would she? When she'd found someone else? Got married? Settled down? Those things would make it much harder. There was never a good time to change your life – but there were times when it felt like the earth turned on its axis in such a way that all you had to do was take a leap. Like when she heard about Morfar's deteriorating condition – something her mother had been keeping from her, knowing how stressed she was about the end of her relationship. When she had finally told her the truth, the decision to move to her parents' summer cabin and care for him had been instantaneous – and fortuitous, as Marta hadn't hung up the towel, she'd burnt it and trodden on its embers.

Jonna continued. 'I – I always thought Morfar hated the language – I mean, it never made sense, really. But there was that thing when you were – I don't know, maybe eight or nine? When your friend Suzie moved to Stjärna, I don't know if you remember…'

'Oh, I remember,' said Ingrid. 'Believe me.'

Her mother sighed. 'Well. Yes. I suppose it must have left an impression. Your father said he'd never seen him like that before. So angry… so wild. I never dreamt he could actually speak the language – considering how he reacted anytime someone spoke it.'

'Me neither. But he seemed to know it very well.'

There was a small exhalation at the end of the line. 'What did he say?'

Ingrid thought back to while she was filling the bath. His voice had changed. 'He sounded young, and he was saying something about a boat, he called me *Küken* – a little bird. Was it maybe an endearment of some kind he used on you?'

'No, never,' breathed her mother.

Ingrid frowned. 'Maybe he had to learn it against his will or something – at school, or later during the war? I know that Sweden was neutral but there was the fear that they might be invaded like Norway or Denmark, wasn't there?'

'Oh yes. A lot of the men were put on standby to train as soldiers in case that ever happened. Being neutral didn't mean Sweden just carried on as if nothing was happening, it was still a time full of fear – watching planes pass overhead wondering if one of those bombs was going to be for you, listening to the news about the world going mad, mass persecutions, concentration camps, starvation… I remember a teacher telling me that it was like hiding away in an attic when there were burglars inside, but the burglars knew you were there, and you were waiting to hear them climb the stairs…'

Ingrid blew out her cheeks. It must have been scary. Of course, Sweden had had to compromise a lot – it wasn't squeaky clean in its neutrality as they'd had to concede a great deal to Germany for the privilege of that neutrality, and so, for the ordinary citizens, it stood to reason that they might have been afraid that their agreement with the Nazis was as 'solid' as the one the Nazis had with Poland, before they crumbled the country in two like a cookie they shared with the Soviets.

'When I was growing up, he hated it whenever anything was in German – even the news. He would walk out the room if the television was on and they were speaking it. I always wondered

– and she was relieved. She looked around the kitchen, which seemed tidier too.

'Not every minute, no, but checking in. Yes, Morfar. It would help us both if you would just stop fighting it.'

He made a tutting sound, then slurped his coffee. 'You're always welcome to visit, Inge, but you don't need to worry about me.'

Ingrid tucked a strand of stray blonde hair behind her ear, then frowned. 'Well, it's my right, isn't it?'

To her surprise, that made him smile. 'I suppose.' Then he sighed. 'At least you're better than Marta. She never shuts up.'

She shot him a look. 'I don't remember getting much of a word in yesterday.'

'Hence why I prefer you to Marta.'

She grinned. So it was going to be like that today. That was good. There were other encouraging signs too.

She was glad to see that he'd kept the fire going. He'd also refilled the water butt, and eaten some toast. She'd wondered what it would mean if he couldn't do those sorts of things himself anymore, and how long it would be before he couldn't.

Still, he was in desperate need of a bath, and from the way his ribs were poking out, it didn't look like he had been eating much besides toast. The doctor had said that when someone had early dementia like him, they often forgot, until their bodies complained. Jürgen had always been a one-track-minded person, who was always too busy to stop and make himself a meal. She'd be surprised if he was eating more than once a day now. It wasn't good.

The truth was for this to work – for either of them – Morfar needed her to come more often. To check on things he might forget, like getting more water, going to the shops for supplies, eating, refilling the log pile.

Which meant, like it or not, that he was going to have to get used to her.

They had been close once, very close. She remembered him carving many wooden animals for her over the years. They were still precious to her, even now. Arctic creatures, foxes and birds, so many birds, and that bear. She still had them all. The bear was always on her nightstand. Keeping watch.

Her grandfather had been different back then. Quiet, kept himself to himself, but he always had time for her. He was a natural hermit, not someone who went for things like midsummer celebrations or family barbecues. He wasn't shy, just reserved. Not good at small talk. But he visited often, and they spent a lot of time together in his garden, planting seeds in the greenhouse, tending the flowerbeds in the spring and summer months, and watching the wildlife as they went on long rambling walks along the lake and through the forest. Morfar was the one who had made her fall in love with their wild northern landscape.

They'd grown apart when her parents moved to Malmö for work. It was normal, she supposed, natural. They still spent every summer at their old cabin, though, and that's when she saw him. The years would fall away, when they were walking in the forest together again, and she would tell him things she never dreamt of telling anyone else. When she got older, some of that ease changed. She was more interested in the boys who came down for the summer, and didn't spare all that much time for her *morfar*. It was normal, she supposed, if a bit sad. He would always have a special place in her heart, however, though she regretted more than anything the distance between them. How little she really knew about his past. Despite what he said about Marta, growing up he'd always let Ingrid do most of the talking. She hoped, somehow, that she could change that now.

But first they were going to have a second try at that bath. And for that there was one thing she knew very well about him – he had the sweetest tooth in northern Sweden.

'I made a cake,' she said, getting the tin out of her bag.

His eyes widened. 'The one with the cherries? The chocolate one?'

'Yes.'

He smiled.

'But first you are going to have a bath.'

He rubbed Narfi's fur, then sighed as the dog looked at him sympathetically. 'I should have known, boy. There's always a catch with a woman.'

She was towel-drying his long grey hair when it happened – he switched to German. It was so fast, and so unexpected, that Ingrid blinked.

'Eh, *Küken*, what are we going to tell Papa about Herr Baer's dinghy? I can't believe it sank like that. Although' – he started to giggle – 'you did run it aground first.'

Ingrid paused towelling his hair. Should she just go with it… try to learn more?

'I ran it aground?' she asked, responding in German.

He swivelled to look at her, then grinned, his voice rising in pitch. 'Well, technically, we both did, I was the one trying to make those waves in the canal, so it was both of us. It always is, isn't it?'

'What?' she asked.

'The two of us getting into scrapes, *Küken*, being twins.'

'Twins?' breathed Ingrid.

He looked at her as if she were mad, then, still in his young voice, said, 'Course we're twins – how hard did you hit your head, Asta, to have forgotten about me?'

CHAPTER THREE

'*Asta?*' Ingrid repeated.

The towel was ripped from her hands. The blood had run completely from his face, making his eyes wild, and starkly blue, as he stared at her in utter shock. 'What did you just say?' he breathed, so softly, so laced with feeling that she actually flinched.

'I – I—' she began, her mouth turning dry. 'You were talking about someone named Asta.'

The look in his eyes was full of pain, and accusation.

He stood up, fast, and put on his clean shirt. 'I don't know anyone by that name.'

Ingrid stared at him, concerned. The change that had come over him was astonishing.

'You said she was your *twin*,' she breathed.

He started pacing erratically, breathing heavily as he beat his hands against his head. 'What are you doing to me? Why are you trying to get inside my head? Stop it, just stop this. I don't want you here – prying!'

'Morfar?' she asked, starting to shake. 'Please, stop it – stop it, you're hurting yourself! I'm sorry you're so upset!'

'Get out!' he cried, picking up her knitted bag and throwing it on the other side of the cabin. 'Get out, get out of my house, now!'

Tears slipped out of her eyes. 'Please, Morfar – can't we just—?'

He actually growled, and Ingrid took a wary step back.

Seeing her fear, his face crumpled. He rubbed both hands across his cheeks. He looked like he was ready to cry.

Ingrid felt as if she were standing on quicksand.

'Please just… go, Ingrid,' he said.

When she made no move to go, he hunched his shoulders. 'Fine, I'll leave,' he said softly, then made his way slowly up the stairs to the small room at the top of the cabin, and closed the door.

Ingrid and Narfi watched him go. Even the dog looked sad.

She had so much to think about as she made her way back to her cabin, through the snowy woods. She switched on her headlamp as she trudged laboriously through the thick snow. In the distance, she heard a lonely owl. Was it night-time already?

She pressed her mittened thumb into the top of her thigh, where the muscle was burning from taking steps in her heavy snow boots. She had city legs still, and they would need to toughen up. She sighed. It wasn't just her body that would need to toughen up if she were to survive here.

She had all these plans, before she moved here, of spending her time wisely, getting time to write stories – finally finish the novel she'd started writing twelve years before, but the strange thing was, the only story she was interested in thinking about was Morfar's.

How could he not have told her that he had a twin sister? Did her mother know – surely, she must? And if so why never mention her at all? A sibling was an important part of a life, but a twin – wasn't that even more special? It was all caught up together, somehow – his aversion to speaking German, this twin – something happened to him, to *them*, she was sure of it.

When she got back to the cabin she phoned her mother to ask about it all, pouring herself a glass of wine, as she sat in front of the telephone, twisting the cord in her fingers. Her mother picked up on the third ring and Ingrid launched into telling her everything that happened.

'No, that can't be right,' Jonna breathed when she mentioned a twin called Asta. 'He told me he was an only child.'

Ingrid blinked. Her wine glass poised at her lips. 'He did?'

'Yes.'

'But it seemed so certain – the way he was speaking, it was like he was a little boy again, and talking to her – it was just… so surreal, and afterwards when he was lucid again, well, I asked him—'

Jonna gasped. 'You asked him?'

'Course I did! I want to know – we have a right, don't we? Well, he just got so upset. At first he was in a rage and then, well, it just looked like he was about to cry.'

Ingrid blinked; it had been torture seeing him like that.

There was silence at the other end, but Ingrid felt a jolt of pain travel from the other end of the line towards her.

Jonna was still searching for some kind of logical explanation. 'Maybe it was because he'd got so confused…'

'No, I don't think so – I think she was real, I don't think you could make up something like that.'

Jonna let out a heavy breath. 'No, maybe not. Do you want me to come – try to get to the bottom of this? Maybe this is too much, my darling.'

'No – no, I'll be fine,' Ingrid refused. She thought it wise not to mention the part where Morfar had thrown her out.

She knew what her mother would do – she would push him too hard, ask too many questions. It would be her right, of course, but it would only make him clam up even more. Ingrid felt that on some level, her own way – responding to his own rhythms – might be the best way to coax it out, gently. She hoped so, anyway.

She thought about the story of the dinghy and a smile flitted about her lips. She wanted to know more. What had happened to them? Why wouldn't he tell her? And why was it that when Ingrid had said Asta's name, he'd almost fallen apart?

Ingrid sat up thinking for hours, watching the play of lights of the aurora borealis from her kitchen window: the deep blanket of stars above the canopy of tall, snow-capped birches in the distance. She stroked Narfi's long soft fur, while he gently snored beside her. 'He's going to be impossible when we go there tomorrow, you know that, right?'

The dog sighed in his sleep.

She took that as a yes.

It was even worse than she'd feared. She was expecting to find him in a similar state to the first few occasions that she'd visited. Swearing and surly. Mean and impossible. Instead she found him, upstairs, crying.

It broke her heart to see it.

'Morfar?' she whispered in horror.

'No, Inge, don't come up here,' he called, stifling his sobs.

She rushed forward, and put her arms around him.

He sat up, slowly. 'Oh, Inge,' he said, looking ashamed.

'What is it?' she asked, sitting with him on the bed. He sat up and put his head in his hands for a moment, desperately looking for a way to make light of something they both knew he couldn't. 'It's nothing, just an old man with some regrets, that's all.'

'Regrets?' she breathed.

'You know they say you should never die with them, but that's life, you're always going to have some.'

She blinked. Her heart started to thud, knowing that she was pushing him by asking, risking having him throw her out of his cabin again, but perhaps now was the time for it, when he was so raw, so exposed. Perhaps he needed a little push? And if not now, when?

'Is this about – Asta, your sister?'

He blew out his cheeks; tears rolled down his face, which he wiped quickly away. 'Inge – please, just don't start this again—'

Suddenly all her promises to tread gently, to go with his rhythms, to not be like her mother, forever questioning, were abandoned, as she pushed hard and fast, the words slipping out in a tumble, to be regretted almost instantly.

'Why? Why have you never spoken about her before? Why didn't you tell us about her – about your life from back then, we have a right to know!'

'*För fan i helvete!* You are as bad as your mother. I said I don't want to speak about it, now drop it!' He was angry, but his lips were trembling, and fresh tears coursed down his old cheeks; the sight was like a blade twisting in her heart.

Ingrid hadn't meant to pry, but this wasn't usual – to have the old man crying like this – she couldn't just let that go. So she swore back.

He looked surprised.

'Yes, I can swear too, I'm not some little child anymore, Morfar – you can speak to me. You can tell me what happened.' A tear rolled down her cheek. 'We were close once, you and I. Can't we be that again? Can't you tell me what's making you so upset? Just tell me, I won't break.'

Morfar stared at her for some time. His lips shook again. 'You won't, but I might.'

She swallowed.

He rubbed his hands over his eyes. 'I haven't spoken about it – in years. I—'

There was a thudding sound on the stairs and Narfi bounded up, looking for them. Morfar stood, wiping his eyes. He looked at the dog, whose limpid brown eyes demanded to know why he had been left behind. The old man patted his head. 'Let's go make some coffee, I need it for this.'

Ingrid frowned, regretting the interruption, but followed after him. She watched her grandfather's long-legged form as it went down the stairs, so very carefully. She could remember him taking them two at a time when she was little. The way he'd throw a smile over his shoulder, his blue eyes twinkling at her, while he waited for her to catch up. He'd never looked old to her before, until now.

As the kettle began to boil, Morfar stood staring out the window, looking utterly forlorn. The sight made her heart clench – what right did she have to his memories – to his painful past; it was *his*, wasn't it? She wanted to know about it more than anything, but not if it was going to hurt him this much – never that. Even her mother, who so desperately wanted him to unburden himself too, would baulk at putting him in pain to hear it – especially with her tender heart.

Ingrid sighed. 'Look. Morfar, we don't have to do this. I'm sorry I pushed, you know, Ben – my ex? – well, he used to call me his stubborn mountain goat. I'm sorry that I was prying.'

He shook his head. 'No, Inge – you're right. I must speak about it. I can't bear to – but I must, somehow. Because when I go – when my memories do – so will she... so will they.'

Ingrid blinked. *They?*

'I just don't really know where to start.'

'Why don't you start at the beginning. Why were you speaking German as a child?' She assumed that was the case, as when he'd been speaking it to her, he'd sounded very young...

He stared at her, almost as if in shock that she couldn't know this, but of course, he'd spent a lifetime keeping these things buried. 'Because, once a long time ago, it was my language.'

Ingrid blinked. 'German was your language – what do you mean?'

He stared out at the forest, but what he was looking at existed only as some inner landscape.

He sighed, rubbed his hands through his hair, and looked at her. 'I mean that a long time ago, I was German.'

CHAPTER FOUR

Ingrid gasped. 'You're German?'

He flinched, as if he'd been slapped. '*No.*'

'No?' she asked.

'I used to be – or at least a long time ago, I – well, we thought of ourselves as German – until they took our citizenship away from us.'

'Who did?' she asked, confused.

'The Nazis.'

Ingrid blinked. 'They took away your citizenship?'

He sat down. He'd forgotten he was making coffee, but Ingrid didn't remind him.

He stared at her for some time, and Ingrid worried that he'd lost track of what he was saying, until he shook his head. 'Inge, it wasn't just our family who lost their citizenship, they did that to millions – those they deemed undesirable, like disabled people, gay people, those with the wrong political beliefs, gypsies – and people like our family, Jews, you see.'

Ingrid stood up in absolute shock. 'W-we're Jewish?' she cried.

Morfar put his head in his hands again and nodded.

Suddenly everything became horribly clear and all those horrid stories she'd heard over the years changed, as it hadn't all happened to some unknown outsider… it had happened to *them.*

Morfar stood up, looking anxious, stressed. 'I know, it's huge. I should have told you and your mother. It just… there were times when it was easier to forget.'

He started to pace around the table, banging his head with his hands, becoming wild, agitated.

'Just tell me what happened. Tell me, Morfar,' she said, coming to gently remove his hands from his head, her heart jack-hammering inside her chest. He resisted at first, and she had to pull as hard as she could, till suddenly they went slack and he blinked up at her as if surprised to find her there. There were red impression marks still on his cheeks.

'Tell you what?' he asked, looking suddenly confused, his eyes glassy, unfocused.

'Morfar?' she said softly.

He frowned, and his anxiety from before seemed to misdirect in his sudden confusion. 'What are you doing here, Marta? *För fan i helvete*, we aren't even blood – you're my son-in-law's cousin, that's nothing to me, really! You don't need to come into my house like this and take over, I am not some frail old man, I don't need you!' he shouted. Then he seized her by the arm and marched her towards the door. 'Go, and don't come back here, until I invite you in – though I'd have to be an absolute idiot to do that.'

'Morfar!' cried Ingrid, tears pricking her eyes. 'It's me – Ingrid – it's not Marta!'

'Pah, you children – you all think the same, you all think that "old" means decrepit. I have shoes older you, some wiser too – out, out, out – I'll see you some other time.'

Ingrid stood. 'No, Morfar, you haven't even had something to eat.'

He scowled, then made his way to the counter, hastily carving up some bread that she had brought the day before, and shoving a chunk into his mouth. Crumbs flew everywhere. 'Happy now? Will you just leave?'

She nodded. 'I'll see you tomorrow.'

He frowned. 'Are you deaf? I just said come *only* when I invite you – and that's not likely to be any time before I die – then, well, you're welcome to come dance over my body for all I care – but for now, get the hell out!'

Ingrid's lips trembled. *I will not cry*, she told herself. *I will not cry*, she silently repeated.

'I'll go, I'll see you later, okay?'

He closed his eyes, sighing deeply.

When he opened them, she was gone.

Ingrid didn't go home. She walked to the frozen lake, and listened to the song of the ice. It was loud, like a beating heart. For some the noise was eerie, but for Ingrid it had always been a comfort, reminding her of her childhood out here in these wild northern woods. She'd always figured that was because her roots were here – dating back thousands of years. But now she had to configure a new aspect to her identity: she was part German? Jewish? How had he kept this secret from them all these years?

She sat on a rock, Narfi close to her side. She was dressed in thermal gear, but it was still cold. Snow was beginning to fall. Up above, the sky was bathed in purple light. It was beautiful, and otherworldly, but her thoughts were centred on the small red cabin in the distance. He'd been so close to telling her everything, before the light in his eyes had seemed to change once more. It was frustrating, and desperately sad. Narfi put his head in her lap, as if he understood the ache in her heart, and she ran her mittens along his furry back.

'Let's go, boy, it's too cold for this,' she said, shivering. Then she stood up and started walking.

It was some time before they finally arrived home, cold and exhausted – but not long after that, Ingrid fell asleep on the sofa, though sleep didn't last long. Her dreams were full of the events of the day, which quickly turned to nightmares, and she tossed and turned. Dreaming of children and parents forced to wear yellow-starred badges. Twins. Trains. Lists of names of people destined for concentration camps. She woke up in a sweat, heart pounding. Her grandfather's tear-streaked face filled her thoughts. It took some time before her heart rate slowed to normal. She spent the rest of the night awake and staring at the ceiling.

Thinking. Thinking of Morfar hiding this secret from them for so long. Why? Why hadn't he shared it with them – it was so much to bear alone – too much to try and take in, too, even now. How could he have borne it all alone?

*

Inge woke in the morning to find thick new layers of snow had fallen overnight.

There were deep shadows beneath her eyes from her restless night. She took her time on her walk through the woods towards the small cabin, all the while trying to summon her courage for when she saw him. But when she got there he wasn't home. His snow boots were gone, as well as his binoculars.

She paced up and down his tiny cabin, filled with fear. There was over fifty hectares of forest bordering the cabin. Until recently, the person who'd known every inch of it better than anyone was Morfar, but now one wrong turn and he could be lost, without food or water and prey for animals. She ran outside, eyes wild.

The sound of a snow plough over the road made her pause.

She waved her arms to get the driver's attention. It was a neighbour who worked for the forestry department. He was a short man in his late fifties with a stocky build, grey eyes, and a serious expression, named Martin.

'Martin, please help!' she called. 'Morfar's gone into the woods. His binoculars are missing!'

Martin frowned, and looked at her like she was mad. He knew her, of course – she'd been coming to the hamlet every summer since she was a child. 'Jürgen will be fine – no need to worry, he knows these woods like the back of his hand.'

Ingrid frowned – was everyone in denial about him?

She shook her head briskly. 'Not anymore. He's getting old – he gets confused now; it's early dementia. He might not realise where he is and I'm really worried.'

He nodded. 'I heard about that but every time I see him, he seems fine.'

Ingrid just stared at him, fighting her annoyance. 'Well, it's when you spend a long time with him that you can see he's not himself – he gets muddled.'

He nodded. 'Okay. I'll put a call through on the radio – we can get a lookout going for him. We have a system in place in case children or animals get lost.'

She remembered. There had been a time some years ago when another of their neighbours' visiting relatives had got lost; it had taken several hours, but they'd found her, thankfully. 'Thank you. Should I come with you?'

'No, don't worry. Besides, with these drifts he couldn't have got very far – and since it's stopped snowing we should be able to track him fairly quickly.'

She felt relief flood her senses. 'You think so?'

He nodded. 'Though there's the—' He broke off, then shook his head. 'Don't worry. I'll come by as soon as I know. You'll wait here in his cabin?'

She nodded. 'Of course.'

She knew what he was going to say – if Morfar had tripped or fallen the risk of dying from exposure in these freezing cold conditions was strong. She couldn't think of that.

She went back inside the cabin, and felt lost. It felt wrong to be here without Morfar, like she was intruding, which in a way, she was. She knew it couldn't be easy for him, such a private soul, to suddenly have people barging in, prying into his personal affairs, forcing him to do things against his will. Growing up, there were times when they wouldn't see him for a couple of weeks straight. He liked his own space. It was why he'd never remarried. Her grandmother had died just after her mother was born, so he'd raised her mother by himself. Jonna always said it was strange – in a way, it was as if he had never been married at all…

She made a cup of coffee and tried to calm her nerves. It didn't work.

'He'll be fine,' she told herself. 'They will find him. Besides, Morfar knows these woods.'

Narfi raised himself off the wooden floor to look at her, his head cocked to the side in concern. She blew out her cheeks. 'I know, boy. I'm sorry.'

Her eyes fell on the mounds of scattered clutter.

Well, there was something she could do to take her mind off things. She tied her hair up with a band on her wrist and got to work. The cabin was a museum of old things. Magazines, article clippings, sketches and hundreds of copies of newspapers. And everywhere there were stacks of unframed paintings. Forest scenes, animals, but landscapes, mostly. Some were unfinished, as if he couldn't quite capture what he wanted to. She put these to one side. She turned to stack some of the newspapers and magazines together, bumping over an old box that was covered in dust at the bottom of a massive pile of clutter. She opened it and frowned. Inside was a hefty stack of sketchbooks. She knelt down on her haunches and opened one. There were beautiful pencil drawings and watercolours. Some were of her as a child, in the forest and her mother. Many of these went back years.

She sat and looked through all of them. It took hours. He'd kept a kind of illustrated diary over many years. She remembered him sketching when she was a child; he always had a notebook in one of his jackets, and a chewed pencil. Though she also remembered that he never showed anyone his sketchbooks, whipping them away when someone asked for a closer look. There were ones that showed the changing landscape of their village, Stjärna, over the years. Others were just of the wildlife – but when she picked up a handsome leather book, her heart skipped a beat. It had gold initials etched into the leather. J.S. She frowned, wondering what the S stood for. A middle name she didn't know about, perhaps?

Inside, the sketches showcased an entirely different landscape, full of canals and city life. And as she flicked through the pages, she gasped aloud, as she found a watercolour sketch of a young girl who looked almost uncannily like Ingrid, except her eyes were slightly bigger, and violet. She was lying on her stomach, staring intently at a large textbook, her blonde hair parted in the middle like curtains around her face.

Beneath the sketch, it said simply: *Asta.*

This was Asta.

Ingrid sat down on her haunches and stared. No wonder he got them confused.

There was a sound from behind, and she turned to see Morfar standing in the kitchen. His binoculars in his hands.

'Morfar!' she cried, standing up quickly, the sketchbook clutched to her chest. 'Oh, thank God, I was so worried!'

He looked furious. 'What am I to do with you? I can't believe you sent out a search party for me, like some lost child, *för fan i helvete*. It's not like I haven't lived here for over forty years – I could find my way back to this cabin in my sleep!'

'Yes, but, Morfar, you know that you have a… condition.'

He looked ready to explode. 'A condition? Pah, I'm so tired of this rubbish, where every little thing must have some stupid label – the only condition I have is old age where I have forgotten more things than you have yet to learn! It will happen to you, too, you know? And suddenly everyone will treat you like an idiot.'

She sighed. 'Maybe, but you could still get confused and lost.'

He started swearing again, and Ingrid said in German, 'Just stop that.'

He blinked. 'What did you say!' he replied in Swedish. He was furious. 'You dare speak to me in that language – here in my house?' His eyes fell upon the mess she'd made. 'What have you done here, why are you going through my things? This is absolutely ridiculous, Inge – you're actually worse than Marta, at least she doesn't snoop! I can consent to the occasional bit of help but this—?'

Ingrid bit her lip, ashamed of herself. 'Morfar, I'm sorry – I just wanted to tidy a bit, that's all – I wasn't looking, but I bumped over the box… and that's how I found this,' she said, and handed him the sketchbook.

All the anger that had taken sudden hold of him seemed to dissipate, and he suddenly stooped, like his knees couldn't support him anymore, and he took a seat at the kitchen bench.

He held the sketchbook open to his drawing of Asta, and touched it, his hands shaking. There were sudden tears in his eyes. Then he glanced up at Ingrid. 'I haven't looked at this in years,' he breathed, touching the sketch with a gnarled, shaking finger. Tears smarted his eyes. 'No wonder I keep muddling the two of you – you look so much like her. Especially now that your hair has grown.'

Ingrid took a seat next to him. 'This was Asta – your twin?' she said.

He sighed, closed his eyes and nodded. 'Yes.'

'Morfar, please will you tell me about her?'

He took a deep breath. Then, at last, he nodded.

'We lived in Hamburg, a city with more canals than Venice – did you know that?'

She shook her head; she hadn't known.

'We lived deep in the heart of the old town. My family had lived there for centuries and if Hitler hadn't decided otherwise, that's probably where we'd all be now.'

Ingrid blinked, realising that he was probably right – that she might not have even been born.

He picked up the sketchbook again, and his hands traced over the initials. 'It was a present from my parents, when I was ten. J.S. For Jürgen Schwalbe. That was our surname – before I changed it after the war. It means swallow, like the bird.'

He let out a low, hollow laugh.

Ingrid frowned. 'What is it?'

'My father used to say that the two of us were like our namesake – you know that swallows seldom rest, they spend most of their lives in flight?'

Ingrid nodded. He'd told her that once before, in the summer when they followed a flock as they made their nests in the forest.

'I sometimes think that with a name like that, it's no wonder our family spent most of our lives on the run. They say that a swallow can cover over two hundred miles a day, and when they land, it's only briefly. They always return to their nests, it's what drives them. Except of course we became birds without a nest to return to.'

CHAPTER FIVE

Hamburg, 1933

The twins arrived back at the apartment on Helman Straße, covered in mud, leaves and twigs. They were laughing, and holding onto each other's backs for support. 'Did you see ol' Polgo's face?'

Asta giggled, her violet eyes sparkling. She raised a hand to imitate him waggling a finger at them. '*If I ever find out who your father is, you horrid brats, I'm going to send him my condolences!*'

They both broke down into more raucous laughter.

'He loves us, really. Imagine how boring it would be to transport people across the canal every day without the occasional visit from a Schwalbe?' said Jürgen.

'Or two?' said Asta.

'Or two,' Jürgen agreed, with a grin.

'In any case,' added Asta, 'Frederick needs us. It's a public service we're doing.'

'Exactly, the city relies upon us.'

Frederick was a stuffed gorilla, and the company mascot on Polgo Hausman's small water taxi. He sat in the window, visible to all who looked down at the Zollkanal from the grand Brooksbrücke bridge.

The twins made it their solemn duty to change his outfit every morning, and there were a few Hamburgers who looked forward to what they came up with – even though Polgo vowed he would skin them alive if he ever caught them. So far Polgo had yet to catch them in the act.

The latest outfit had consisted of their mother's old brassiere and a shift. It was too good to pass up, and they waited along the riverbank to get a glimpse of Polgo's face, which was a picture.

'Our best yet,' said Jürgen.

'Saucy Frederick,' said Asta.

Which elicited several more giggles.

The pair hadn't countered on Polgo's apoplexy, though. 'You little heathens! I am running a respectable business!' he'd screeched, leaping from the boat and wading across the canal towards them, as the pair ran, laughing, along the stretch of the towpath, skidding on a mud bank, and slipping away into the vast network of bridges that crossed the city. He was no match for them.

They were still laughing when they heard a strident voice calling their names inside the apartment.

'Twins! Come here, now!'

They immediately stopped laughing, and started hatching an excuse, something that would explain where they'd been. 'Shall we say we were set upon by robbers again, *Küken*?'

'No, we used that with the cook and it got so complicated last time, I didn't even blame her for telling on us.' They shared a laugh. The lie had indeed got so convoluted that it was like an adventure tale – pirates, robbers, missing gold… it had been thrilling. Until the cook lost patience and chased them around the apartment with her rolling pin. Jürgen started to giggle. '*If I catch you I will put you in my pie!*'

Asta's eyes danced. 'Frau Fisher is not like Mother, who is too smart to be fooled for long. We'll need something simple. We'll say Tookie escaped and Herr Wilhelm offered us a reward to find him.'

Jürgen shrugged. It was boring, but it would probably work. He frowned. 'And we rolled in the mud—?'

'Because... he had a paw stuck in some ropes by the river...'

They nodded together. It would do. Well, until their mother asked after Herr Wilhelm's toy poodle.

They shuffled inside, towards the sound of their mother's voice, the perfect excuse ready in place.

'Where have you been?' she demanded. She was a small woman, with dark blonde hair, and fierce black eyes which seemed almost to snap at them.

'We – you see, Herr Wilhelm's dog—' Jürgen began.

Their mother held up her hand. 'On second thoughts, I don't want to hear it – especially one of your long, winding tales. Not after what has happened today.'

Asta and Jürgen shared a look. Had Polgo found out who they were – had he phoned their parents?

'We can explain, Mutti... um, we didn't mean to take your brassiere,' said Jürgen.

'Well...' hedged Asta. 'I mean, we did, but it was an old one – it had a hole this size,' she said, making one as big as her head with her hands to emphasise, never letting a chance to exaggerate escape, despite the fact that her mother wasn't exactly a heavy-breasted woman.

'And we found it in the rag bag,' lied Jürgen. They'd used one of her good ones – thinking Frederick deserved to look his best.

Mutti blinked. 'My brass— no, it's not about that,' she said. 'Though I wish the two of you would stop and think about what you're doing – you can't get away with this sort of thing anymore. It's far too dangerous.'

'What's dangerous about it? I don't think he minds that much. I know he *says* he wants to skin us alive, but we have seen him laughing – even when he chases us – and the punters love it.'

Mutti stared at them, realising they were each speaking of different things. 'What on earth are you two talking about?'

'The stuffed gorilla. What are you talking about?'

'The stuffed gorilla?'

They tried to explain, but it was hard with her frowning so fiercely.

Mutti pinched the skin between her eyes. 'God help me,' she said, and she looked so crushed they both felt an overwhelming stab of guilt. 'Come into the sitting room, your father is home early – we need to speak to you both, it's important.'

They followed after her in surprise. Papa was never home early. 'Is he sick?'

It was funny but as a doctor he was always the last person to look after himself when he was ill, always too busy looking after everyone else to take time off.

'No, he is fine. He came home early because of the news.'

'The news?' asked Asta.

Their mother nodded. Her face was grave as she made her way to the sofa where their father was sitting. The twins paused in surprise. Their dapper father, always so well-groomed, with his perfectly styled hair and starched shirts, looked dishevelled. His hair was a mess, from where he'd been rubbing his hands through it, his clothes were wrinkled and there were deep shadows beneath his eyes. But it was the look in them that caused both twins to swallow in sudden fear.

'Sit down,' he said quietly. 'There's something we need to tell you.'

Jürgen closed his eyes. This had happened to his friend, Hans. He was sure of it. Now he had two fathers. His real one and someone he now had to call 'Uncle'.

'You're getting a divorce,' he accused them, his blue eyes wide. Asta gasped. 'No!'

To their surprise, their parents smiled for a moment. 'I wish it were that simple, in a way,' said their mother.

The twins blinked at each other.

'No, my dears. It's much worse than that… and for people like us – Jews – as Hitler has been made chancellor,' said their father.

The twins shared wide-eyed looks. They knew about him, of course. The leader of the Nazi Party who had been making promises that he was going to turn things around for Germany. The man who blamed the Jews for everything that had gone wrong since the First World War – instead of the actual war that had caused mounting debts in reparations to many countries, not to mention the stock market crash that had occurred just four years earlier. Yet, for some reason, people believed that the Jews were to blame. When the twins had heard these claims they had always thought he seemed like a crazy, angry man, looking for someone to be crazy and angry about, and that people would see that. But maybe not.

Jürgen frowned. 'But—' He looked at their mother. 'He doesn't mean *us*, though – I mean, we celebrate Christmas.'

'We aren't even really Jewish, are we?' asked Asta. 'It's not like we ever go to synagogue with Granny. Surely he just means to make life hard for those Jews who don't really see themselves as German? I mean, it's not nice, but maybe they just need to adapt a bit more…'

Mutti shrugged. 'Maybe.'

Asta wasn't alone in that prejudice – it was a feeling shared by a lot of the more westernised Jews, that the problem was a case of not blending in enough. She'd heard her parents talk about it before – even her neighbours too. About how the very Orthodox ones were different to them… Later, they would realise how wrong that was and in time Asta would grow intensely ashamed of this prejudice, but at that moment it was just something she'd been taught – and she took comfort in the idea that Hitler's dark plans and ideas for the future might not apply to *them*.

Their father looked at them, and shook his head. 'Somehow, I doubt we'll seem more German to him even if we nail the Nazi flag with a cross on our door.'

That night Jürgen lay in bed, listening to the sounds of their parents as they spoke long through the small hours. Their voices were anxious, and the mood inside the flat was tense. He couldn't sleep. It was past two in the morning when he called out to Asta in the bed opposite. 'You still awake?'

'Yes,' came her quiet voice. 'Can't sleep.'

'Me neither.'

'Want to play cards?'

'Now?' Asta sat up to look at him in surprise. She could just make out his tousled dark head.

'I don't know – maybe.'

'Mutti and Papa will murder us if they find us up.'

'I doubt it. They're up too.'

Asta swung her legs out of bed. He was right, of course. 'Okay,' she said, switching on the small bedroom light that sat on a low table between their beds. There had been a time, after they'd turned nine, that their parents had suggested that perhaps they should have their own separate rooms now they were growing up.

'You might want some privacy,' suggested Mutti delicately. 'You know, for when you undress and that sort of thing.'

'We turn our backs, Mutti, what more privacy would we need than that?' Jürgen had asked.

'Well… when you're older things might change and you might need a bit more than that.' Then she sighed, muttering something about why was Papa never home to explain boy things to his son, while her face turned a bit red.

But the suggestion had only made them upset. 'But, Mutti, what if I wake up in the middle of the night and need someone to talk to?'

'Yes, and how will I sleep without listening to Asta's snoring. I couldn't!'

'Besides, who needs privacy from their twin?' demanded Jürgen.

'Exactly,' agreed Asta.

'Well, maybe one day you'll change your mind…' their mother had said. 'It's not a bad thing to have some space to yourself, it doesn't mean you love each other any less.'

'Course it does,' Asta had cried, clutching Jürgen with tears in her eyes, while the boy sobbed and said he would just break the wall between them down…

Mutti had sighed. 'I give up – have it your way, but we will revisit this matter when you are twelve, all right?'

'No!'

She'd sighed again, and left muttering about being ganged up on… and needing a drink. 'You two are worse than all my patients combined.'

Mutti was a head nurse at the University Hospital Eppendorf. She organised a team of over a hundred staff. Their father was an orthopaedic surgeon and he worked in the same building. He fixed people's bones for a living.

The twins played cards until dawn that night, listening to the sound of their parents speaking in the front room and the noises they made when putting the kettle on for yet another cup of coffee.

As Jürgen uncovered a Jack and an ace, giving him the winning hand to Asta's three, seven and two, he called, '*Siebzehn und vier.*'

As he looked up at her the dawn sun was painting the sky the colour of apricot. The wintry air was cold and crisp and the clock on the bedside table struck five thirty; they were already late for Polgo and the gorilla.

Asta looked at the clock too and frowned. Then she picked up the cards and shuffled them. 'Another round?'

Jürgen nodded, feeling a deep ache inside for something he couldn't put a name to. Something had shifted since they'd returned home the day before. It would only be many years later when he realised it was the moment they'd begun to put their childhood behind them.

They never did dress the gorilla mascot in Polgo Hausman's water taxi again.

CHAPTER SIX

At school, the Jewish teachers were seen huddling together and speaking anxiously. There were a few children whose parents were in the Nazi Party, who had begun to walk around the place as if they owned it. Like Udo Van der Welt, who told his friends that the teachers would soon be out of a job.

The end of the school day couldn't come fast enough for Jürgen. After he left the boys' grammar school, he waited for Asta outside the girls' secondary school, a five-minute walk away. They took the long route home, walking past the canals, their breath fogging the air in front of them. Neither of them noticed the cold as Jürgen told Asta all that had happened.

'Of course, that wimp, Udo, never dared say that the Jewish teachers were out of a job to their faces. Just told a few of us at break – he was looking at me when he said it, though, like he was hoping for a fight.' Jürgen balled his hands into fists. 'I was close, I'm not going to lie – but I thought I wouldn't give him the satisfaction. So I just whistled, as if I knew something he didn't, and said, "We'll see," like I knew better. I could tell it made him furious because he kicked over the rubbish bin. Luckily the biology teacher saw and he made him pick up all the rubbish by hand – and it was full of grotty things from lunch!'

'Good,' said Asta, shortly. But she had a faraway look, her face turning hard and cold. She crossed her arms, hunching over in the wind.

'What's with you?' asked Jürgen.

She looked at her twin and her violet eyes glittered. 'Karen told me that she can no longer be my friend. Apparently, her parents are friends with Udo's and they were told that the time had come to choose a side.'

Jürgen's eyes widened in shock. Karen had been her best friend since kindergarten – well, besides Jürgen.

Asta nodded, looking glum. 'Her mother said continuing a friendship with "those twins" would be "unwise".'

Jürgen grinned. 'Well, it's never exactly been wise to be our friend. Not unless you enjoy visiting the head teacher every few weeks.'

'Yes,' said Asta, who didn't return his smile for once. 'But this time it's because of who we are – not for what we've done.'

'That's worse.' Jürgen kicked a stray bottle out of their path; it rolled onto the street and made a satisfying crash. They couldn't help who they'd been born.

At school, Udo had become insufferable. His smug face was there whenever Jürgen crossed the threshold, and he was always speaking of how things were about to change – how soon they wouldn't be allowing Jews into 'his' school. Jürgen did his best to ignore him but it was hard.

He bided his time, then one day, during a biology lesson, he found his moment.

It had meant using the last of his savings but it was worth it to buy Hennie.

He hugged the glass jar to his side, as he unscrewed the lid, creeping softly from his seat, while the teacher's back was turned. Then he upended the jar with Hennie inside straight onto Udo Van der Welt's hair.

Jürgen was already back in his seat by the time Udo had begun to scream and claw at his hair, jumping off his chair so fast it crashed onto the floor.

'Get it off, get it off!' screamed Udo.

No one made a move. Not even the teacher.

When Udo started to cry, Jürgen finally stepped forward, to scoop up Hennie into his outstretched hands.

'All that fuss over a spider,' he tsked at Udo.

Udo's fear-filled eyes flashed to hatred as realisation dawned.

'They'll expel you for this. I'll make sure of it – I know it was you.'

'They'll have to prove it was me first,' said Jürgen.

'Who else would have brought a tarantula to school?' he shot back.

Despite Udo's threats, none of the other boys snitched on Jürgen, even though one of them must have seen him with the jar. There are few things worse in the schoolroom than a snitch.

Still, he was called into the head teacher's office, and of course they found the jar which held the spider he'd recaptured. He wasn't expelled, but he soon wished that he was.

The head teacher, Herr Weimar, closed the door, then leant against his desk, pinching the bridge of his nose.

'I've just had a visit from Frau Van der Welt, who is most distressed about this stunt you played on Udo. She wants me to expel you... is that what you want?'

Jürgen shook his head. His school fees were expensive, and his parents made a lot of sacrifices to send him here. They would be livid.

The head teacher sighed, then took off his glasses, and rubbed his eyes.

'Then, I have to ask you, boy, are you stupid?'

Jürgen blinked.

'It is not a rhetorical question.'

'Um, I—'

'I must surmise that you are indeed stupid or woefully naive,' said the head. Then he picked up a file. Jürgen could just see his name on top. It was worryingly thick.

The head teacher opened it and sighed. 'It's full of pranks – mischief... dressing up the school cat.' He gave a small snort. 'I remember that. Stealing the janitor's keys... ah, and yes, how could I forget the day your sister came disguised as the new pupil, "Anton". It seems you had a few of the teachers fooled for most of the day...'

Then he slammed the file shut. 'These things, Jürgen, these pranks, need to exist in the past, do you understand me?'

Jürgen shook his head.

'You seem to not be getting something that is rather obvious.'

'What?' Jürgen asked.

'Things are changing and I can tell you one thing,' he said, touching the file, 'time's up.'

'Time's up?'

Herr Weimar let out a big sigh. 'For acting like an idiot. There's zero tolerance for people like you in this country – for Jews. You'd have to be a blind idiot to try and make it so easy for people to come after you.'

Then he put his glasses on his nose. 'So, I ask you again, are you an idiot?'

Jürgen swallowed. 'No, sir.'

'Good. Your detention will consist of cleaning the school bathrooms.'

Jürgen's eyes widened.

'Every day for a month.'

*

'It's probably the only way he could get away with not expelling you,' said Asta, wisely, on their way home from school.

Jürgen looked at her. 'That's not true! I'm sure there's a lot of things I could do besides cleaning toilets – you have no idea how filthy those boys can be. And when they find out it'll be even worse – they'll make it unbelievably disgusting!'

'Probably,' agreed Asta. 'But I don't think giving you lines or making you stay behind would have mollified Udo or his mother – they want to see you either humiliated or expelled.'

'I don't see how they have the power to do that – not yet anyway.'

Asta nodded. 'That's the problem – there could still be a "yet".'

Jürgen balled his fists. 'It makes me want to get back at Udo all the more for this. The little wimp. You know that he smashed an egg into Hans's hair and called him a "filthy Jew" the other morning? There was no punishment for that. Or when he tripped another boy whose mother is married to a Jew down the stairs?'

Asta nodded. 'A month – two months ago – he would have been given the cane, now they're frightened of him – and his parents.'

Jürgen nodded. 'I wish I'd been expelled instead.'

Asta shook her head. 'Don't say that – that's when Udo wins.' Then she looked at him with a grin. 'So, tell me again about how he screamed? Did he wet himself?'

Jürgen grinned in response, a dimple appearing in his freckled cheek. 'Like a girl – or worse, actually, even you don't scream that badly. But no, he didn't wet himself, unfortunately. Maybe next time?'

And the two laughed so hard they could barely breathe when they entered their flat.

When they got inside, their father was waiting for them, and the laughter died quickly in their throats, the air turning to lead as it sank into the pits of their bellies.

'Did you have a good day?' he asked Jürgen coldly.

'Er—' began Jürgen.

'Well, it sounds to me like you did – as I was called out of surgery to discuss your antics at the school.'

'Papa – I—' Jürgen began. His eyes were wide with fear.

'It was my fault, well, my idea to buy the tarantula,' said Asta. 'Punish me, not him!'

Papa shook his head, then took a sip of whisky. He looked tired.

'You kids – it's time you grew up. We're hanging here by a thread, don't you understand? It's not the time to act like fools.'

They blinked.

'But, Papa,' said Jürgen, 'it was just a silly prank and Herr Weimar has said that now I must clean the bathrooms for a whole month – I mean, that's not fair, Udo Van der Welt tripped a boy, who fell on his arm—'

Their father stood up. 'You know, maybe I'm the fool. I am quite sure that I never gave you the impression that this world was fair but if you haven't been listening to the news – if you haven't figured out that things are about to get a whole lot more unfair, well… then I don't know what to tell you. Except, maybe… *think*. Use your head. Maybe your brain will start working when you start cleaning those toilets.'

Then he turned on his heel to leave, saying over his shoulder, 'And if I ever get interrupted during a surgery for something like this again, cleaning toilets will be the least of your worries.'

As predicted, the boys turned the bathrooms into a virtual pigsty, bringing in things – from marbles to dolls' heads – to block the pipes. They smeared mud on the walls and piled rubbish into the sinks at the end of each day. As the news of his punishment spread, Jürgen started to go in an extra hour earlier to clean, and he always had an audience, with lots of the boys arriving earlier too to be a spectator and offer some advice. 'Don't forget to really put your elbows into it this time,' said one as he used the plunger to sift out a doll from one of the toilets, masking his nose with his other hand as the foetid smell rose. He flung the doll's head into the bucket then frowned, giving a low whistle.

'What?' asked the boy.

'It's mad – come see.'

The boy hurried forward to look inside, then pulled a face at the soiled doll's head covered in excrement.

'It's just a doll's head,' said the boy.

'But it looks just like your mother!' said Jürgen.

Luckily the janitor intervened before a fight broke out. 'Out – out of here, boy, get to class.'

Then he smacked Jürgen over the back of his head. 'You want to get another month of this?'

Jürgen shook his head as he moved on to the next blocked toilet, the bile rising in his throat. 'No.'

'Then keep your stupid trap shut from now on.'

Which he did. It was the longest month ever, but by the end of it even the boys had stopped coming in early and few bothered taking the time to make the bathroom more of a mess than it already was. The joke had become stale.

But not for Jürgen, who had learnt his lesson at last.

In April, things went from bad to worse. The news came on the radio that the schools were closed for an extra month, and at first Jürgen and Asta, like all the others, were excited at the prospect of an extended holiday. Except that when they returned, both their schools were now run by the Nazi Party. And Like Udo Van der Welt had predicted back in January, all the Jewish staff had been dismissed. Including Jürgen's head teacher, Herr Weimar, who was married to a Jewish woman, and was now being called a 'half-Semite'.

In fact, it was uncertain if the twins would even be allowed to attend the schools themselves. Things had started to escalate since March, with storm troopers marching into cities and terrorising the Jewish population in an attempt to segregate them from the rest of society. They'd attacked shop owners, and those in civil service, dragging them into the streets and making them perform humiliating acts. Local police were powerless to stop them and when news of their behaviour leaked into the overseas press, painting the Nazis in less than a favourable light, it only made them persecute the Jews even more. On 1 April, there was a nationwide boycott of Jewish-owned business, with the word 'Jude' or the Star of David painted on windows. They marched through towns, inciting hatred and terror which led to spurts of violence. The boycott didn't work, as people continued to shop at the businesses in the days that followed, but the tone had been set, and six days later a new law called the Law for the Restoration of the Professional Civil Service dismissed Jews from public service unless they could prove their non-Jewish parentage. Similar laws that affected lawyers and doctors soon came into effect.

At home, the mood was apprehensive. Both Mutti and Papa could be faced with dismissal… and then what would happen to them all? Neither of them could claim non-Jewish grandparents.

In the end, President von Hindenburg intervened suggesting that these new rules shouldn't apply to those Jews who had fought in the First World War, and Hitler reluctantly agreed.

'So, you'll be able to keep your jobs, then?' Asta asked her parents, sitting across from them at the dinner table, their chicken and sauerkraut untouched. Papa had been in the war; he'd fought with his two brothers, but only he had survived. His only surviving sibling was his sister, Trine, who lived now in Denmark.

'For now,' agreed Papa, stabbing a piece of chicken with his fork. 'But your mother might not.'

They stared at her in surprise. 'I don't think it applies to the spouses of war veterans. It's okay, I might be able to get a job at the Jewish clinic – a former colleague who works there has hinted that there might be an opening if I want to come on board. But at least one of us will definitely get to keep their job. It's a good thing – a relief,' she said, though it sounded like she was trying to convince herself of that.

Papa looked at her in disbelief. 'Is it?' He shook his head, and put down his fork, which clanged onto his plate, then stared out unseeing at the streets of Hamburg below their apartment. 'You've worked hard for that hospital – and you're excellent at it but despite that, you must leave, just like that? Just because we don't have Christian grandparents. Maybe it would be better if we had no alternative – like the Rubensteins.'

The Rubensteins were their neighbours – both worked in the civil service, government office jobs, and now were looking at emigrating to England.

'You can't be serious,' said Mutti, who had picked up her wine glass only to set it down with a thud, slopping red liquid onto the crisp white linen. 'Hana Rubenstein is beside herself, she's been crying every day since it happened. Her whole life is here – and she can't even speak English properly. All I have to do is work for another hospital. In some ways it will be better – less responsibility. They're only going because her husband can, and they have a friend who is willing to put them up – but can you even imagine how horrid it will be for them – it's not like the English are that fond of Germans, after the war…'

Papa snorted. 'Worse than here? As foreigners, they will have more rights there than in their own country. As long as he gets the right visa and pays his taxes, they will be fine. I think we should think of doing the same.'

Mama blinked. 'Leave Hamburg?'

He stared at her. 'Germany.'

'And go where?'

'Denmark, maybe. We can go to Trine – she's already suggested it; she has a small cottage by the sea, but she has a big barn which she has offered us.'

Mutti's eyes widened in shock. 'A barn? You can't be serious! We don't need to flee – we aren't destitute, or about to be like the Rubensteins, we don't have to go! I don't want to leave my friends, give up working…' She started to cry, her gaze falling on their stylish flat in the heart of the city, with its polished her-ringbone wood, high ceilings and touches of luxury from fine art to hand-made antiques. '… to live in a barn.'

The twins looked stricken. They didn't want to leave either. This was their city, their home, with its vast network of canals. Things were bad for now, but surely they would get better?

Papa sighed. 'I don't relish the idea either but we might have to at some point. Maybe it's better if we did it fast. It's just… I've been thinking it's like a bone, a clean break often heals the best – but if you keep injuring it, the longer it takes to recover.'

CHAPTER SEVEN

Since Asta could remember, Jürgen was usually found with a sketchbook in hand. He was forever drawing something he'd seen: scenes of daily life in Hamburg, from canals to people at cafés and restaurants or sitting on benches. He drew dogs roaming free, as well as Asta and their adventures. There was a playfulness to his scenes, a way of looking at the world and finding the humour, along with the shared humanity.

He kept a daily sketchbook, like his idol, Adolph von Menzel, had. 'You know, Asta, they say he had eight pockets in his overcoat and they were filled with sketchbooks – he said he couldn't understand how an artist could be without one.' Menzel was known for his paintings and his patriotism, but it was his sketches and his work processes that Jürgen respected most. Like Menzel, Jürgen's drawings were full of empathy, particularly for people who were finding it harder to be acquainted with luck.

On their tenth birthday, Papa and Mutti, presented them each with a single gift. It was unusual, as often in the past there had been several for each, but times were tougher, and more uncertain. Yet it was this very simplicity that made each of their gifts so special. Asta's was an introduction to veterinary science – a first-year anatomy textbook for university students, and Jürgen's was a handsome leather sketchbook, that had his initials stamped in gold foil. J.S.

Jürgen began to fill his immediately, sketching his sister, as she pored over the anatomy textbook with fervour.

She was arranging different coloured pencils around her while she began taking notes, a look of satisfaction on her face, as she studied an illustration of the muscle network of a dog.

He grinned, catching her feet, ankles crossed, while she lay on her front. 'You know, *Küken*, you are a bit weird, really.'

She had a pink pencil in her mouth – the perfect shade for tendons – as she looked up at him. She didn't get offended. Her violet eyes danced. 'I know, but then, I suppose we are all a bit weird, deep down.'

He nodded. She was probably right.

He stifled a smile as she began to learn each and every muscle, bone, and tendon. Later there would be colour-coded notes, which would be stuck up all over her wall, or placed into the pocket of her school jacket, so that she could test herself.

And then soon – like the way she had once studied several maps of all the hundreds of Hamburg's canals – she would know it all by heart.

Jürgen looked up as a shadow moved over his sketch of the former Jewish teacher, Frau Hinkel, who had passed by the school gate, shoulders weary.

'See, you've got it all wrong,' said a whiny voice that Jürgen recognised as Udo's. He looked up and the boy was peering at his sketch with intensity. Jürgen made to stow away his sketchbook, but the boy was quicker, and snatched it, taking out a pencil from his pocket. 'I'll fix it for you, shall I?' he said. 'The nose should be at least two or three inches longer – and you missed the bump,' he said, looking up at Jürgen. 'You all have them,' he said, and drew a cartoonish mountain over Frau Hinkel' s nose. 'Also, the eyes – they have small beady eyes, like rats, like you…' he said, drawing a line to cut the woman's eyes in half.

Jürgen stood up quickly, his hands balled into fists at his side.

Thankfully, before anything could escalate, a teacher named Herr Staeler intervened. He snatched the sketchbook from Udo and looked at it.

'I was just fixing it,' said Udo, a smirk on his face. Frau Hinkel's face, despite his graffiti, was recognisable. The teacher shrugged, then nodded, and handed the sketchbook back to Jürgen. 'Good job,' he told Udo, his eyes daring Jürgen to object.

Jürgen didn't say anything, though his eyes spoke volumes.

'Leave, Schwalbe,' dismissed the teacher, finally looking away.

There was more talk that year of moving but for the moment it was only that. The twins' parents were often arguing, stressed and anxious.

'I flat out refuse, this will blow over and then what – we will have smashed up our lives for nothing,' argued Mutti.

'I promise you, if that is the case, if it's all nothing, we can move straight back,' implored their father.

'Don't be silly, we won't get any of this back – not our jobs – it was a miracle I got in at the clinic as it was, with so many Jewish doctors and nurses out of work, or our home – besides, what do you want the children to do – go to school in Denmark, learn a whole new language while we live in some barn in the middle of nowhere?'

'Is that really such a bad idea?'

'To live in a barn? She keeps her horse there – and she hasn't even offered to get rid of it.'

'She will, I'm sure.'

'Mmmh,' said Mutti, who wasn't convinced. 'Besides, it's cold in Denmark.'

Papa snorted. 'It's not much different than here. It's beautiful too.'

Mutti shook her head. 'Could we even get work there? I wouldn't know how to be anything but a nurse – and would they let us when we don't know the language? It's just too much to decide. I still don't think we need to yet. Six more months, then we'll make that call – if things get worse.'

But six months came and went and there was no more talk of leaving. The twins were relieved. They didn't want to have to move. Though one sunny June afternoon, Asta changed her mind.

Jürgen found her at home, crying on her bed. 'Hey – where were you, I waited for you outside your school but they said you left early, what happened?'

From her prone form on her small single bed, Asta groaned. 'I don't want to talk about it.'

Jürgen frowned, then took a seat next to her, almost on top of her knees. 'Budge up,' he said.

She didn't, so he hovered over them. She sighed, then shifted over. 'Go away,' she sniffled.

'Nope.'

She flung herself the other way around, and from under the curtain of her light hair, she asked, 'Did they do that thing with the rulers to you yet?'

He frowned. 'Rulers?'

She nodded, tears filling her eyes. 'Frau Klein, our biology teacher, measured my head. She told me it's smaller than an Aryan's – that it shows how weak Jews are and how... *inferior*.'

Jürgen frowned. 'Did she measure the others' heads?' he asked.

'No, I'm the only Jewish girl there.'

He made a huffing sound, like he disagreed.

'What – it's true.'

'Yes, I know that's true – but how would she know your head was smaller than any of the others' unless she measured theirs too?'

She frowned. 'Well, she's a biology teacher so maybe she knows how big Aryan heads are.'

'And they're all exactly the same?'

'I don't know.'

'Let's ask Papa.'

'No!'

'Why not? He's a surgeon – I'm sure he knows more than some biology teacher.'

'A surgeon of bones.'

'So – they have bones in the head!'

Asta wiped her eyes; she wanted to be like Jürgen, to just dismiss what her teacher had said, but the woman had been so sure, so convinced. Asta was someone who lived her life in facts, in science, in biology. So it had hit her harder, because she so admired the woman. The teacher was even rather sympathetic, patting her shoulder afterwards and saying, 'It's not your fault you were born inferior – it's just a condition of birth, you couldn't help it. Other than that, I think you are quite clever, really.'

Of course, that had only made things worse.

She didn't know exactly why she didn't want Jürgen to tell their father – perhaps in some small way that didn't quite make sense, she feared he would see her as inferior too.

Unfortunately, their father was on call that night. At dinner, though, Jürgen was not to be deterred.

Their mother paused, a piece of mashed potato poised on a fork before her mouth as he relayed the tale despite Asta's scowling face.

Then she blinked. 'She measured your head?'

Asta nodded, not meeting her mother's eyes.

'And she said it made you inferior?'

Asta didn't respond.

Jürgen interjected. 'You know it's nonsense, Mutti – she didn't even measure the other girls!'

'Because they are Aryan, she didn't have to,' said Asta.

'I see,' said Mutti, putting her fork down. Tears splashed down Asta's face and onto her plate.

'I'm sorry, Mutti.'

Mutti blinked. 'You have nothing to be sorry for. I can assure you that there is nothing inferior about you at all.'

Asta didn't say anything. Mutti stared at her for a long time. Then she said, 'Tomorrow you're coming to work with me for the morning, and in the afternoon, we're going to find you a new school.'

Asta looked up in surprise. Their mother's face was grim, determined.

'In the morning, we're going to visit my old hospital and the children's ward – where we will measure some heads ourselves, and you'll see that your teacher is nothing but an idiot. Then in the afternoon I will have the satisfaction of telling her so before we enrol you both.'

'Both?' asked Jürgen in surprise.

'Both,' she agreed. 'To the Jewish school – at least there you'll get treated with some respect – and I can be sure they won't fill your head with any of this sort of nonsense. It's bad enough that people out there believe this sort of rubbish, I will not stand by and let them force it down my children's throats too.'

'We'll get to be at school together?' asked Asta in delight.

'Yes.'

Their mother was true to her word. The next morning, they went over to the hospital in which for the past twenty years Mutti was head nurse, and she was quickly indulged by one of her former colleagues and allowed to measure the heads of several young girls in the children's ward, as well as four nurses and an intern,

Mutti proved her point. By then she hadn't needed to – Asta had already started to see that what Jürgen had pointed out the day before was true, but it was nice to have it confirmed, to expose the lie once and for all.

'Everyone's head is different – it's not the size that makes it worth something, it's what you do with what's inside of it that counts,' said Mutti.

'But I still don't understand why she would tell me that – if it's all just rubbish?' said Asta. 'She likes me – she wouldn't want to upset me!'

'You can love a dog, Asta, but never think of it as an equal. I think that she wants it to be true – your brother had a point. She would never measure the heads of the other girls in your class because then she might have to doubt everything she'd been told… and right now, these lies, these slurs, they're holding everything together, for the people using it to rise to power.'

The twins were enrolled at the local Jewish school due to the sheer force of their mother's will – that and the sympathy of Rabbi Bloch. They were past capacity but when Mutti explained what had happened, he said they could make things stretch a little wider to accommodate them.

For the twins, the new school was a reprieve. After a year and a half of education that was becoming increasingly about the Nazi Party – that left them feeling like outsiders while they were forced to listen to incentives that encouraged the non-Jewish youth to become model German children and join the Youth League, where lessons on what made someone seemingly inferior was because they were like them, and Jewish, or had some other 'flaw' had become daily life – the new school was like coming up for a breath of air.

Here they could speak loudly, laugh or say what they felt. Their new friends were like them; many hadn't even known they were 'Jewish' in any real sense, until Hitler told them they were.

'My grandfather was Jewish, apparently,' said a boy named Otto on their first day. 'I mean, my mother was adopted so she didn't know until we were told we had to prove our ancestry.'

'Same thing happened to our priest – he was told he couldn't be one anymore because someone in his family had once been Jewish,' said another girl, named Sara.

'A priest?' Asta asked in shock. 'Even that's not Christian enough?'

'Apparently not.'

For a time, it was possible to forget about Hitler, and their worries. 'He won't be in power forever,' said their mother, 'and then those stupid laws will be gone; they've lost too many valuable people – doctors, lawyers and the rest – they'll have to change it back.' They hoped that was the case.

It certainly felt like life was improving. The twins came home from school with smiles every day. They weren't the same children who'd once come home laughing and pulling pranks on Polgo Hausman's water taxi; they were older, and warier, but the longer they spent in their new school, making friends like themselves, the happier they had become. Which gave their parents comfort.

'It was a good call, that school,' Papa said one Saturday as they walked to the park. They'd just finished their ice creams and for a while they could almost feel as if things were about to return to normal.

On the way home, they passed their old neighbour, Geoff Rubenstein. He looked like a shadow of his former self. He'd lost weight and his hair had turned completely white. His clothes were old, dirty and frayed.

They stared at him in shock, while Papa clutched his arm. 'It is good to see you, my old friend, but I must admit, I am surprised – I thought you'd gone to England?'

'Pah, that fell through – my cousin couldn't vouch for me, he needed to be earning enough for us all. Times are tough there, too. We're looking at other options now.'

'But are you all right – where are you staying?' asked their father, concerned.

'We're with my sister – her husband served in the war so he still has a job. Hana – my wife, she's doing some sewing and washing – we're getting by, we're better off than many, don't worry. Besides, we're going to America, I have family there – it's going to be fine. It was nice to see you,' he said, stopping and smiling at the children like he always used to on the stairs of their apartment – usually after he handed them each a sweet from his pocket. Peppermints or toffees.

He handed them each one now. 'Still can afford these, so it's not all bad,' he said and he winked.

He wasn't the only one forcing a smile on his face.

On 15 September 1935, new laws came into effect, known as the Nuremberg Laws. They forbade marriages and relationships between Jews and Germans and officially stripped the Jews of their German citizenship.

Papa became obsessed with keeping their passports safe. 'They can't take these from us,' he kept saying.

Finally, even Mutti agreed that the time had come to look at moving.

Unfortunately, there were half a million Jews in Germany thinking of doing the same, and many countries had begun making the process increasingly difficult.

'We still have our jobs,' said Mutti. 'We're okay.'

Their friends felt the same way, including a fellow doctor, who had taken a job selling medical supplies to hospitals – because he hadn't fought in the First World War and wasn't allowed to practise medicine unless it was in a Jewish hospital. 'It's not all bad, my hours are better and besides, Hitler is focused on expanding Germany – and rebuilding the economy, so at some point they'll see sense.'

Papa had looked at him incredulously. 'I don't think he will.'

'Oh, Fritz, you worry too much,' said Mutti, patting his knee.

Germany invaded Austria and got away with it, with not so much as a slap on the wrist. It seemed that no one wanted to enter another world war. Nineteen thirty-eight brought with it new laws that were going to make life even harder for them. Jews were forbidden from practising medicine, but Papa got around this by getting a job at the Jewish hospital with Mutti. It was not even a third of the salary of what he had before.

'We're lucky,' Mutti told the twins. 'At least we have jobs.'

The twins knew that their parents wanted them to believe that was the case. Late at night they heard them talking about their aunt, Trine, in Denmark.

'Do you think we should try to get hold of her – try to get her to help us, perhaps she can vouch for us?' Mutti asked Papa.

Asta heard them speaking on her way to the kitchen, and paused behind the door in the sitting room.

'I don't want to worry her,' said Papa, 'besides, we haven't registered our paperwork yet.'

It was a horrible predicament – they couldn't apply for a visa without showing the authorities their passports – and that would ensure that theirs were stamped with the official 'J'. And there was the possibility that the visa could be denied and then they'd never be able to get out of the country.

She heard Mutti's anxious voice. 'She's sent two letters already. I think we can safely say that your sister is worried.'

'I thought you didn't want to go to Denmark?'

'That was before!'

'Okay, okay, I'll phone her,' he promised.

Asta left then, wondering if they were going to leave for Denmark after all. But in the days that followed they heard nothing more.

All Jews were now required to have a new middle name, Sara for females, and Israel for males – these were to be added at the registry office by law. Also, a large J was to be stamped inside their passports. Papa refused – especially the latter.

'I won't do it, Frieda – we agree to this and then whatever rights we have will be taken away.'

'Rights? We don't have many left – and without these new documents we won't be allowed to work at all!'

'Think, Frieda, if we do it we won't be able to leave. That's why they want the passports stamped, so that Jews can't pretend to be Christian and go to Switzerland.'

Papa didn't settle into his new job, like Mutti had done, it was hard for him to find peace in it – as he had one eye so firmly on getting them out of the country, hiding away the passports he'd refused to hand over.

In the end, though, the authorities came for them.

It appeared that Papa had made a scene at the Jewish clinic where he worked, when an SS officer came in asking to see everyone's documentation and he refused to show them.

The twins were on their way home when their world imploded. One of the nurses – who they knew only as Frau Kaplan – rushed over to tell them the news. She came running up to them in the street, her face red and streaked with tears. She was out of breath. 'Oh, my dears,' she gasped, clutching at them. 'You can't go home.' A fresh set of tears began leaking down her face. 'They've taken them both.'

'Our parents?' breathed Asta, her knees buckling. Frau Kaplan held her up. Her curly hair was glistening with sweat; she must have run all this way to tell them.

'Taken them where?'

'To Dachau, the labour camp – for refusing to change their documentation.'

Asta and Jürgen gasped. 'No – just for that – they can't have taken them!'

'I saw it myself. Your mother gave me a look to tell me to run here, knowing you'd just be getting out from school. The police are going to come for you next, I'm sure of it – I don't know where they send the children, I think it's some sort of camp somewhere else, but don't let them take you.'

She handed them some money. It wasn't a lot. 'I'm sorry, there was no time to get more – I heard them say that they would be going to your flat today to find you both, and to search the flat, so I couldn't even risk getting your things, in case they found me there.'

Asta clutched Jürgen's hand. 'We can't go home?'

Frau Kaplan shook her head. 'No, I'm sorry, it's the last place you should go now. I'd take you home with me, but they could look for you there.' She swallowed. 'They would know that I'm friendly with your mother and could figure out quickly that I came to get you. They could make trouble for us all. I'm sorry, I think it's best if you find somewhere safe to go. Somewhere they won't know. If you came with me, or any of your parents' hospital friends, there is the chance that they could find you and take you away too. Technically, you've broken the law too – as you haven't registered your documents either. I'm not sure they would be as harsh with you but…' She broke off.

They nodded. There was the chance they would. Who knew what they would do? They weren't kids anymore – sixteen was old enough to be prosecuted, wasn't it? It would be some time before they realised that she'd saved them, that she had risked a lot to protect them, but right then, they were told to run, and Frau Kaplan watched them dart away, before she, too, turned to go back to work. Hoping that no one had seen her leave.

CHAPTER EIGHT

They spent the night in Polgo Hausman's water taxi. He still kept the keys in the same place, and with the winter season fast approaching he wasn't running it as frequently anymore. It was freezing cold, but they shivered from more than just the cold.

'I keep feeling like we need to go back there, that it's all just a misunderstanding,' said Asta. 'That Mutti and Papa are there waiting for us and worried like hell.'

'Me too,' said Jürgen. His arms were wrapped around his knees. All they possessed were the clothes on their backs, which were easily identifiable as school uniforms.

Someone was bound to notice and ask questions.

'I think if we could just get into the flat – or find out more…' he said.

'You heard what Frau Kaplan said, though – they were coming for us, and going to search the flat. I doubt they'd give up that easily.'

He nodded, tears beginning to course down his cheeks, which he dashed angrily away. 'We should have taken Papa's side when he wanted to emigrate, then we wouldn't be in this mess now. We'd be in Denmark or somewhere safe, together.'

Asta nodded, wiping away her own tears. 'Mutti wanted to go a few weeks ago – she wanted to look into getting a visa. If Papa wasn't so stubborn maybe we wouldn't be here now either.'

Jürgen's head snapped up in anger. 'So, it's his fault that they were taken?'

'Wasn't it?' she asked softly. 'Couldn't he have avoided this just by letting us change our paperwork? He made us hide our passports – that we never even used; he was saving them for what, for things to get worse than they already are? All he did was talk! Mutti said that Trine sent two letters asking if we were coming. Even she was worried about us. And now look at us – we're stuck – our documents are at home, probably to be found by those damned SS, giving them the proof they need and making it harder to deny that he was planning something. What's worse is they're there and we can't even use them – how far are we going to get without them?'

Jürgen stared at her for a long moment. She was right, of course. But it felt horrible blaming their father, when he was only trying to protect them. Asta dashed away a tear and groaned. 'Of course, it's not Papa that's done this – *they* did – *they* forced him.'

Jürgen nodded, then stood up to pace within the small interior of the bridge. 'We'll have to get them. Tomorrow. Papa hid them well, so I don't think that they will have found them that easily.'

Asta raised a brow. They'd managed to figure out that their father hadn't had his documentation altered… and come looking. Besides, the one thing you could never accuse the Nazis of was a lack of attention to detail, of not being thorough enough…

Still, there was always the chance that they hadn't found the documents. The advantage the twins had was that with any luck, they didn't yet know about the hidden passports. She nodded.

'Yes, tomorrow, we'll go.' There were other more pressing concerns too. 'Either way, we need to go and get more clothes, food. Hopefully by then they would have moved on.'

Jürgen nodded. 'And Trine – Papa's sister – the one who lives in Denmark. We'll need her address too. I just know it is somewhere near the sea – Elsinore.'

Asta blinked. Then slowly began to nod. He was right. Of course he was – it was time to leave Germany. Past time. They would be going to Denmark.

They left the boat well before dawn, not having slept a wink. They were overtired, hungry and desperately sad and anxious by the time they arrived at their street. They kept to the shadows, stationing themselves by a set of bins outside the apartment block across from theirs. It was a well-practised move from years of being pranksters and hiding away from Mutti and their old cook. Even so, when they saw two officers stationed outside their building, it was all they could do to stop themselves from crying out.

Asta leaned back against the wall, fighting for air, well out of the officers' sight. 'They're waiting for us,' she breathed in horrified realisation.

Jürgen nodded, then tipped his head to the right. 'Let's go.'

They crept away as silently as possible, only daring to take a proper breath when they were several streets away.

'Now what? Can we go to the school, maybe someone can help us there?'

Jürgen nodded, and they made their way to the school, only to gasp when they saw a group of officers waiting outside there too.

'That can't be for us – surely?' she asked.

'I think it is,' he said, backing away slowly.

Unfortunately, he kicked a tin can, and an officer looked up from the school, and frowned.

'Run!' cried Jürgen, and they did, darting back up the street as fast as they could. The officer tore after them. But they had a decent head start, and the twins knew the back alleys of Hamburg better than most. They flew up a street, and entered a side door of a building that appeared locked but they knew from experience wasn't – the padlock wasn't threaded through properly. A minute later they heard boots outside the door, and they held onto each other tightly, hands clasped over their mouths. Then they heard the sound of those boots hastening away. It was some time before they unpeeled themselves from the door, and made their way out through the front of the building, racing into the city of canals.

Using some of Frau Kaplan's money they bought themselves cheap clothing from a charity shop, and a takeaway frankfurter roll from a stall near Polgo's water taxi.

They were exhausted and scared. 'I wish we could just go to Granny,' said Asta. Their mother's mother lived not two streets away, and there she had warm beds, food, and no doubt a comforting place where the twins could process what had happened.

Jürgen sighed. 'I know, but you heard what Frau Kaplan said – we can't go where they'll know to look for us.'

They spent their second night aboard the water taxi, and it was the first time they managed to sleep. In the morning, they regretted letting down their guard, as they rose sometime well after dawn to find Polgo Hausman staring at them with a look of horror on his swarthy face.

'It's you,' he breathed, as they scrambled to their feet, eyes wide with fear.

'I – er – we—' began Asta, her eyes darting to the door, signalling a message silently to her twin, who nodded.

He was a short man with a rounded belly, dark hair and full lips. He made to stand before the door. 'Not this time.'

Asta closed her eyes in horror. 'Please,' she cried. 'Just let us go – we won't bother you again.'

He raised a brow. 'You know I should turn you both in – this is breaking and entering.'

They breathed in. 'Please, Herr Hausman, we don't mean any trouble…'

To their surprise, he laughed. 'You two? Your middle names are trouble.'

They were silent, and he frowned. He acknowledged, 'At least, it used to be. Tell you what – why don't you tell me why you are both sleeping in my taxi and then we'll decide what to do with you both, hmm?'

The twins shared a look; they didn't know if they could trust him or not but they had no choice. He was bigger than they were, tending towards the burly side, and though the twins were young and fit, and could easily have outdistanced him in a race, up close they weren't exactly a match for him. Up close it was strength that mattered, which is why they'd always avoided being caught, till now.

'Did you get into an argument with your parents, is that it? Caused too much trouble back home and they threw you out?'

They shook their heads.

'Our – our parents were taken,' breathed Asta.

Jürgen looked at her in surprise, but then nodded. They might have run from Polgo and terrorised him in the past, but that was because he was the sort of man whose anger seemed more like hot air. They'd seen him laugh just as hard as they had at some of the outfits they had put on his mascot, Frederick, the stuffed gorilla.

Polgo Hausman blinked. 'Taken?'

They nodded. 'My father resisted having the names on his documents changed so they arrested him and my mother.'

Hausman stared, then closed his eyes for a moment as he realised. 'You're Jewish?'

'Yes.'

'But – couldn't you go stay with family? Why are you here?'

'We were warned that if we went home the police could take us too.'

Hausman swore under his breath. 'It's like the world has gone mad,' he said. Then he looked at them. 'Well, you can't stay here.'

They nodded. Asta reached for their small pile of belongings.

Hausman frowned. 'I don't mean on this boat – I mean here in Hamburg.'

They looked at him in surprise.

He sighed. 'I always knew you two would cause me more trouble.' Then he said something in a language they didn't understand. Switching back to German, he said, 'I can help you get out of the city – maybe take you to family somewhere else or to friends? Where do you need to go?'

'Denmark,' said Asta.

He blinked. 'Jesus.'

They swallowed, but he just shook his head. 'It's fine. That just might take some time.'

They stared at him. 'You'll help us?'

He stood thinking for a long time. It was like he was trying to decide whether he should risk his neck or not, which they could well understand.

'Yes.'

'But why?' asked Jürgen.

'I – well, I'm a bit like you – though all I have to do is keep quiet about it. Unless someone betrays me…'

They frowned, and he shook his head. 'I'm not Jewish.' He sighed. 'But, well, they've decided that people like me shouldn't exist either… that we shouldn't be allowed to love who we love.'

They stared, but he didn't offer up any explanation.

'I can get you as far as Elmshorn, I think. It'll be in a few days, so you'll have to stay here till I get things ready. There's someone I know who can probably take you through the border.'

Asta was touched more than she could say. 'Thank you, Herr Hausman.'

Jürgen nodded, clasping the man's hand, too choked to speak. The twins looked at each other. Behind them was their beloved city, with more canals than Venice. It was home, it was everything they'd ever known, and now they were going to leave it all behind. Asta dashed a tear away. Would they ever see it again? Would they ever know what home was again?

CHAPTER NINE

Snekkersten, Denmark, December 1938

Trine paused, jamming a pen between her teeth, as she looked up from the copy she was editing. She wondered, once again, why it was that the journalists always felt the need to put too many commas into things. For people so consumed with facts, you'd think that they would appreciate the value of a full stop once in a while. And it was quite possible they believed that the semi-colon was something to do with the foreign office.

She sighed, and fixed another problematic sentence. It was written by Henrik Jensen, a young up-and-coming reporter who did everything on the run, from eating, to speaking, to dressing and, of course, checking his work. She was sure he hadn't quite meant that Malmö had a new dime syndicate that was taking over the streets... she changed the word 'dime' to 'crime', and grinned. Still, she enjoyed finding the mistakes, and fixing them. Unlike her predecessor, who had quit on the spot after one of the features writers described an exhibition of the beloved visual artist Anna Ancher's work as 'pleasant' several times in the same piece. She'd thrown a thesaurus at the features desk, which had hit someone on the head. Sadly, they still hadn't quite got the memo about overused words... though Trine was quite sure no one ever used the word 'pleasant' again.

She fixed another stray comma, and took a sip of cold coffee. She needed to get through everything before the morning's deadline, which was when the *Elsinore Gazette* would go to print.

A noise outside, though, caught her attention. Her view took in the still ocean, where a lonely seagull flew past. Her eye roamed from the water to her barn door, which seemed to be juddering on its hinges.

She frowned, then picked up her shotgun, and went to put on all the items she'd only recently taken off after the short crossing to her drive. She'd kept the weapon close ever since she'd decided to walk out on her marriage, five years before – just in case Uwe came back and tried to change her mind.

From his dog bed, a golden retriever named Bjørn jumped to full alert, padding after her. The snow had been cleared earlier in the day, and Trine was careful not to make a sound. What anyone might want from her barn was anyone's guess, but thieves in winter weren't unheard of, even out here.

She gritted her teeth, then kicked the door open wide, where it slammed into the wall, making a loud crash.

There was the smallest intake of breath, and the hairs on her neck told her two things. She wasn't alone, and whoever it was was frightened.

Still, Trine did not lower the shotgun. There was no telling what a scared person might do. 'Show yourself,' she warned. 'Or I'll shoot.'

Nothing happened, and Trine kicked the door again. There was another sharp intake of breath, and Bjørn stopped growling, inching his shaggy blond self forward.

'No, Bjørn,' shouted Trine, but it was too late. He'd gone past her to a small lump in the heart of the barn. Just beyond, the dun-coloured mare, whose eyes were rolling in fear, stamped her hooves. And suddenly from behind the rearing horse a figure emerged, clothed in what looked like filthy rags, with long matted hair.

Trine blinked, then lowered her weapon.

It was a young girl.

She stood up, unsteady on weak legs. Her eyes seemed glazed and feverish. Her lips were dry and cracked.

'I-I'm sorry,' she said so faintly that Trine struggled to hear. 'I don't want to cause any trouble.' At last the words penetrated. Trine frowned. The girl was speaking German. She stared at her in shock.

'If you don't want to cause trouble why are you in my barn?' asked Trine, sharply. It had been some years since she'd spoken the language, despite it being her native tongue, so she was a bit rusty.

The girl stared at her, not saying anything for some time. Her eyes were huge, haunted.

'I – I was cold, it was late, and I didn't know if I should wake you—'

'Wake me? Why would you come wake me?'

The girl swayed on her feet. 'It took so long – to – to—'

'To what?'

'To find you,' she said, weakly. Then she folded in on herself like a crumpled shirt, into a total faint.

Trine stood for a long moment, frozen. Bjørn was barking wildly and the mare was hovering far too close to the fallen girl for Trine's liking. Finally, with shaking limbs, she set the shotgun down. She calmed the mare, easing her away from where a stray hoof might cause even more damage to the poor girl lying on the floor. Then she knelt down and picked the girl up, hoisting her over her shoulder. Her arms and legs shook from the effort, despite the fact that the small bundle in her arms was painfully thin. Trine was feeling every bit of her fifty-year-old self as there was a painful twinge in her lower back when she straightened up.

'I might regret this in the morning,' she told Bjørn. She wasn't only referring to her back.

It took some time to get the girl inside, as she kept mumbling feverishly and crying out.

Trine put her in her small bedroom, then went to fetch some water. When she returned with the glass she heard the girl mumble something and she began to thrash wildly on the bed.

'Shhh, shhh,' said Trine, coming to sit by her.

She put the glass on the bedside table and stared at the girl. She was even younger than she first imagined. Possibly only just fourteen, but not more than sixteen, surely?

She frowned. Then looked at the girl sharply as the girl's words penetrated, repeating a name, 'Jürgen.'

She lit a candle and brought it closer to the girl's face, and her heart started to pound in sudden fear. It couldn't be, could it?

The light fell on the girl's face, and it was as plain as day. Trine clutched a hand to her chest in shocked recognition. 'Asta?' she asked.

CHAPTER TEN

Hamburg, 1938

Polgo Hausman was as good as his word. Three days later, he returned, with food, clothes and a plan.

'I can take you as far as Elmshorn. From there, a friend of mine will meet us and take you both to Silkeborg.'

The twins were surprised that they wouldn't be going by boat, and asked as much. Polgo had shaken his head. 'It would raise far too many questions, trust me. Besides, this boat won't go far on the open water.'

They left at dawn, on a Sunday. The twins saw the last of their city through the back window of Polgo's small cream-coloured Volkswagen, which looked a bit worse for wear, the interior cracked and faded by the sun, the paint scratched from what looked like an attack by wolves.

'My blasted dogs,' said Polgo, in explanation. 'They would eat it if I let them – it's their dog bed during the day.'

Asta began to sneeze as soon as she climbed into the back seat, and was soon covered in long brown hair.

'It's perfect,' she said. And it was. Not that the twins had ever been particularly impressed by material possessions, but they had come from a rather wealthy home, and the sort of cars their parents' friends drove were high-end luxury vehicles. But right now, the beat-up runabout might as well have been a Rolls-Royce, to them. He handed her a tissue from the glove compartment. 'Allergic?'

She nodded. 'It's fine, don't worry.'

Seeing her now-streaming eyes, he winced. 'Sorry, there's a clean blanket back there you can lie down on. That might help.'

'It's okay, Küken loves animals, she wants to be a veterinarian some day – despite the fact that she's allergic to most of them.'

Asta shrugged. It was true.

Polgo looked from Jürgen to Asta, and they saw the expression of surprise, mixed with something like pain, but it was soon gone, and he smiled. 'Well, I hope you get to fulfil your dream one day.'

Asta looked down. Would she ever be able to, really? Would she ever have the kind of life that allowed for things like dreams again? Right now, all she wanted was to be able to see her parents again, to have a heart rate that wasn't racing as if she'd spent the whole day sprinting, and a full night's sleep – to feel that peace again that she'd known as a child, before someone had decided that everything about her and her family was somehow 'wrong'. Those were her dreams now – and they meant more than all the old ones combined.

Polgo cleared his throat, and started the engine, which spluttered into life in a series of wet coughs, before progressing on to a gentle idle. 'If we get stopped, you are Anna and Frederick – my niece and nephew,' he said, pulling out two birth certificates. 'These are forgeries – and they aren't particularly good ones, I'm afraid. There was someone who owed me a favour. A retired secretary from the home office – they should, hopefully, fool the local police but questions might get asked if we're stopped by the SS.'

Jürgen frowned. 'Why?'

'Because they're trained to spot that sort of thing.'

At the twins' blank stares, he continued. 'It's the paper – it'll give you away, it's not the same, the ink too – they're on the lookout for just that sort of thing.'

Asta took a breath. It would buy them time, but that was all. Hopefully it would be enough.

'Thank you,' she said.

He shrugged. 'Don't thank me yet.'

He switched on the radio, and backed onto the street. The station was reporting the news, and the broadcaster spoke of a world that seemed vastly different to the one they lived in. There was music, and the sound of excited speaking. Then a long ramble about their great Führer and the progress that had been made, and the beautiful country that they lived in.

A muscle flexed in Polgo's jaw, and he switched the radio off with his fist. 'Damn propaganda – how people swallow this nonsense is beyond me, they'd twist in shame if they heard what's being reported about us overseas.'

'What is being said?' asked Asta, looking at him, a small flare of hope in her eyes. It was illegal to listen – and you could be sent to a camp or put to death just for doing it.

'The truth – but I wouldn't hold your breath,' he said, pointing at the radio. 'They have a way of twisting things to suit themselves, and they just keep getting away with it.'

Jürgen was silent. It was true, what had been happening had been going on for years… no one had said or done anything to challenge it. Though that wasn't true – those who had – those who'd tried – had found themselves in prison or worse, put to death. Perhaps Polgo meant the world – or Europe – no one was coming forward to stop him.

As if Polgo could read his mind, he nodded. 'No one wants another war – so they're just giving in to him… even after he annexed Austria, I thought… surely now they'll have to act, but no.' He shook his head. 'And it's not like we can either.'

The twins stared at him. They hadn't, if they were honest, thought about how much the Nazis had affected the ordinary citizens of Germany, not really, but they knew it wasn't easy for them either. 'I've known people branded as traitors – people I used to take across the canal – businessmen, journalists, good men and women, friends – but they squash anyone who dares to go against them. The stories I've heard…' He broke off. 'Well, let's just say that they're not having an easy time either.'

He was thinking of one of the men he used to transport across the canal every week. Ludwig Gendal, an editor of a well-known Hamburg tabloid. He was a fat, jolly man with a handlebar moustache, and a shining bald spot. He used to laugh uproariously whenever he saw the latest outfit the twins had illegally dressed the stuffed gorilla Frederick in, and the two would talk about politics, books, and culture. But over the years, as the Nazi Party gained more ground, he became thin and withdrawn, and like the twins, who stopped breaking into Polgo's taxi to dress the mascot, after a while he disappeared too, until they found his body in the canal one day. Some said it was suicide, but Polgo never thought so. The last time he'd seen him, Ludwig had said something about a duty of care to the public, and that Polgo must be sure to check the paper the next day for details. Polgo had – the front-page story had been a puff piece about Hitler's rise to glory. They'd killed him and whatever he'd planned to say.

Ludwig wasn't the only one. Books by anyone who was critical of the party were burned. Intellectuals and free-thinkers had found themselves imprisoned at worst or without a job at best. You could find yourself in dire straits or lose your life simply by disagreeing, so it was safer, far safer, to go with the flow, to not question, to buy into the belief that Hitler was their saviour, the one who had turned the economy around. There was no denying he had, but at what cost? In the end what had it been worth, if Germany had to pay the price of it for ever?

Polgo changed the channel. Classical music was playing. Mozart. None of them listened.

The roads were quiet, but every car they passed made Asta jump.

Polgo looked at her from the rear-view mirror. 'Listen to me, both of you. That's not going to work.' He sounded angry, but there was something else beneath that anger. It was fear. Fear for the two of them.

Jürgen and Asta looked at him in surprise. 'W-what do you mean?' asked Asta.

Polgo held the steering wheel steady with his knees, then pulled up his sleeve.

Jürgen saw what looked like a faded black stain. The skin, faded to a dull gunmetal grey. A tattoo.

He blinked. Only criminals had tattoos, didn't they? Or was it sailors too?

Polgo saw him staring, and nodded, as if he could read Jürgen's mind. 'I didn't always operate a water taxi. When I was around your age, I was in and out of trouble so much that I make the pair of you look like saints. Two years. Ebrach Abbey,' he explained.

It was a young offenders prison.

'Anyway – like I said, it's not going to work if the two of you look as guilty as sin.'

Asta's eyes widened. 'We don't.'

He raised a brow. 'Yes, you do. You startle at every little noise. You follow every car as if someone is going to jump out and stop us,' he said. He frowned, then hissed, looking in the rear-view mirror, 'If you value your lives, start smiling right now.'

To their credit, they did.

'Now laugh,' said Polgo, who laughed as if someone had said something wildly funny.

The twins plastered fake smiles on their faces, and pretended to laugh even as their hearts clamoured inside their chests as they left Hamburg behind, while a car with the Nazi flag on either side of its mirrors sped past, its brown-shirted occupants nodding at them in return.

They pulled over at a gas station inside Elmshorn, a town on the small river Krückau, a tributary of the Elbe. It was an hour's drive north of Hamburg.

A brown delivery van with gold lettering that said HERMAN & SÖHNE was waiting.

'Herman will take you the rest of the way; it'll be a circuitous journey, based on his delivery route,' said Polgo, getting out of the car, and helping them with their small bundle of belongings towards the truck.

Herman was a large man, with blotchy skin, yellow straw-like hair, heavy shadows beneath grey eyes and a nicotine-stained beard. 'Polgo,' he said, by way of greeting. He didn't smile or hold out a hand to shake.

Polgo hadn't expected it. There hadn't been a lot of hand-shaking back in prison, where he'd met Herman. Polgo had gone the way of the straight-and-narrow, Herman, not quite so much. Still, he was resourceful, and dependable to a degree.

'Thank you for doing this.'

Herman shrugged. 'You know me, Polka, as long as the price is right… I'll muck shit all day.'

A muscle flexed in Polgo's jaw. 'Charming.'

Herman sniggered. '*Ja*, that's me, full of life's charm. Lay the grease on me.' Then he held out his palm, and Polgo placed a thick envelope on top.

Herman opened it, then sniffed. 'Fine.'

'You'll let me know – once they're safe?'

'*Ja, ja,*' said Herman impatiently, opening the glove compartment and putting the envelope inside. Then he rolled the car window down, and spat black tobacco, which trailed down the side of the van door, onto Polgo's boots. Polgo had to stop himself from jumping back. People like Herman loved to prey on any imaginary weakness. His fists clenched at his side.

Herman smirked, his teeth blackened with the tobacco juice.

His fun over, not getting the reaction he wanted, Herman sniffed. 'We'd better get a move on, get your kisses over with.'

Polgo kept a smile fixed on his face. 'Just a second,' he said, then drew the twins a little away from the vehicle. 'Look, there's no other way to put it, he's an asshole, but he should get you across the border in one piece, which is the thing I'm most concerned about.'

Jürgen clamped a hand on Polgo's shoulder. 'It's fine, that's all we care about too. Is there any way we can repay you the money at least?'

Polgo shook his head. 'Just stay alive.'

Jürgen nodded. 'We'll do our best.'

Polgo turned to Asta as Herman started to blast the horn. 'I wish I could take you myself but this is for the best – he delivers across the border into Southern Jutland, so no one will ask too many questions.'

Asta looked at him, and felt tears smart her eyes. After everything that had happened, Polgo had been the closest thing to a friend they'd had – it was hard to believe only a week had passed since he'd found them hiding on his boat; it felt like a lifetime.

'Thank you for everything.'

He nodded, then patted both their arms. 'Thank me when you're there and you're safe,' he said again. 'Good luck.'

They nodded. Herman honked again, and the loud horn made the twins jump.

'Get in,' he told the twins, who hurried over, everything they owned in a small bag in Asta's arms.

They watched Polgo reverse, his old cream Volkswagen speeding down the road. 'Get in the back,' called Herman, 'and don't touch the food – if I catch either of you stealing, I'll go Chinese on you,' he said, then made a motion with his palm as if he were slicing off a hand.

Asta itched to tell him that the Chinese weren't the only ones who did that but she kept her mouth shut.

They nodded, and Jürgen turned to open the van door at the rear. Only to gasp.

There were people already inside.

Jammed alongside tins of sweetcorn, peas and carrots, bully beef and jars of sauerkraut and paper packages full of cured meat, were four adults. Closest to them was a thin man, in wrinkled clothes and an oversized brown jumper. He stared back at them, dark eyes blinking, and frowning. He had liver-spotted olive skin and thinning grey hair, with long side curls on either side of his face, which he tugged at anxiously. He was wedged in next to a woman with reddish hair, tied up with a silk scarf. She had bulging brown eyes, protruding teeth, and a mouth that had deep lines on either side of it. Despite this, there was a kind of faded elegance to her, like an old rose. Her scowl, however, deepened as she stared up at the twins as they got inside. Behind them was another couple, a plump woman with a dark eyes and black scarf tied around her head, and a man with short curly hair, apart from his own long side curls, and glowering back eyes.

The tall man closest to them came forward first to close the van door after them, and to welcome them as the truck backed out onto the open road, offering a tight, forced smile. 'Welcome,' he said. 'I am Hershel Blocman.'

The twins introduced themselves. 'Asta and Jürgen Schwalbe.'

'Good to meet you,' said Hershel. 'The man at the back there is Lars. The sisters are Ruth and my wife, Esther,' he said, indicating the scowling woman next to him in front. The others nodded their heads in greeting, their smiles not reaching their eyes.

But the woman named Esther just shook her head, her expression full of scorn, which they soon realised wasn't necessarily directed at them. Her Polish-Jewish accent was strong, and Asta could see that she was wearing what seemed like several days' worth of clothing all at once. Instead of greeting them or introducing herself, she glanced from them to Hershel, venom in her mouth as she spat the words, 'What is this idiot thinking – that for the right price, he'll try to smuggle all the Jews out of Germany, along with what…' She picked up something next to her. '…jars of sauerkraut, what a fool!' Then she muttered, 'It won't be the jars that shatter – it'll be us, when this all goes horribly wrong.'

CHAPTER ELEVEN

Snekkersten, Denmark, December 1938

Trine watched Asta as she slept.

The girl tossed beneath the covers, her dark blonde hair a matted, sweaty nest, her skin flushed from fever. She was delirious, and mumbling, though it was hard to make out what she said. Some words were uttered over and over again, like Mutti, the German word for mother, and Jürgen.

Trine took a small, clean sponge, and dribbled water over the girl's cracked and dry lips. Then felt her forehead, which was hot to the touch.

She frowned and checked over Asta's thin frame for anything that might explain her fever. Trine had been a volunteer nurse in the First World War and had been stationed just outside the Somme in France, in a makeshift field hospital, that she still sometimes dreamt of at night – sometimes she was sure she could still smell it. It never really left her.

The trenches had made her stomach iron-clad, although the experience had broken her ex-husband, Uwe, turning the good-natured man she'd married into a violent drunk. The man she'd married had never come back from those godforsaken trenches. She didn't necessarily blame him; it had come as a shock when he was conscripted, like so many other residents of Southern Jutland, to fight for Germany. It was one of the reasons they'd moved to Elsinore after the war. What neither of them had realised was that the past comes with you, unless you fight like hell to let it go.

Her little brother, Fritz, was Asta's father, and he'd served in the war as a medic. It was he who had told her to leave Uwe, not long after he'd married Frieda. 'Come back to Hamburg, you can live with us, divorce isn't the scandal it used to be…'

Which wasn't strictly true, people still talked, not that Trine cared, but she'd still had hopes that Uwe would change back, that there would be some day, some moment when he returned to who he used to be. She sighed as she stared at Asta; if she had, would this have been her fate too – escaping one kind of hell, only to find another as they were doomed to try and escape their own country?

Bjørn sniffed the girl, his golden head nudging her as if he could urge her to wake by sheer will.

Trine patted his silken head. 'She'll be all right, boy, we just need to give her some time, I think. That and some medicine.' There were no lesions, bites or scratches. 'Probably some kind of bug or flu,' she said aloud, as she continued to examine her niece.

'Oh, Asta,' she breathed, her heart in her mouth, as she watched the feverish girl thrashing in the sheets. She fetched a bowl of clean water and a towel, and bathed her forehead. She moved down to rub the flannel across the girl's neck, where an ugly red scar made her pause.

It looked like a knife wound – and like she hadn't got it that long ago either. The skin was still raw and pink. What had happened to her?

She swallowed, thinking of her brother, and the rest of their family back in Germany. 'If you're here, where are the others?'

*

It was a long night. Trine spent most of it in the chair next to her bed watching the girl, while she finished the rest of her editing. Bjørn chose to keep the girl company, stretching himself against her hip. She patted the dog's head and glanced at the clock on the bedside table. It was just after 5 a.m. The sun would only rise for a brief hour in the afternoon during winter but still, the lights across the harbour gave the illusion of dawn. That and the sounds of life outside beginning to stir in the old fishing town. She liked it here; it was quieter than in the city. Here she felt like she could breathe.

She checked on Asta, who was sound asleep, and frowned. She put on her boots, and squared her shoulders. It was time to ask for a favour. Bjørn lifted his head up off the bed. Trine put a finger to her lips. 'Stay here, keep watch.'

Then she put on her heavy parka and waterproof, fixed her woollen fishermen's cap over her long grey hair, and, flashlight at the ready, made her way out into the cold December morning.

Lisbet Sørensen opened the door in her floral pink nightgown, with the sort of scowl that Trine was sure had terrified the children she used to teach. The retired schoolteacher had short, steel-grey hair and sharp blue eyes, which widened when she saw her friend.

'*Hej?*' she said, then seeing Trine's face, frowned. 'Do I need to fire up the getaway car?'

'Not yet,' said Trine, a small smile on her face. Despite Lisbet's stern appearance, she was an ideal friend – not particularly sentimental, on the surface at least, but she was loyal to a fault. Lisbet had made the last five years – since she'd walked out on her marriage and moved here – bearable, and they had a habit of walking along the beach in the mornings together.

'Coffee?' she offered.

Trine nodded. '*Tak.*'

To her credit, Lisbet didn't ask too many questions as she handed her friend a cup of coffee a few minutes later. She simply listened and nodded as Trine explained what had happened.

'She's got a fever – I'm not sure how serious it is – and she's malnourished, which can't be helping.'

'No,' agreed Lisbet. 'Malthe can make her his first round – I'll go wake him now.'

Malthe was Lisbet's husband, and the local doctor, who refused to take up retirement.

Trine nodded. 'Thank you. As far as I can tell there's no sign of sepsis or infection…'

Lisbet's eyes widened. 'That poor child.' Then she shook her head, staring out at the stretch of sea in the distance, but seeming to see something else. 'I can't believe she showed up in the middle of the night like that.' Her expression hardened, and she sighed, inclining her head toward the small radio that was on the windowsill. 'I suppose I can, really. She's been driven out – like the others, most likely.'

Trine nodded. 'Yes.' A single word, but one that didn't, couldn't convey the horror and magnitude of what had happened recently in Germany.

The papers were full of it. Reporters at the paper she worked for had covered it too. It was news that shocked the globe; millions around the world had woken up horrified to learn about Hitler's latest treatment of the Jews. The November Pogroms – or Kristallnacht as it became known – was the most horrific event reported so far, and the shockwaves were still being felt. As thousands of Jewish-owned stores, homes, buildings and synagogues were invaded by SS forces and attacked with sledgehammers, destroying over seven thousand businesses, assaulting and arresting over twenty thousand Jewish men, who had been sent off to concentration camps. It wasn't enough that their citizenship had been taken away from them; they were to be broken and punished for ever daring to exist.

In Trine's own paper, the headline had read, GERMANY'S DISGRACE.

Her hands shook as she put the coffee down. She had tried to telephone her brother, Fritz – tried to find out what was going on. Offering, once more, a place for the family to stay. She'd sent several letters to him over the years – ever since Hitler had been made chancellor, suggesting he consider immigration, but his response had always been the same. 'We will, just not yet.'

That 'yet' had arrived, hadn't it? But still she never heard anything… till Asta appeared at her door out of the blue.

Her own parents were long since dead, and when she hadn't heard back from Fritz – and found that the phone line had been disconnected – she'd tried her sister-in-law's parents, but there had been no response from them either. The only thing she'd heard about her family was the arrival of her niece, half-starved and delirious, hiding in her barn the night before.

She stood up, tried to push back the fear. 'I need to get to the office, else the paper won't be able to go to print – would you mind looking after her while I'm gone?' she asked Lisbet.

'Of course, go – she's in good hands, I'll fetch Malthe now.'

Trine fidgeted on the train ride into Elsinore, feeling torn; should she have sent someone with the pages instead – what if Asta woke up without her being there? She knew Lisbet would take care of her, but after everything the girl had been through, it felt horrible to leave her like that. As it was, she hadn't seen her niece and nephew since they were eight or nine. Where was Jürgen? It seemed so strange to see the one without the other. Fear sat heavily in her chest when she arrived at the printer's, where the typesetters were already beginning to pull their hair out.

'What kept you?' grumbled an old man named Karl with arthritic joints, who'd been setting the plates for the *Gazette* since he was a boy of twelve. He had a rolled-up cigarette lodged on the side of his mouth that he moved from one side to the other, as he sized her up with pale blue eyes as sharp as a tack.

'Overslept,' she said. It was simpler to lie.

He raised a brow, but didn't say anything. She was usually here just before dawn, especially on a print day. He shrugged. Karl wasn't the type to pry.

Despite Trine's worries, the morning moved quickly and she talked him through the changes. He'd already pre-loaded some of the pages, and they went through the copy together, with help from his assistant, a young man with short brown hair and a lazy smile named Oleg.

After a few hours, Trine was finally able to leave, before putting in her application for a few days' personal leave.

Her boss, Henk Garsman, was shocked. 'A holiday? You?'

She'd once come to the office with a temperature of forty-one degrees and a nasty cold. Henk had wished she hadn't – particularly when it laid him low a few days later and he couldn't move from his bed. It made him wonder just what kind of superwoman powers she had to be able to work when it was a labour for him to simply breathe…

'It's a personal matter – some things I need to take care of.'

He frowned, pushing up a pair of wire-rimmed spectacles as he peered at her with his deep brown eyes. 'Is it Uwe – do you need someone to come—'

'No, it's nothing like that – it's a family thing, my niece, she's not well.'

He nodded. 'Take all the time you need. We can manage.'

She raised a dark blonde brow, and he grinned. 'This paper has run for sixty years without you, Trine Anderson, and we muddled along somehow – we can get a temp for a while.'

She narrowed her eyes. 'Anna Herstman?' she asked.

He sighed. 'Anna Herstman.' Anna had been their last sub-editor, the one who'd thrown a thesaurus at the features department.

He seemed to reconsider. 'Actually, I'll send her the pages at home.'

Trine nodded. 'Probably safest,' she agreed.

Back at the house, the smell of soup made her mouth water. The windows were steamed over, and the air was rich with the scent of garlic, caramelised onions and freshly baked bread.

'You didn't have to do this,' she said by way of greeting to Lisbet, unwinding her scarf from around her neck, and placing her shoes on the rack by the door. Though she was grateful – Lisbet's vegetable soup, made with beef shin, tomato and lentils, was the one of the best comforts in the world.

Lisbet shrugged. 'I know. There's fresh bread too. I always like to have something to do, you know me.'

Trine did. '*Tak.*' She knew that she'd made it more for Asta than her and that touched her. 'How is she?'

'Still sleeping. Malthe says she has bronchitis. Like you said, she's half starved – all the bones on her ribs are showing; she probably hasn't eaten anything much for days.'

Trine winced.

Lisbet looked at her. 'She's going to be all right, don't worry.' Then she picked up a small pad where she'd jotted down some notes. 'Malthe's left some instructions for you – though he says with your experience, most of it you'll already know. Lots of rest, fluids, that sort of thing. He'll come and check in on her again in a few days. But she should be fine.'

Trine thanked her, grateful for the vote of confidence. It had been some years since she'd cared for anyone besides herself, and the dog. And Bjørn looked after her more than anything.

Lisbet turned the gas down on the hob to let the soup simmer, then dipped a spoon in the pot, blew on it, tasted it, then added more salt. 'She was speaking German – in her sleep, I don't understand it much, even after all these years with you trying to teach me, but she kept saying one word over and over.'

Trine frowned. 'What?'

'Jürgen.'

'Oh,' said Trine, and pain flashed across her face. 'That's her twin.'

Lisbet's eyes widened. 'Her twin,' she breathed. 'Oh…'

Trine nodded, fear clutching her heart. 'They were inseparable.'

After Lisbet left, Trine went to check in on Asta. She was sleeping more comfortably, probably from whatever medication Malthe had given her. She was still flushed with fever but she had been put in a clean nightdress by Lisbet and had been given a wash, for which Trine was grateful.

Her hair, though, was still a dank and matted mess.

Malthe's instructions were to spoonfeed her soup and water and to crush her medicine into the food. There was an awful lot of it, which he'd left on the bedside table, with instructions written in Lisbet's neat schoolteacher's hand.

Bjørn lifted his golden head and yawned, his heavy tail thumping the bed at seeing her. She smiled, and patted his head. 'You haven't left her side, eh, boy? I think she'll like you when she meets you. Come on, let's go, you have needs too,' she said, and he jumped off and followed to the kitchen, where she left the door open so he could do his business, while she filled a bowl with water and went to fetch towels, shampoo, and a brush. It wouldn't make Asta feel much better, but it would help Trine – like Lisbet, she too found it hard to be idle.

A bark from outside made her pause, and she popped her head round to investigate. Bjørn had his lead in his mouth and he darted toward her hopefully.

'Oh, Bjørn, I'm sorry, not today.'

There was the sound of footsteps and Trine startled; they were coming from the direction of the barn, but whoever was there remained in shadow. Bjørn let out a low bark that soon turned into a joyful yipping sound when he recognised who it was.

'It's just me – sorry,' said Oliver, a young man of around seventeen with short blond hair and green eyes. He was Lisbet's son.

'My mum sent me over – told me that I should look at the animals. I've checked in on Millie already and fed her.' Millie was Trine's horse. There wasn't much call for a horse out in Snekkerston, but considering Uwe had threatened to shoot her when she said she was leaving him, the horse had come with her. Oliver rode her on the beach sometimes.

'I can take Bjørn for his walk.'

Trine leant against the door of her house, and smiled her first smile of the day. 'I swear that woman is a mind-reader, thank you.'

Oliver grinned. 'I don't mind. Bjørn and I are old friends.'

'That you are,' she agreed, as Bjørn did his best to jump into the boy's arms, like he had when he was a pup. Oliver laughed at the dog's antics.

Then he looked at Trine, and his face suddenly turned serious. 'Is it true – what my mother said, about your niece?'

'What part?' asked Trine.

'That she's here – that she escaped from Germany?'

Trine nodded. His eyes were full of questions, but she had no answers, for either of them. Perhaps he realised he was prying, because he looked away, giving Bjørn his attention.

'I hope she gets better soon,' he said, then fixed the lead onto the dog's collar, and the two started to walk towards the harbour.

'Oliver?' Trine called.

He stopped, and looked back at her,

'My niece – well, I don't know what's she's been through – but I can imagine that—'

'It's a lot,' he agreed.

She nodded. 'She might need a friend, someone her age.'

He nodded. 'I can be that.'

Trine washed Asta's long dark blonde hair, rinsing it with a jug of warm water over a basin. There were twigs and mud and all sorts of things tangled up into the strands, and she had to replace the water twice. Part of her was worried about waking her, while another wished she would, so that she could get answers to all the burning questions that were tormenting her. Where were Fritz, Frieda and Jürgen – why was Asta here by herself, and so thin, so sick, so starved?

What had happened?

But she didn't wake, and Trine was left alone with her thoughts, as she diligently teased out every snarl and snag in her niece's hair. It took ages, until finally it lay around her pillow in a soft, clean halo, drying quickly in the heated room.

Oliver brought Bjørn back not long afterwards, and the dog settled next to Asta, giving the girl several sniffs, at her new fresh scent, before resting his head on her lap.

Trine smiled, then stretched. The night before she'd slept in the chair; tonight something a bit more permanent would need to be arranged. She lived in a single-roomed cottage, so it would have to be the kitchen bench. She got up and fetched a pink-and-green patchwork quilt that she'd made several winters before to pass the long, dark hours, along with a pillow from her wardrobe. She was just about to leave, when she felt a prickle on the back of her neck; she turned around, and blinked in shock.

Asta was awake, and staring at her hard. She sat up, like a wounded, frightened animal, touching the nightdress, and looking around in distress. She was half-delirious, mumbling, and terrified. Nothing she said made sense.

'No, stay in bed,' called Trine, as Asta crawled out of the bed, frantically searching for something. She knelt beneath the bed, looked behind the door.

'Asta?' asked Trine, coming forward slowly, her hands raised in peace.

The girl whirled around, swaying on unsteady feet. A hacking cough ripped through her tiny frame, and she bent over, almost double.

Trine rushed over to help her.

'Mutti,' cried Asta, calling for her mother, then seemed to look uncomprehendingly, glancing around. 'Where am I?' she asked, blinking. 'Who are you?'

'It's me, Asta, your aunt, Trine,' Trine replied.

'I need to go, Mutti, I can't stay in bed,' she said, not hearing, not understanding. 'We just left him, I have to go find him,' she said, looking up at her, with her eyes glazed, and full of tears. They spilled over, coursing down her cheeks. 'Oh God, we just left him. I screamed and screamed for him to turn back, to stop… but he wouldn't, he just wouldn't,' she moaned, her thin body shaking with fierce sobs.

Trine felt her body go cold, her knees start to shake. 'You left who, Asta?'

Asta didn't say anything, she just sobbed all the harder.

Trine shook her softly. 'Tell me.'

Asta stared, unseeing, at her.

'Jürgen.' Then her face crumpled again. 'Oh, Mutti, he – he's dead.'

CHAPTER TWELVE

Elmshorn, 1938

'Esther, stop it,' hissed the tall man who'd introduced himself as Hershel as the van backed out onto the road for the next leg of their journey. They were heading across Germany, towards Southern Jutland, which bordered Denmark. He had long grey curls either side of his face, known as *peiyes* in Yiddish, which marked him out as a Hasidic or Orthodox Jew.

'You'll scare the kids,' agreed Ruth at the back.

The man called Lars, another Hasidic Jew, shook his head. 'But she's right. We paid good money for this, everything we owned. I knew he was a stinking, thieving liar… but I didn't take him for a damned idiot.'

'Well, what do you expect?' snapped the Ruth. 'He is the only one who agreed to take us. No use complaining now, especially after what happened.'

'What happened?' asked Asta.

Esther looked at her in shock, as her patterned scarf slipped further away from her hairline. She pulled it back, impatiently, adjusting it with a clip.

Privately Asta wondered if they were so worried about being caught, shouldn't they try to blend in more? They seemed so concerned that the twins' presence put them in danger – but with their fake birth certificates and normal attire, surely they stood a better chance as their appearance didn't announce who they were before they even opened their mouths?

'You aren't serious – you really haven't heard?' she breathed. A hand came up to clutch at her throat. Asta could see, just at the edge of a neckline, several thick clumps of what looked like rows of necklaces. Had she put on every piece she owned?

Asta shook her head, and Esther and the others began to speak, almost all at once. 'A few nights ago, the SS organised a nationwide attack – a pogrom – against all Jewish-owned businesses,' said Lars.

Ruth began to quietly cry. 'Oh, poor Ida.'

Esther whispered to the twins, 'Her friend, he owned a stationery shop. They killed him,' she said simply, and the stark horror of that washed over them.

'So much glass, so much blood,' said Hershel sadly. 'A night of crystal – that's what they're calling it because of all the broken glass – and all the broken lives. I heard the commotion – I used to work as a lawyer before they changed the laws so I'd got a job in my friend's shop, a tailor's. Well, luckily, we'd closed for a break. As I was coming back I saw the SS – saw them dragging out men and women… we heard tell they were taking people to detention camps in the east.' He sighed and closed his eyes. 'Concentration camps. I managed to get home by sheer plain luck and that's when I told my wife, Esther, that we need to get out, *now.*'

It was the same with Lars and Ruth. He ran a tobacconist's in Hamburg. 'Luckily, Esther phoned just in time, and I slipped out of the back door,' he said, looking up at his brother-in-law. So much of their escape had been about luck that day. 'How come you didn't hear about it?' he asked the twins. 'I mean, it was everywhere – even on our horrible censored stations.'

Ruth nodded, and looked at the twins in confusion. 'If not that – why else are you leaving Germany?'

'Well, our hell started a week earlier,' said Jürgen.

Asta nodded. 'See... they took our parents to Dachau – the labour camp – for not changing their paperwork. That's what one of the nurses at the hospital where they both worked told us.'

Hershel was surprised. 'They were still allowed to work?'

Asta nodded. 'Our father served in the war so he was allowed to practise medicine until the laws changed again but they got around that by taking jobs at the Jewish clinic; our mother is a nurse. I think they knew it was only a matter of time before even that loophole was taken away – even so, he refused to change his passports and paperwork.

'Well, anyway, the nurse that came to warn us, told us that the SS were looking for us too – to take us, perhaps, we weren't sure... so we ran away, we didn't hear anything about the pogrom. We're from Hamburg too,' she added.

Esther swore. 'Filthy bastards.'

'Your parents didn't think to use the Kindertransport?' asked Ruth.

'What's that?' asked Jürgen.

'Well, in Europe and other places where news has been spreading about Hitler and his plans – his hatred of the Jews – there have been so many refugees seeking asylum they're starting to organise refugee transports of Jewish children. They can't help everyone, but they're trying their best to get the children out to places like England,' explained Hershel. 'The churches are big drivers for it.'

Ruth nodded. 'That's what we just did. We have a friend, a priest, who lived near us – he arranged for a family to take our boys. Soon they will be on their way to England. Imagine, even the Catholics want to help us! Couldn't your parents have done the same – a friend in England, maybe?'

The answer was of course, obvious, considering the twins were sitting in the back of a van with them.

'We didn't know anyone there,' said Asta, simply. 'Besides, up until the morning they were taken, our parents still believed that things would get better.'

Esther sighed, then to her absolute shock, she reached over to squeeze Asta's hand in sympathy. 'Oh, *zeeskeit*, sweetheart. It wasn't just them – we were all like that. No one considered that the alternative was true. That things were only just starting to get worse, and now...' She didn't say what they were all thinking: now it might be too late.

'Shhh, don't speak like that,' reprimanded Ruth. 'This is it – this is our chance. We just have to trust it.'

Esther raised a brow. 'I think for that to happen we'll need a miracle.'

'Well,' said Ruth, her dark eyes teasing, 'I'd say Jews were long overdue a break, wouldn't you?'

And to the twins' surprise, all of the adults began to laugh. When Herman banged on the wall from the driver's side and shouted at them to keep it down, they pressed their hands into their mouths and laughed harder still. The twins didn't. For two people who had spent half their lives pulling practical jokes, they couldn't think of anything less funny than this group of people desperately wishing for a miracle to save their lives.

They made one stop in the night, and to their horror, it was to collect even more passengers. Their driver, Herman, didn't let them get out or relieve themselves. He simply scowled, and shoved them back with a thick red arm, ushering in another couple with his other. 'Too many eyes, come on,' he said, as a frightened couple of around the twins' grandparents' age climbed inside the crowded van sometime after dawn. This time, Esther didn't give them a hard time, but she looked mutinous all the same.

The couple's names were Sofie and Goran Rosenberg. Unlike the others, they weren't Orthodox Jews, nor were they from Hamburg but the countryside around it.

Somehow, they all made space for them amongst the tins and jars and brown paper packages of cured meat.

It wasn't long before they too were sharing their story. 'Goran hasn't worked for three years; he was let go, like so many others, I suppose. We've got by through my sewing. But they stopped that – when they found out that some of my clients were gentiles, they took away my sewing machine. What right did they have to it? It was my mother's…'

'Thieves,' spat Lars. 'That's all they are. They took money from my tills too – I mean, how do they even justify any of it?'

'Because to them we are not people,' said Esther.

'What animal sells tobacco?' asked Lars.

And they grinned.

'You're right, though,' said Sofie. 'It's not logical. I heard they've got these pamphlets that tell you how to spot a Jew, and what to be afraid of – they're making us out to be monsters.'

'It's true,' said Asta and told them about what had happened at her school – how the teacher had tried to make her think that she was inferior due to the size of her head – and how incredible her mother had been, not simply dismissing it, but actively proving to her how ridiculous that theory was. Asta bit her lip and looked away. Jürgen held onto her tightly. It hurt to mention their beloved *Mutti*, to wonder where she was, what was happening to them.

'They're the monsters,' said Esther.

Jürgen and Asta nodded.

'It used to be so different, I never felt like an outsider – like anyone thought we were less. Most of our friends were "gentiles",' said Sofie, curling her fingers into air quotes. 'And then one day we were these outsiders, something to be scorned, and mocked or feared.'

'Oh, well, you're lucky, of course, that was simply not the case for us,' said Esther, touching her headscarf. 'I don't think we've ever really been treated all that well. Polish Jews – and Hasidic to boot, we weren't even treated well by our own kind – they saw us as something beneath them, like people stuck in the past – and now…' She broke off. 'Well, it made no difference, did it? We're all fleeing from our own homes in the middle of the night.'

Asta looked at the floor. Esther was right. It was true – hadn't she once looked at them – the more Orthodox Jews who refused to give up their old-fashioned ways – as the 'problem'? Hadn't she only a few hours ago judged them for refusing to change – to give up their head coverings and side curls? She could see how silly it was thinking that her family or any others who didn't display their religion were 'more German'. The line separating them was made of thread. No matter what you felt in your own head or heart, the Nazis painted them all with the same tarred brush.

No one said anything. What was there to say? They'd all learnt about the cost of prejudice, and how damaging it really was.

Sofie opened up a satchel; inside were two cake tins. She lifted the lid off a green tin with a triangular pattern along the rim, which was full of small pies. 'They're chicken and mushroom,' she said, handing the tin round. Esther pressed one into each of the twins' hands. 'Eat, eat. You two look half-starved,' she said, with a frown.

At Sofie's frown, Esther explained, 'They're not ours – in case you think you're thinking of judging us for that.'

Sofie looked up, aghast. 'I – I wasn't.'

'Esther!' barked Hershel in reproach.

She put her head in hands for a moment. 'Forgive me, I feel so much stress it is leaking out of me, sitting like acid bubbling beneath my skin turning everything I say sour. I just meant…' She gave an apologetic half-smile, half-grimace. 'If they were mine, they'd probably be a bit fat... there's no way I would ever be accused of having children who look hungry.'

Sofie nodded. 'I understand.'

Asta looked at Esther in sympathy. 'My *mutti* would probably have reacted the same way, don't worry.'

Goran agreed. 'Sofie is like that too. The grandkids are always saying, "*Bubele*, enough..."' He smiled, then looked at the twins. 'Who are your parents?' he asked, looking at Ruth and Lars, who shook their heads.

'Not ours. Esther would be flat on her back if she said that to my face about my children.'

Jürgen shook his head. 'They're not here,' he said, and the twins once again repeated their story.

Goran frowned, like he didn't know what to say.

Suddenly there was a loud bang, as a tyre went over something, and the van swerved off the road, hitting gravel and skidding uncontrollably. They held on to each other, fighting to contain their terror as the van, at last, came to a stop. Esther breathed into her knees, panting heavily. There were white finger marks on Jürgen's hand from where Asta had clutched at him.

After several anxious minutes, they could hear loud, angry voices. It sounded like arguing. There was someone else there – someone with Herman.

'Quick,' whispered Lars, pulling a large blanket from the back and throwing it so that they all grabbed a corner to huddle together beneath it.

Jürgen looked at Asta, her hand clutched in his. What good would the blanket be if someone checked? They were like children playing hide and seek, thinking no one could see them if they had their eyes closed.

Asta's heart began to beat so loudly in her chest it was a wonder that whoever was outside, barking at the driver, couldn't hear it.

A pair of boots seemed to make their way towards the rear, and there was a bang on the back of the van. They all jumped.

Asta thought she might be sick.

There was a rattle, and Esther clutched onto her tightly – later there would be red lines on her hip from where she pressed her hands against her skin, but right then she felt nothing. They all held their breaths, watching the inside of the door through the small holes in the knitted blanket, as the handle moved. Then someone said something, low and muffled.

Finally, they could hear Herman's drawling, sarcastic voice. 'I have a delivery for Frau Grudel, in an hour – her husband is in the Party – he's a rather senior officer. It's for a shindig they're having tonight to celebrate. Will I tell him that his men will have to wait, because you were checking his stock? I believe he is patient man, oh wait… no, he's not. So, I'll be sure to mention your name. Officer Smidt, is it?'

There was the sound of someone swearing softly, a veiled threat to 'get that tyre sorted immediately, and not keep Grudel waiting,' and then suddenly, blissfully, the booted heels started to retreat.

They dared not release the breaths they were holding until the van started to move again. The blanket was torn off them, as Goran jumped up and vomited the chicken pie he'd wolfed down only moments before on the side of the door.

No one said anything. They all understood.

At some point, despite their fear, despite wondering if the officer was following them, and wondering just where in Germany they were now – not being able to see a thing, with no windows or word from Herman, with the monotonous, never-ending drive, and the stuffy air – the twins fell asleep on each other's shoulders.

*

Asta woke up with a start a few hours later, as the van swerved on the road, then started to reverse, as if the driver had made a wrong turn. As the van continued on its way, they wondered what the time was. 'How long have we been driving?'

'Almost two days for us,' said Esther to their surprise.

It was hot, the air stale and rank from the press of bodies, combined with the overwhelming stench of dried vomit. They were thirsty, having finished their water hours before. Lars was the first to give in and open a jar of pickles, and take a sip of the water inside, which he passed along. 'If he's not even going to let us stop for water or to relieve ourselves, well, then he can't be surprised.'

Asta and Jürgen took a small sip of the pickle juice, Herman's warning riding strong in their minds. But it was the press of their bladders that was the most urgent. Asta crossed and recrossed her legs, uncomfortably.

The men had created a makeshift bucket from a box, which they lined with sheeting, and she didn't know what might be worse, using that or making a mess on the floor. The smell was already bad, and there was nothing to do but close her eyes when someone used it as there was nowhere to turn to offer any privacy.

Jürgen squeezed her fingers. 'I'll make sure no one sees if you use it,' he whispered.

She squeezed his hand in return. It would be impossible, but she appreciated him saying it nonetheless.

She was just gearing herself up to risk it, when the van came to a sudden, grinding halt. They all gasped. There were rapid footsteps, and then the door was pulled open fast.

'Change of plan,' said Herman, wrinkling his nose at the smell that wafted out to him, a stench that incorporated sweat, urine, unwashed bodies, vomit and fear. 'Get out.'

They all blinked up at him, shielding their eyes in the early afternoon sun. They were parked alongside a long stretch of open woodland.

'How long are we stopping for?' asked Esther. 'It would be good to stretch my legs for a bit.'

'Stretch them forever,' he snapped. 'Didn't you hear what I said? I *said*, change of plan – you'll be stopping here. It's close enough,' he said.

They all blinked at him in shock, as his words dawned on them in horror, and as one they turned and stared at the forest that swept out from them.

'Where are we?' asked Asta. 'Are we across the border?'

He scoffed. 'Are you stupid – you heard what happened – as soon as I'm in Flensburg, they'll come for me. There's no order for Grudel, and by the time they realise that… well, they'll come to investigate.'

At their looks of confusion, he explained about the officers. 'They'll be waiting for me at the border, I can guarantee it. No doubt they've telephoned ahead. You want to be killed?'

Hershel frowned. 'Where have you taken us then?'

'Just outside the Marienhölzung forest,' he said.

'What?' cried Lars. 'You can't be serious – we're miles away.'

'Barely – a few hours' walk perhaps.'

'Are you mad?' said Esther, looking from him to the forest behind. There were tall beech, spruce and alder and it went on for what looked like miles.

'Where is this?'

'North Germany, in the Schleswig-Holstein area – not too far from the border,' explained Goran, as the other men started to argue with Herman. Hershel looked ready to throttle him.

'Look, I don't know what you want from me but this is the best I can offer.' Then he swore, muttering something about ungrateful pigs as he made his way back to the van, saying over his shoulder, 'I've got you this far – that way is Denmark,' while pointing through the woods to the right. 'If you keep walking you'll get there.'

He was gone before Goran could even tell him that his sense of direction was wrong; if they went the way he'd pointed they'd just enter further into Germany.

The adults were still arguing, and Asta and Jürgen were getting impatient. 'We need to get off the road. Now, follow us,' said Asta, heading towards the trees.

There were a few cars that passed, looking at them oddly, with their assortment of luggage, and their strange dress.

'The further we go, the better – or like that idiot says, stay out here and make it easy for them – it's not exactly like we look like regular Germans out for a stroll.'

Hershel touched his side curls, and nodded.

'Come on,' said Goran.

The temperature began to drop as they made their way into the woods, rushing as fast as they could into the unknown.

They would need that miracle now more than ever.

Goran had a book of maps, which he unearthed from his satchel sometime later. 'I brought this along, in case this happened.'

Asta and Jürgen weren't the only ones who were impressed.

Not long afterwards, he'd plotted out a route. 'It'll take us a couple of hours, I think. We'll have to stay off the main roads as we go from this forest into countryside.' He eyed the older members and said, 'Maybe a bit longer. If we make it that far, we'll cut through the border to Frøslev. I'm hoping that there will be less patrols, if we do it after midnight.'

'How sure are you?' asked Lars.

He looked up at him. 'I have never been less sure of anything in my life.'

Which wasn't at all reassuring.

Lars swore and kicked a rock out of his path. 'Yet we are meant to follow you because you have a book of maps?'

Hershel clamped a hand on his brother-in-law's shoulder. 'Do you have another suggestion?'

When he kept quiet, Hershel shrugged. 'Well, then – we will use the only one we have. Hopefully, whoever patrols around here takes a break at night.'

They were already tired, hungry and thirsty from their ordeal in the van. But they'd been walking for close to an hour when they heard the sound of running water. Asta and Jürgen raced towards it, cupping handfuls of the cold, fresh liquid into their mouths. It was sometime after they'd slaked their thirst, and washed their faces and hands, getting rid of a week's grime, and longing for a proper rinse, when they heard the sound of dogs barking.

They turned to each other in horror.

CHAPTER THIRTEEN

Goran was pale, his hand shaking as he cupped it around an ear.

Then he tested the wind by licking a finger and seemed to visibly calm, muttering, 'Upwind, they're on the other side of the river, thank God for that.'

'How do you know that?' demanded Lars, who looked sceptical. 'It sounded like they're coming from the right to me – what if we run straight into them?'

Goran frowned at him. 'If you go right, you will. Trust me: I worked as a forest ranger for twenty years, before they told me I couldn't anymore. I know how to keep us safe. Grab your things, quickly – once those dogs catch our scent, we'll be done for.'

Asta's heart thundered in her chest, thinking how lucky they were to have Goran with them. She'd agreed with Lars – it had seemed to her that the sound was carrying from the right.

The twins followed quickly after him. The others didn't move as fast. They had more to carry, and Asta fought the urge to scream.

'We need to get moving, that way!' Goran pointed ahead.

The air was cold and crisp; their breath made clouds of steam as they hurried, hampered down by their possessions. They didn't dare leave them behind, as it would announce who they were just as well as their actual appearance.

Their booted feet crunched onto dead leaves and mud, and they kept their chins tucked towards their chest as they raced into the wind, their eyes alert, startling at every sound, every rustle from the forest, which stretched before them.

They'd been running for ten minutes when Goran at last allowed them to stop. It wasn't just the older folk wheezing and struggling for breath. Even Asta and Jürgen held their knees as they gasped for air. Jürgen helped Sofie, who he'd fairly dragged along with him.

Goran opened his rucksack again, and brought out a battered pair of binoculars. 'There,' he said, pointing a gloved hand in the distance.

They frowned, until he passed it around, and they could see a small wooden structure far away. There were patches of frost on its roof.

'Is that a cabin?' asked Sofie, hopefully.

'It's just a pergola – it helps to keep out the rain and the other elements,' he explained. 'It's a simple structure for campers. I think it will serve us well for now.'

The sun was beginning to set as they walked the rest of the way between the tall woods. They heard the caw of a crow, and watched as a squirrel darted across their path, as they approached the structure. It was very basic, with no walls but at least it had a roof, and it offered, for now, at least, a place to rest.

'What if the dogs come this way?' asked Jürgen.

'It's unlikely – they were heading away from where we were, but at least from here, we'll be able to see them,' said Goran, handing over his binoculars again, and Jürgen realised they were on higher ground, looking down towards a valley. 'These are good lookout points,' he explained.

No one said anything for a while, then of all people, Esther looked at Goran and said, 'It was a piece of good fortune, the day Herman picked you up – thank you.'

They all nodded.

Goran inclined his head, then took out something wrapped in green canvas and tied with leather strings, which he began to unravel, to reveal what looked like some kind of kit for starting a fire.

'You're welcome – but it's no lucky accident, if that's what you're wondering. It's one of the things I paid every last cent we had for.'

They looked at him in confusion and he explained.

'When Herman said he'd take us – Sofie and I – across the border, I said if anything went wrong, this was where he should leave us. Well, actually I asked for Klues Forest, which is further up, but I suppose this is as close as he could get us. It's not where I would choose to cross the border – especially at my age.' He ran a hand through his hair, looking weary. 'Trust me. They're not my woods, of course, but with my experience, well, we have a chance.' Then he looked at the map again, and said, 'Though, whoever it was with those dogs turned us around. I'm thinking a change of plan; midnight might not be best – let's wait here and start again at dawn. We'd be best to keep to the more densely forested path as much as possible, and avoid as many urban areas and open countryside as we can. So we'll head towards Klues… and then on to the border town of Kruså, God willing' he said, as if thinking out loud.

Asta blinked. She'd thought that Herman was just pure evil, taking Polgo's money, leaving them on the side of the road to fend for themselves, but this made her feel a little better.

'Herman *knew to take us here?*'

'He knew.'

Then he looked up at them all, puffed out his cheeks, and rubbed his eyes. 'This was going to be near impossible, if it had been just Sofie and I…'

Sofie nodded. 'My knee is badly damaged – I should have had an operation but it was hard to get treatment and the Jewish clinic was so full,' she said.

They looked at her and Goran nodded. 'If it wasn't winter or we were all fighting fit we could cross over to Denmark in a few hours, but with the patrols and our age and number – it's likely to be double that or even longer as we're going to have to be very careful. I didn't factor in all of you.'

No one said anything. None of them had factored in the others either.

Sofie touched one of his bags. 'Also. We might have to take turns in the tent.'

'At least you thought to bring a tent,' said Esther, pulling out a toaster from her large carpet bag. 'I don't know what I was thinking with this!'

Despite everything, they all laughed uproariously. 'What?' asked Esther. 'I like this toaster, who knows how well they make things in Denmark?'

Which made them all laugh harder still.

As night fell, and they were greeted by the sound of an owl from one of the nearby trees, Goran switched on a flashlight, which he handed to the twins.

'Asta, Jürgen, will you look for dried twigs and leaves, anything to start a fire?'

'Won't that be dangerous?' asked Jürgen. 'A fire, here?'

Goran nodded. 'Yes. But the temperature is dropping substantially. We'll need it – even if we all huddle together there's a danger we could get hypothermia – these woods get freezing at night. It's a calculated risk we'll have to take.'

The twins shared anxious looks. They weren't alone in wishing the odds were more in their favour, but dying of hypothermia while trying to escape wasn't something they wanted to try either.

They combed their nearby surroundings looking for dry twigs and leaves, but most of it was wet and swollen from the weather. They kept searching, the flashlight's beam casting its rays low to the ground. It was nearing midnight, and above their heads the moon was bright amongst the stars.

The cold, cloudless night displayed a blanket of stars, and with the wind whistling amongst the trees, it was beautiful. It seemed somehow unfair that the world could still contain so much beauty after all that they had been put through – all their pain and fear, all their anxiety for their future – but then, the world had stopped being a fair place for the pair of them long ago.

After twenty minutes, however, they had a change of luck, and found a stack of firewood beneath a tarpaulin alongside a metal drum.

'Probably something the rangers use to keep warm,' said Jürgen wisely, as they began filling their jumpers with the wood. It was good to have this moment to themselves. To talk freely, and to process all that they had gone through so far.

'Polgo is going to be so mad when he finds out that the driver left us,' said Asta. 'I wish there was some way we could let him know we're all right.'

Jürgen nodded, adding another piece of wood to his pile, ignoring his concern that they weren't all right, not yet. 'Come on, let's head back.'

After a while he said, 'I was thinking,' looking at his twin, her face drawn in the harsh flashlight which highlighted the deep shadows beneath her eyes, 'what are the chances of us all getting across safely?'

Asta frowned. 'We can't think like that, Jürgen.'

He stopped walking. Some animal skittered past in the dark, possibly a rat, thought Asta. The sound of insects increased in volume, loud and humming, alongside the howling whistle of the wind.

'We *have* to, Asta. You heard what Goran said – about how much longer it will take to cross than it should. I like them too but two of them are really old – older even than our own grandparents – you saw how hard this was on Sofie. And the others aren't exactly young either – if we have to get away fast, how quickly would they be able to move?'

'We did it today, Jürgen – we got away just fine from those dogs,' said Asta, feeling disloyal.

'We got lucky,' said Jürgen, his mouth set in a thin line. 'We were on the other side of the river, and those dogs hadn't caught our scent – otherwise…' He broke off. 'Well, let's just say, I'm not sure we would have made it.' He sighed. 'Not with Sofie anyway.'

Asta frowned. She didn't like where this conversation seemed to be going.

'I mean, we're young, fit, we could even… I don't know, climb the trees if we needed to.'

'What are you saying?' asked Asta. 'You want to leave them behind, after all they've done for us?'

'What have they done?' he asked.

Asta's mouth fell open in shock – it wasn't like her twin to be so obtuse, so unfeeling. 'Without Goran, we'd probably have been caught by now – put on the first transport to Dachau or some other godforsaken concentration camp where they send the children…' It was a horrific thought – but she faced it nonetheless. If the Nazis had decided that the best place to send the Jews they didn't want was these holding camps, why stop at the adults? Besides, they were sixteen now… hardly children anymore.

Jürgen made a dismissive sound. 'Goran is really smart, I don't mean him.'

'Well, we can't pick and choose who we want, Jürgen – then we're acting just like the Nazis, choosing who you deem "good enough". He wouldn't leave the others and neither will I.' She shot him a dark look. 'How far would we have got without Goran – are *you* a forest ranger? Do *you* have a map or things to make a fire? A tent? I don't even know which direction Germany or Denmark is from here,' she said in a low hiss, near hysterical. What Jürgen was suggesting was insane.

'Calm down, *Küken*. I can't believe you'd compare me to those monsters. I'm not saying anything. I'm just worried – it's the Orthodox ones, I mean, Jesus – Hershel and Lars with those side curls – and they're both wearing bloody yarmulkes – while we are trying to flee the country! Not to mention the women with those headscarves.'

Asta could feel the blood starting to flood her cheeks. She wasn't often angry with her twin, or felt like she didn't know him, but the things he was saying were genuinely making her mad.

'That's exactly the sort of horrible prejudices we used to have – all of us, at home, Papa, Mutti – thinking we were better than them,' she snapped, whirling around to face him, several logs falling to the ground in her anger and disappointment.

Jürgen grabbed her shoulders. 'That's not what I mean – yes, we were pigs for thinking those things – and fools, but what I am saying, if you'll calm down, *Küken*, is that if we're going to cross the border, we can't all do it looking like we're runaway Jews!'

She glared at him, then suddenly, all at once, her anger fizzled out. He was right, of course he was. 'Well, we can't just leave them.'

'I know – I just – it's going to be tough, is all I'm saying. I don't really want to leave them, I'm just—'

She felt her heart soften. He was just scared, that was all. So little of this was within their control now. They were going to have to put their faith in a bunch of strangers, one of whom looked like she could barely walk to the shops on a high street, let alone the many miles it would take to make it across the border. As for the other four, well… he was right, they couldn't leave them, which meant they were going to have to ask them to disguise themselves.

'Somehow we're going to have convince them that there's no way they'll get across looking as they do. I mean, they must realise that, somehow – it's not like they'll blend in.'

It was a horrible thing to ask someone to disguise their religion in order to survive. It was not the sort of conversation any child wanted to thrust on an adult. But it was unavoidable.

As if reading her mind, Jürgen said, 'They either take this seriously enough to realise that they will have to do something they are not comfortable with or we will have to decide to do something we aren't comfortable with, *Küken*. We will have to choose each other – and go our own way; you're my only family now, and I will not have them risk your life. I'm sorry if that makes me sound prejudiced or selfish or whatever, but that's just how it has to be, okay?'

Asta looked at him, saw the tears tracking down his face, then nodded. He didn't like the idea any more than she did. She nodded.

When they got back to the shelter, Goran made short work of the wood and a fire began to crackle within minutes. They waited for the flames to grow and for the warmth to spread.

'I'd give anything for a cup of tea,' whispered Esther, holding her long, thin hands out to the flames.

'Or a cup of coffee,' suggested Sofie, rubbing her eyes, and stifling a yawn. It had been a long day. A long few days and weeks, really.

'We should take it in turns to keep watch,' said Hershel. 'Rotate between the men, that sound fair?'

They all nodded.

'I'll take the first watch,' he offered.

'Before we turn in,' said Goran, looking up at him, then feeding another log to the flames, 'I'm sorry to say this but—' He stopped, seeming uncomfortable. For all that he'd taken charge over the past few hours, it was clear that conversation wasn't his forte.

'Look,' he tried again. 'Forgive me, but for us to have any chance – we can't look as if we are Jews on the run,' he said. The twins shared relieved looks; of course, Goran and Sofie must have been thinking the same thing as them... they were glad they didn't need to be the ones to say it. 'I don't mean to cause offence, I respect you all – but right now—'

To their surprise, Esther sat up and nodded. 'You're right.'

Lars looked like he was going to object, but she held up a hand to silence him. 'God will forgive us, but first we must help ourselves. We'd hoped to have been through the border into Copenhagen by now,' said Esther. 'We never thought we'd have to be... refugees.'

Then she opened her carpetbag at her side, and fetched a pair sewing scissors, which she handed to her husband, who took them as if it were a viper about to strike.

'I shouldn't have to do this,' Hershel said. 'It's against all human decency – against all the laws of the Torah.' He took the scissors and did nothing.

'Can't you tuck them away, beneath a hat?' asked Jürgen, having a change of heart at the older man's suffering.

'He could hide it under a hat,' suggested Goran, 'but then if we're stopped and he is asked to remove it...'

Esther scowled, then snatched the scissors from him. 'Then they put him in jail or worse.' And before he could say anything she'd opened the blades wide, and snipped off one of his side curls.

He'd ducked, but it was too late. The long lock of grey hair fell onto the ground, and he stared at it, mute with shock; the pain on his face was hard for Asta to watch.

'There – if there is anyone to be struck down it will be me, for the crime of trying to keep my husband alive,' said Esther, going around to do the other side, with tears in her eyes, and a shaking hand. Hershel nodded, and closed his eyes – the other was gone before he'd even shut his eyelids.

Esther took the scissors then looked at her brother-in-law. 'Now your turn, or do you want me to do it for you?'

'No,' said Lars, and he took a deep sigh and snipped his off too. Asta was heartbroken to see the tears in his eyes.

It was Ruth who removed her headscarf first, revealing shiny black hair tightly wound into a bun at the nape of her neck.

Goran looked at her. 'You know you could do that in the morning; it is freezing now,' he said to lighten the mood.

'Better I get used to it sooner,' she said.

No one said anything, but they all nodded. Somehow, it seemed she wasn't just speaking about her appearance, but the change that was happening to them all – the one they had been forced into, against their will. They either faced it now, or they turned back. Esther took hers off next, revealing reddish-brown curls.

No one said much after that, and Hershel took the first watch, for their new dawn. The men and women went to bed shivering, and cold from more than just the loss of their coverings.

Asta woke with Jürgen shaking her arm. '*Küken*, wake up, they've heard people – hikers, probably; it's time to get going.'

She sat up, rubbing her eyes. Her back was sore from sleeping on the cold floor of the shelter, her hip frozen and numb, as she hadn't moved once during the night; she'd just fallen into a deep sleep, despite everything. It was the first time she'd been able to lie down properly since they'd been aboard the canal boat, and she'd sunk into a dead sleep, but she was wide awake and alert within seconds, pushing herself up off the ground, grabbing her small bag.

The others were already waiting. Goran was doing his best to mask the evidence of the fire which had grown cold now. He kicked it apart, using a large bunch of leaves to disguise it.

'Obviously, any trained dog will still find it but it might look like it isn't that recent.'

They nodded. Everything Goran did, they were realising, was with the aim of being careful, to manage risk.

In the daylight, Asta almost didn't recognise the others, as the men had abandoned their yarmulkes, their side curls burnt in the fire the night before, and the women looked strangely naked without their headscarves.

Hershel was busy filling in a mound of earth, which looked almost like a small grave. He kicked the last of the mud and twigs over it. At Asta's puzzled expression, he explained, 'We've got rid of anything that doesn't make us look like we are day trippers – out on a hike, or camping for night or two – especially if they stop and check us.'

Ruth had red-rimmed eyes, and Lars was trying to console her. 'There were family albums and other mementoes that we were forced to leave behind. We'll just have to make new memories,' said her husband, clutching her hand tightly.

'At our age?' she asked. But she nodded, and seemed to stand up straighter. 'Of course, you're right.' Asta saw her stuff a handful of photographs into her brassiere. Seeing her looking, Ruth wiped her eyes and said, 'Just a small handful to remember everyone. I suppose that's all I need, isn't it?'

Asta nodded, then looked at Jürgen, her heart in her mouth. They didn't even have that – not even one photograph. What she wouldn't give for even that – because what if they never saw their parents again?

Asta looked away; perhaps Esther had read her thoughts because she gave her shoulder a squeeze, and said, 'I can be the most sentimental of all, but the way we remember is here,' she said, touching her heart. 'No one can take that away – no one, you hear me?'

Asta nodded, sucking in her top lip, and catching hold of herself. Then she blinked in surprise as she stared at Esther. She looked as if she'd lost half a stone overnight; gone were her multi-layers, and Asta couldn't see the lumps of jewellery beneath her neckline.

Esther shrugged. Then touched the bag at her hip, in silent explanation.

The twins nodded at each other. This might actually work.

They'd started their walk in the cold dawn air, feet slipping in mud and wet leaves. The wind howled up a storm, bitingly cold, and rushing at their ears, making them walk with their heads down. It was a struggle to hear each other, and it was only when Jürgen shook her arm that she realised that he was trying to get her attention.

She looked up and frowned, only to gasp aloud, her heart starting to thud – there, not ten metres away, was a group of officers with dogs who were snarling and snapping against their leads.

They had walked, silently, straight into a spider's web.

CHAPTER FOURTEEN

Ruth started to shake and Esther looked ready to faint. Polgo's words inside his small, beaten-up Volkswagen, his concerned eyes staring at her from the rear-view mirror, echoed suddenly in Asta's head. 'For this to work, you're going to have to become actors.'

Startled, they'd stopped walking, but Goran quickly said, 'Keep moving,' as the officers hadn't, as yet, made a move towards them.

Asta swallowed and elbowed Jürgen. 'Tell everyone to smile – quickly, pass it on.'

Esther looked like she would rather vomit, but Asta quickly explained, with a casual smile fixed in place. 'We have to act as if we are a normal family on a hike. Do it, Esther,' she hissed, and suddenly, the older woman did. The others followed suit.

'More natural,' hissed Jürgen. 'Like we're having fun, not like we're cornered rabbits. Relax, walk slower,' he said – because Ruth and Sofie had begun to walk very fast. 'Remember we are not in a hurry.'

Suddenly, one of the officers stepped forward, blowing into his hands. He was tall and thin with bright ginger-coloured hair.

'*Morgen*,' he greeted them. 'It's cold enough,' he added. 'Can I ask what business you have here?'

Hershel was the one who answered, in a voice quite different to how he normally spoke – it was posh, Berlin-sounding; gone were all traces of his faintly Yiddish-accented diction. 'Losing a bet, officer,' he said with a grin.

The others echoed Hershel with nervous smiles.

The officer looked nonplussed. 'How's that?'

'Well, you see, last Christmas, my grandchild Jürgen, here, dared us that if I got the wishbone in the chicken that we'd do a hike – the whole family, on the first day of December. Well, as it's hard to get the whole family together in that month, we decided on November… anyway, that's not the point. See, he bet me that I couldn't handle the Nazi youth camp training in the wild, and as I'd had too much sherry, I said of course I could. Well, anyway, he said that if he got the bigger piece we all had to go so he could put me to the test, and like an idiot I agreed – and *mein Gott*, he was right. Totally unprepared, I slept in a tent for the first time since the war…'

Jürgen tried to look as if this wasn't news – to be fair, the twins were made for this sort of thing. 'He was a medic in the army. I mean, he's good at rolling bandages, but he couldn't even light a proper fire! Took him forty minutes.' Then he grinned. 'Course, I can do it in five. I have all the badges,' he bragged. Which was perhaps a mistake.

The officer, who had been smiling and nodding, frowned. 'You are in the Hitler Youth – but where is your uniform? Surely all young boys your age wear them at the weekend?'

Jürgen swallowed, and it was Asta's turn to lie. 'My fault.' She rolled her eyes. 'Oh he's so proud of that uniform, just loves to wear it everywhere, he wouldn't even let the maid, Sara, iron it when he first got it – remember?' She nudged her twin like it was a big joke. He shrugged.

'Course not!'

The officer with the dog came over to see what the hold-up was. '*Heil Hitler*,' he greeted, and the six of them reciprocated, trying desperately to make it seem as if that was natural.

'Sara?' said the other officer. He had dirty blond hair and a thin moustache. 'That sounds like a Jewish name.'

Asta nodded, then put on a whiny, snotty voice. 'Oh yes – she was, well, a half-Gentile anyway, but Mother was right in getting rid of her. I mean, no one wants *that* around the house, do they?' Then she shuddered as if in revulsion. 'I mean, around food and things…'

The officers both seemed to nod. Asta could feel Esther's ire bubbling from here; she hoped she would control it.

'Anyway,' Asta carried on, 'like I said, he was being insufferable telling me that I couldn't make it in the boys' league like him, even though the girls' one is almost as good, and of course,' she said, forcing down the bile as she did, 'I'm very happy to grow up and be a good…' She racked her brains, trying to remember everything she'd been told at the girls' school in Hamburg, everything she'd overheard. '…mother of German children – but' – she laughed – 'he's still my twin, and I can still beat him at any race.'

'Liar,' said Jürgen.

Asta just grinned.

The first officer, the one with ginger-coloured hair, seemed to be warming to them, but seemed also to think that now was the time for a lecture on a woman's place. 'It is not your job to beat the men in your life, *fräulein*, but to help them be the leaders they were born to be.'

Asta managed, somehow, not to snarl, and put on a serious face. 'Oh, yes of course, I know that – but that is why I will push him, you see – he can't be allowed to lose to a girl. I can't help teasing him sometimes, but I do know he's better than me,' she said between gritted teeth, wishing she could kick both officers in the shins and run away.

Finally, he laughed. 'I like this one,' he said, then looked at the first officer. 'Real spunk – we need that in girls too. Reminds me of Gisela – my own sister, she's a rascal.'

Asta's knees almost buckled.

'So, what did you to the uniform?' asked the other, the one with the thin moustache.

'Well, I tried it on, and then I teased him by dressing up like him. See, I put my hair up,' she said, demonstrating – the resemblance was very close, 'and I told him I was going to go compete in the races...' She grinned. 'Anyway, he got very mad and tore after me. We wrestled and I got mud all over it; unfortunately he'd only packed that one for his visit to our grandparents,' she said, looking at Hershel, who grinned in return, nodding along in agreement.

'So, I'm in his bad books,' Asta finished.

'Very bad books,' said Jürgen.

The blond officer frowned. 'The uniform is a solemn symbol; I hope you have learnt your lesson – it is not something to be mocked.'

'Oh, I have, sir.'

They were still staring at them when Sofie clinched the deal by opening up her bag, and taking out one of the two tins – this one green with a red-and-white striped lid. Inside were biscuits. 'Would you like one?' she asked.

'My thanks,' said the blond one, taking a large golden biscuit. 'My God, this is lovely, try it,' he said to the other, who reached for one, his eyes widening as he chewed. 'That texture, so rich, what's in it?'

'Lard,' said Sofie. 'It's blessed,' she joked.

'That it is,' he replied. 'Well, good luck with your journey, you might want to stick to the path,' he said. 'There's a place a few hundred metres that way where they have a coffee station. Tell the other rangers there Officer Krill sent you.'

'Thank you,' they said, and left, hardly daring to breathe, shocked that they had managed to pass as Gentiles.

After a while, when their hearts had finally stopped thundering in their ears and the officers were no longer in earshot, Sofie looked at Asta. 'I can't believe you said that – about your "maid" Sara.'

Asta nodded. 'I know, I'm sorry, I just thought—'

'No, child, don't get me wrong, it was brilliant.'

'Why was that brilliant – she sounded like some horrible racist!' cried Esther.

Hershel shook his head. 'She sounded like one of those privileged German Youth League girls who have been taught to hate Jews. It was probably what saved us. He was on the fence till then,' said Hershel. 'Trust me, I was a lawyer, I could see it – that was the moment he started to believe.'

Lars shook his head. 'Nothing like a bit of racism to form a bond,' he said, sarcastically.

'I almost thought I'd die when she said that, I was so shocked,' said Esther. 'I actually forgot for a moment that you were Jewish yourself.' She laughed. 'Who knew you two were such good actors?'

Jürgen smiled. 'We're not good at a lot of things,' he said, 'like mathematics or playing by the rules.' He grinned. 'But pulling pranks, well, that's our speciality.'

They all returned his grin, but nervously.

Jürgen looked at Sofie, and said, 'Those cookies – that was very clever too – but why did you say the lard was blessed?'

To their surprise, she laughed. 'Because I make it with *smaltz* – Jewish lard, and it had been blessed, by a rabbi.'

They all howled with laughter.

When they were quite sure the officers weren't nearby, Goran led them away from the path, doing more of the heavy thinking that they'd been growing accustomed to from him. 'If we head the way they suggested, it is still technically on the route I planned, and we'd still cross the border – perhaps later this afternoon, depending on how many miles we can cross today. However, I don't relish the idea of drawing more attention to ourselves. We had a lucky escape. I wouldn't want to push it.'

'But we pulled it off,' said Esther, with a frown.

'Yes, because – and I'm sorry to say it – we did most of the talking,' said Hershel. 'Three of us have accents that no amount of pretending to be a Gentile is going to disguise.'

Esther blinked. 'I don't have an accent – I wasn't even born in Poland.'

'You do,' said Asta, slightly shocked at her. 'I'm sorry – but you do sound like you speak Yiddish or come from Poland, and I'm sure they will be looking for that.'

Esther frowned.

Ruth and Lars looked like they wanted to argue, but Goran held up a hand. 'I don't want to fight, I'm just trying to think of a way to get us out of here in one piece, all right?'

Hershel frowned. 'I agree – we don't all sound the part. I can put on a posh German accent, though, like I did before. I was used to the prejudice, trained to spot it as a lawyer. But, well, I am wondering – isn't it sometimes easier to hide in plain sight than way out off the beaten track?'

Goran shrugged. 'You aren't wrong – but I do think the accent is a concern. So we'll take a vote?'

Almost everyone agreed with Goran, apart from Hershel and Jürgen, the latter having seen the sense of the lawyer's words. 'I feel like the officers would expect to see us, and wouldn't think to question us again, that's all I'm saying.'

'But what if we're forced to speak – I can't do what Hershel did – I didn't even realise I sound different,' said Esther. Then she paused and frowned. 'I roll my *r*s a bit, I hear it now, a little, *ugh*, but even so – I can't unlearn how to talk in a day, can I?'

'No, you can't,' said Goran. The others nodded in agreement, and they diverged from the route the officers had suggested, taking a wilder path.

They walked through the empty forest. Asta's thin city boots had split apart at the toe, and the cold from the leaves and mud from the ground turned the skin swollen and soft. Seeing her dilemma, Sofie, who was hobbling herself, each step an agony, sacrificed a long woollen scarf. 'Tie it around that boot; it won't dry your feet out – for that we'll need a fire, and a rest – but at least no more water will get in,' she said, helping her to make a firm knot.

Asta was touched, considering how much pain the older woman clearly was in. Like Asta, none of the others had proper hiking boots. This was another reason, Goran pointed out, that it was a good idea they didn't stay too near people. Their story had worked, possibly due to the surprise factor, and the quick thinking of Hershel and the twins, but how long before any of the rangers or officers – who were patrolling the area, no doubt, for just such a possibility of Jews fleeing into Denmark – started wondering why a group of people who'd apparently been preparing for a camping trip for a year hadn't thought to wear any sensible shoes?

After two hours' walking, Esther begged for mercy. 'I'm sorry, please, I am not used to this pace, I am exhausted, can we stop, just for a moment?' There were tears in her eyes, and she was pinching the skin around her forehead. 'My head is pounding.'

'My knee could use a break too,' said Sofie, who looked like she was on the verge of collapse.

Goran frowned. They hadn't got very far as it was – what should have taken an hour or so had been twice that, which made their predicament all the more dangerous. It was clear he wanted to press on but his face softened when he looked at her. He hesitated.

Then sighed. 'Okay, just for an hour – enough for a small rest, and to eat something, and then we really must carry on.'

Esther released a sigh of relief. 'Yes, please, just a moment.' Then she pointed up ahead at a nearby running stream. 'Let's get some water, then we'll be able to think. There's no use pushing on if we drop down later.'

Hershel and Goran shared a worried look that Esther didn't see. Possibly that a few hours' walk was nothing. The longer they stretched it out, the greater their chances of being found.

Asta and Jürgen went to collect water in a tin can that Lars provided, then they sat down gratefully around the fire that Goran built, feeding the small flames into the log pile they'd found near the shelter the day before.

Asta blew onto her hands, trying to warm them up, and gratefully took a seat on a fallen log. She was frozen and her feet were throbbing in pain due to her thin, impractical shoes; she could quite cheerfully have curled up right then and had a nap, but the pressing need of her aching feet drowned out all else. She unwrapped the scarf around her thin leather boot, which was soaked in mud and leaves, the smell boggy and foul, and curled her knee up to her chest as she tried and failed to undo her sodden laces. They'd swollen from the water and heat of her feet, and the knot she'd tied to keep them tight around her ankle was proving impossible to loosen. Her fingers were stiff and plump from cold, and as much as she tried she couldn't get the knot undone. Like Sofie, she felt close to tears.

'Hey, *Küken*, give it here,' said Jürgen, picking her foot up and plopping the muddy boot on his knee, where his nimble fingers made quick work of the stubborn knot and laces. She looked up at him gratefully, and he winked at her. 'You loosened it for me.'

He pulled off the offending shoe, only to pull back, wrinkling his nose. 'Good lord, that's nasty.'

She pulled a face. 'Sorry,' she said. 'It's the muddy water.' She withdrew her foot, and peeled off a thick wool sock, only to swallow as some skin came away revealing a large, painful-looking gouge.

Jürgen's face turned from revulsion to concern. 'Geez, that looks bad, *Küken*.'

Hearing him, Goran came over to investigate. 'Those shoes are just no good for this,' he said.

Asta raised an eyebrow. 'Well, it's not like I knew I would be doing a hike, Goran.'

He nodded, then frowned. 'That's going to be a problem, though.'

Asta shook her head. 'I'll be fine. I'm tough as old boots.'

Jürgen grinned. 'Course you are.'

Sofie, however, shook her head. 'Asta, if you leave it like that it'll get infected.' She looked at the others. 'Has anyone got any iodine?'

They shook their heads. Esther sighed, and put her head in her hands. 'I thought to bring all my jewels, and a stupid toaster, but not medicine. I'm a foolish old woman.'

Asta reached out for her hand. 'Well, if we had electricity and bread, I know what I'd want more.'

'A hole in the head?' asked Esther, and they all grinned.

Asta looked up at the others. 'I will be fine. I think if we can just let my socks dry out a bit and I'll pour some water over my feet to clean them – that will help.'

Sofie sighed, then lifted her long black skirt, and unrolled a thick woollen stocking to reveal her knee.

They all gasped. It was swollen – almost double in size to what it should be. The old woman's hands shook, as she touched it and flinched.

Esther looked at her in horror. 'You can't walk on that!' she cried.

'I'll be fine,' said Sofie, who tried and failed to roll the stocking back over the swollen joint.

Hershel shook his head. 'I think we'll just have to rest for today, you can't walk like that.'

Sofie shook her head. 'I'll be fine.'

Esther touched her shoulder. 'It's not just you. I can't.' She was holding her head. 'It feels like my brain is going to explode. I can't even see straight.'

Goran sat down, nodding, admitting defeat. 'We'll camp here tonight,' he said.

CHAPTER FIFTEEN

Sofie handed around the last of her biscuits, and Jürgen took out a brown paper package that was filled with smoked German sausages, and another full of cheese. 'Courtesy of Herman, the not-so-magnificent,' he said, with a grin.

Esther looked, then gasped aloud. 'But that's pork,' she said, shocked, as Jürgen broke off a piece and put it into his mouth. The others declined as he tried passing it around.

'I know,' said Jürgen, 'but we don't have a lot of food, and we need to keep our strength up.'

Lars, who'd been sitting next to him, stood up suddenly, a frown between his eyes, and made his way to the stream, walking fast.

Jürgen blinked, following him with his gaze. Esther looked at the boy. 'He's a very devout man, Jürgen, but I'm sure he'll calm down.'

Jürgen felt wrong-footed. 'I'm sorry… I didn't even think.'

Sofie patted Jürgen's arm, but Ruth frowned at the boy. 'Well, you should. You don't think he's been asked to do enough? You know what the Torah says about hair on the side of men's heads – if you cut it you let the devil in? No, of course you don't because clearly you were never taught about your own religion! Yet knowing what he did, and that there was no other choice, he did it. But this – this offal – he does have a choice over. How stupid are you to offer a man like that pork?'

She stood up on with all the dignity she could muster, touched her head, then frowned as her hand encountered uncovered hair, and went to join her husband, a scowl on her face.

Esther made a tutting sound after her. 'Sometimes it's hard to remember you're supposed to be the grown-ups.' Then she closed her eyes, and touched her chest; they could hear her muttering a silent prayer in Yiddish. Then she held out her palm. 'I'll have some – it's not as if there's anything else.'

It was sometime later when Lars and Ruth returned, both looking sour.

Jürgen tried to apologise once again, but the man wouldn't look the boy in the eye. He flung something onto the ground instead. It was bloody and covered in mud.

'It's a hare!' cried Esther, sitting up straighter to see the bloodied creature.

There was still a small piece of sausage on her lap, which he seemed to glance at with disgust. Esther's hand came out quickly to mask the offending item.

'But we have no hunting gear – how did you manage that!' said Hershel, looking impressed.

Lars narrowed his eyes at them all, then spat. 'He was injured, in a trap. I put him out of his misery. There is always the option to look for food. The Lord provides – if you are willing to work, to use your brain; the Devil offers the easy way out,' he said, giving a pointed look at Esther, and glaring at Jürgen. Then he began to skin the hare in a few quick movements. Esther opened her mouth, perhaps to ask how he'd learnt to do that, but closed it again. She looked at the bit of sausage like it was poison.

Feeling mutinous, Asta picked it up and shoved it into her mouth. 'Delicious,' she said, looking at her brother. 'I seem to recall that the Lord helps those who help themselves.'

The look Lars shot her afterwards was one of pure venom, and she almost regretted her behaviour.

As Lars prepared the meat for a spit using twigs, Goran looked at him, and shook his head. 'You should hope that whoever's trap that was doesn't come looking for his dinner.'

Lars placed the fire-sharpened stick through the animal's flesh, then put it above the flames. 'No, they'll just see that the animal escaped.'

Goran stared at him for some time, his eyes dark and incredulous. Lars intercepted the stare and snapped, 'What?'

'Are you an idiot?' asked Goran.

Lars's eyes flared in sudden anger. 'What?' he hissed.

'I said, are you an idiot? You took a hare out of a hunter's trap. Someone who lives around here, maybe, or a ranger, even – or someone from border patrol,' he said, indicating the many hectares of wood. 'And left a bloody trail for him to follow.'

Lars made a huffing sound of dismissal. 'Pfft, what trail – it's not like I dragged the creature here!'

Usually mild-manned, Goran looked ready to hit him. 'Get up,' he said.

'What?' asked Lars, looking from the meat that was beginning to roast, to look at Goran in disbelief.

Goran strode around the fire, towards the path where Lars had come from. Then he knelt down and picked up some leaves and sniffed. 'See?' he said, roughly, holding out the pile towards the other man.

'What? I see some old muddy leaves. You know what, Goran? You can drop this macho act now, I'm getting tired of it.'

Goran blew out his cheeks in frustration. He shoved the leaves towards Lars's face, rubbing one of them with his fingertips, which came away smeared with blood.

'Blood droplets – and I can guarantee they are evenly distributed from wherever you took the creature to here. Fresh blood,' he emphasised.

'So what!' said Lars. 'Do you expect me to be impressed?'

Goran bunched his hands into fists. 'No, Lars, but I expect you to use your brain – if there is a tracker or hunter out there they will know that you helped yourself to their trap!'

Ruth shook her head. 'How could they possibly know that?'

Goran stared at them as if they were idiots. 'No animal tracks. No smudged blood or disturbed leaves from paws – but what they will see is two pairs of human footprints. A wounded animal that gets itself free – well, they might let it live to see another day – though truth be told, most wouldn't want it to suffer with a broken paw, but I can promise you that if they know that you have taken their kill from their trap they will hunt you down, like the thief you are.'

'Surely not?' said Esther, who'd paled.

Goran looked at her. 'Are you willing to take that chance?' He shook his head. 'I'm sorry, but it's time to go.'

'What?' exclaimed the others at once.

'But I thought we were spending the night,' cried Ruth.

Goran began to kick over the fire, to Lars's outrage. 'Hey, stop that! I'm cooking here!'

Goran shook his head. 'You have this fool to thank if whoever's trap that was comes looking for that hare. We'll be in trouble, and we'll have a hard time trying to explain ourselves.'

'But surely they won't come back for what's in the trap straight away,' said Asta, who thought she might cry at the prospect of putting her wet socks and shoes back on, and walking on her poor, swollen feet. 'I mean, don't they check only every few days?'

'Not always,' said Goran. 'And I, for one, do not want to be some sitting duck in case they come here and find us roasting their kill, which is what this fool is asking us to do,' he spat, his anger suddenly overcoming him.

Lars had clearly had enough, and he stood up quickly, and took a swing at him.

Hershel and Jürgen dove at Lars, holding him back. Esther had jumped up with Asta, in case it turned into a fight, but Goran just stared at Lars, then wiped a trickle of blood from his lip. 'You should have just taken the boy's meat,' he said. 'You're a fool.'

'Well, if I'm a fool I think that's it, then – time to go our separate ways.'

Goran shrugged. 'Fine by me.'

'No,' cried Esther. 'You're both acting like idiots. You know that the pork was a step too far – none of us were actually starving. Let's just let it go, we need each other.'

Lars tore his arm out of Hershel's grip, then went back to the nearly extinguished fire, and started to rebuild it again. 'Ruthie and I will stay here.'

'Lars,' said Ruth, in a shocked voice, blinking her dark eyes, and staring at Esther in horror.

'We will rest – and in the morning when no trapper has come here looking for his imaginary kill, we will continue,' said Lars, not looking at the others.

Hershel frowned. 'But you don't know the way!'

Lars scowled. 'There's signs. We'll be fine. Or you could stay with us – your *family*.'

Hershel looked at Esther and the two exchanged concerned looks. 'Lars, come on now – just drop this – we need Goran. He's the one with the map, for goodness' sake. We need each other.'

'No,' Lars said. 'I don't need someone telling me what to do – making me give up my *peiyes* – no. But you made your choice – water over family – whatever, good luck, have a nice life.'

'Lars!' barked Hershel. 'You're being selfish, acting like a scolded little boy. Even Jürgen didn't act like that, even though he had every right to feed himself. Act like a man.'

Lars swore, and Esther shook her head. 'Please, Lars, don't be like this.'

'I'm not being "like" anything.'

Hershel shook his head. 'Come on, Esther. If Goran is right, well, we can't wait here for some trapper to find us. Lars, come or don't come – we are not choosing a stranger over you, we are choosing to live – and to get away from a potentially dangerous situation.'

Lars scowled but said no more.

Esther and Hershel waited a full five minutes in a thick, soupy silence, Ruth darting anxious glances at them, until finally they both reluctantly joined the rest of the party and rushed after Goran.

It was tense, and the mood remained low as they continued on their journey without Lars and Ruth. Goran didn't say anything as he moved silently through the late afternoon, cutting a path through the tall spruce. The only sound was the occasional whimper from Esther, and the soft moans that were coming from poor Sofie as she attempted to walk.

'We should go back,' Esther kept saying. 'I shouldn't have left Ruth. Sofie can't even walk.'

'I'll be all right,' said the other woman, who clearly didn't look it.

Hershel looked just as torn, but he kept shaking his head and repeating, 'They made their choice.'

Asta stumbled along as best she could with Sofie, who could barely move. They were hardly getting anywhere. She looked at

Jürgen, and could see how conflicted he felt, how responsible. If he'd kept his mouth shut, kept those sausages to himself, all of this might have been avoided.

They hobbled on for half a mile until a sound chilled their bones, and they stopped stock still. It was a blood-curdling scream. They turned to each other in their fright when they heard something, even worse.

A gunshot.

CHAPTER SIXTEEN

'No!' cried Esther, her hands covering her face. 'Ruth! That was Ruth, oh my God.'

'It might not be,' said Hershel. Esther looked at him, and he shook his head. They'd all heard it – a woman's scream.

'D-do you think it was the hunter?' asked Sofie.

Goran nodded. He didn't look at all happy. He hesitated, looking at Hershel and Esther. 'I don't think it would be wise to turn back.'

Esther stared, touching her red-gold hair, and her unadorned throat. Then she stopped. 'It was only one shot.' She turned and looked at her husband with hope in her eyes. 'Ruth might still be alive.'

'And in the hands of someone who will take her to an officer – and send her to a camp. It will be swift now that there's a crime,' Hershel argued, ever the lawyer.

'What crime?' cried Esther, tears coursing down her cheeks. Sofie tried to hold her, but she wouldn't let her.

'An accomplice.'

'For a stupid animal trap?'

'That and trying to cross the border.'

'They can't charge her for that – not until she's actually done it!' she said.

He shook his head. 'That's not how it works – intention is also a crime.'

She shook her head violently. 'I am going back.'

'No!' cried Hershel.

'Shh, be quiet, all of you,' hissed Goran. 'You're making a racket. Sound carries with this wind.'

Asta and Jürgen clutched each other's arms.

They all shut up quickly. But it was too late. There was the sound of dogs barking not far away.

'Run,' hissed Goran, who raced ahead through the trees, only to come to a grinding stop.

The two officers they'd encountered before – the ones who'd questioned them, when they were pretending to be on a family camping trip – were heading towards them. The blond-haired one with the thin moustache was holding onto a struggling Ruth, his hand across her mouth. The red-haired officer who had given Asta a hard time pointed a shotgun at them all. But there was also a third man, a stranger, in full ranger gear, who came into view.

Asta's heart thundered painfully in her chest.

'Ruth!' screamed Esther, rushing towards her sister.

The red-haired officer pointed his shotgun at the sky and fired, and Esther came to a screeching halt.

Jürgen looked at Asta. 'Run,' he whispered. She stared at him in shock, but he grabbed her hand, and started to flee.

'Are you mad?' she cried to Jürgen, as they tore off away from the group. Their movement caused the others to panic as well. Goran dragged Sofie with him, as they too fled.

Jürgen didn't answer, he just ran, and Asta followed, their sixteen-year-old legs finding the energy required. Adrenaline pumped through Asta's body and she was no longer concerned about her sore feet, consumed by the desperate urge to get away.

One of the men tore after them. Asta glanced behind her and saw that it was the red-haired man. The other officer and the man in forestry gear were hot on the heels of Goran and Hershel. In their panic, they'd each hared off in separate directions.

Gunshots flew overhead, and Asta and Jürgen ducked. Asta looked at her twin, who slowed for a second, but then kept going.

'I'm fine, keep going, he won't catch us.'

She nodded and they raced, as far and as fast as their legs could carry them.

Asta didn't see the rocks on the path as she slipped, and fell down hard, onto her hands, grazing her palms, and skinning her knees.

'Asta!' cried Jürgen, rushing to help her. She sat up quickly, head pounding, only to frown in shock, but it wasn't her own injuries that made her cry out, it was his – the entire left side of Jürgen's face was covered in a thick coating of blood.

'Your face!'

Jürgen felt it, and looked shocked. In their rush of adrenaline, he hadn't even sensed the wound. His hands shook as he stared at the blood on them, then he felt the back his head, where more and more blood was oozing out in a viscous flood.

'You've been shot,' she cried, jumping up to look at him, only to gasp in shock as she was suddenly lifted off her feet. It was the red-haired officer, and before she could scream, he had pressed a knife below her throat. With his other hand, he pointed a pistol at Jürgen, who'd picked up a log with every intention of using it to break the man's skull.

'I have one more shot here, you filthy dog. You'll be dead soon from that wound in your head – so you decide,' he said, pointing the knife ever closer to Asta's jugular. 'I slit her throat, and put you both out of your misery, or you put that down and she gets to live.'

Tiny drops of blood were forming on Asta's neck from the sharp knife. She couldn't see Jürgen for the tears in her eyes. It couldn't be true – Jürgen was fine – he couldn't die from that shot, could he?

'Drop it, Jürgen. I'd rather go to a camp, so long as I'm with you, we'll be fine.'

Jürgen nodded, then dropped the log.

The red-haired officer stared at him.

'You think you're both clever, don't you?' he said, anger flaring in his eyes. 'Making up those filthy little lies. We realised there was something not right about your story when we didn't find you back at the coffee station. Started to get suspicious…'

There was a sound from behind, and they saw the park ranger making his way towards them. In the second that the officer looked away, Jürgen grabbed hold of the log again, leapt towards him, and cracked it over the man's head. But he didn't act fast enough, as the officer fired just before he hit the ground.

Asta watched in horror as Jürgen fell backwards, blood blooming out of a bullet wound in his side, his face turning white.

'Jürgen,' she cried, racing towards him, only to have the wind knocked out of her as she was swept her off her feet by the ranger who threw her over his shoulder. She twisted and struggled against him, hands reaching out for her twin, but the ranger didn't stop, as he trod silently through the forest.

'Let me down,' she screeched. 'Jürgen!' she cried. Her captor twisted her around, as easily as if she were a sack of potatoes, and clamped a hand over her mouth.

'Listen,' he said, in heavily accented German. 'Shut the hell up, or you'll get us both killed.'

She blinked, tears falling from wide eyes, but she kept her mouth closed in shock.

'He's dead, okay?' he said, and she screamed once more against his palm.

'Stop that,' he hissed and she did. 'There's no point in going back.' He put her down, only for her to begin to bolt straight back towards her twin. But he caught her easily, and shook her hard. 'He's dead,' he repeated. 'I'm sorry. But we're alive – we must keep it that way.'

Her face crumpled into desperate sobs once more. His hands were at his hair, like he was ready to rip it out in frustration. For a moment, it looked like he might leave her, then he scowled and threw her once again over his shoulder and started to run.

At some point, he'd slowed down to a walk. Night had fallen, and he finally let her slide off his shoulders. She stumbled, and he caught her. 'You should have let me go back.' Her face was stamped with heartbreak. 'You had no right to take me.' Then she gasped, as the shock and the horror and the agony of it all hit her, and she sank to her knees. 'I don't want to live if he's dead.'

To her surprise, he sat down next to her, closer than was necessary. 'You have to,' he said, simply.

Angrily, she brushed the never-ending tears from her eyes, and glared at him. She looked at him properly, perhaps for the first time. He wasn't as old as she'd first thought. Possibly somewhere in his early twenties. Just really big – tall and muscular. He wore a knitted cap, and had a thick blond beard covering most of his face. His eyes were sharp, and very blue.

'Why?' she snapped. 'We were born together, we can die together. Sounds right to me.'

She blew out her cheeks. The thought of living in a world without Jürgen was inconceivable.

'You were twins,' he said, understanding.

Her face twisted in pain at the use of the past tense, and she sank her head between her knees.

He patted her shoulder awkwardly. 'Look, we stop – just there,' he said, pointing at what looked like a hut up ahead.

She looked up at him, frowning. It was getting harder to see him in the fading light.

'Why are you helping me, who are you?' she asked.

'Come,' he said, pulling her up once more as if she weighed nothing.

'Where are you taking me?' she demanded.

'Out of the cold, somewhere safe, that's all,' he said. 'Come on.' And he took her arm, steering her towards the small hut.

Asta followed the strange man into the hut. 'Who are you?' she asked again, trying and failing to get the image of Jürgen lying in a pool of his own blood out of her mind.

He shut the door behind her, making her jump. The hut was small and basic. There was a rolled-up sleeping bag in the corner, as well as some tools mounted on the walls.

'Kalle Blomkvist,' he said.

'You're Danish?'

He nodded. 'I work for the forestry department but I also help to manage the border.'

She stared, then frowned. 'So, you're working with them – the Nazis?'

He shrugged. 'Yes and no, I work for Denmark.'

'So why don't you just hand me over to them?' she hissed. 'To those officers, why carry me here?'

He rubbed his hands together, then began to start a fire, keeping an eye on her at all times, watching her every move, as if she were preparing to run. He wasn't misguided. Every inch of her wanted to run away, straight into the arms of danger, to find her brother.

'To keep you safe.'

She looked at the floor, angrily, dashed away more tears. 'You had no right to take me away.'

'No,' he admitted, adding another log to the flame. Then he straightened, and took off his heavy coat, revealing a woollen jumper beneath. 'But then, what right do they?' he shot back.

She blinked. 'What do you mean?'

He stared at her for a long while, but didn't answer. Eventually, he said, 'You're Jews, right? That's why you wanted to get into Denmark?'

She didn't say anything. Even now, she wasn't sure that she could trust him. What if this was all some elaborate way to get her to admit to it? What was the penalty for crossing over into a country as an illegal?

'We have had many refugees,' he explained, then he sighed. 'Here,' he said, indicating what she presumed he meant to represent the Danish-German border. 'Newspapers are full of the stories of the refugees. It's a problem.'

Asta frowned. Such a small word to describe such a wealth of prejudice.

'They feel sorry for people like us – but not sorry enough to want to make room for us. They think we will come over and steal their jobs, take up their land – they never think that we could help, bring needed skills…'

'I know,' he said. 'They forget that another language doesn't mean another species.'

She looked away, surprised at his view. 'But you work in border control.'

'Which means I have seen it for myself. It's not easy to ignore someone's humanity when it is staring you in the face.'

He got up, and fetched a blanket from the small sleeping area on the floor. 'Here,' he said, handing it to her, 'you're shivering.'

She took it but didn't put it on. She didn't feel like she deserved to be warm, not when Jürgen was lying somewhere in the forest, cold… and possibly dead. She stood up, the blanket slipping from her fingers. 'Look, thank you, but I need to go back, I can't leave him there. Even if he is de—' She stopped, unable to say the word. 'I have to go back, I can't leave him.'

He shook his head. 'You can't go.'

'Why not?' she said, anger giving her strength as she crossed over to the door. He jumped up and barred her from leaving.

'There's nothing left for you. The other officer – he would have radioed for more people, they wouldn't just leave your brother lying there in the forest – they will have taken the body with them.'

Asta winced at the word 'body' but clenched her jaw. 'I need to go – I can't let them take him. If he's d-dead, I'll need to bury him.' Her lip shook.

'They won't give his body to you – they'll lock you up first. He doesn't deserve this.'

'What?' she said, eyes flaring. 'You don't know anything! My brother deserves everything!'

He nodded. 'That's what I mean. I saw him – he was brave, he knew what he was doing. He saw his chance to protect you, and he took it. It cost him his life.'

Her face crumpled, and she wobbled. He caught hold of her.

'I caused his death.'

'It was his choice – he risked himself for you and if you go back there's every chance that you won't survive – maybe not now but they could put you to death for breaking the law. Either way, your brother died so that you could be free – it would be a pretty horrible sacrifice if he did it for nothing.'

She looked up at him as she slipped from his embrace onto the ground; the shock of his words struck her dumb. But he was right, and the horror of it, the sheer, awful disgrace of it, the impossibility of the truth being that she had no choice but to leave the person she loved the most in the world with those monsters. She began to sob then, and found she couldn't stop.

CHAPTER SEVENTEEN

The next day, Asta was woken by the smell of bitter coffee. She'd fallen asleep on the hard, cold ground, and for a moment, between sleep and wakefulness, she'd forgotten. It winded her, the realisation, and she gasped, clutching at her stomach, as if she'd been kicked. Her eyes were swollen and painful, and she sat up, and simply held the cup Kalle was offering her, not saying a word.

'Where is it that you are going?' he asked.

She stared at the tin mug in her hands. It was burning her palms and part of her thought, *Good*; it was good to feel the pain – pain was what Jürgen must have felt. When she set it down, it felt in some small, stupid way like yet another betrayal.

'To Denmark,' she said with a frown. Surely that was obvious?

'Yes, I know,' he said, his pale eyes staring at her deeply. He was sitting cross-legged from her, surprisingly flexible for such a large man. 'But was there a plan – somewhere you were going to go once you got there?'

She nodded. 'My aunt, Trine.'

He looked relieved. 'That's good.'

Then he frowned. 'If you have family there couldn't you have just got a visa?'

She shook her head. 'There was no time.' And she explained about her parents. She thought, sitting there on the hard wooden floor, that she would simply say a few words, but somehow, she found herself talking, telling him more than she normally would. She broke off, stopping suddenly, after she'd got to the part where the nurse had come to warn them not to go home.

'Why did you stop?' he asked.

She frowned. 'I was babbling, sorry.'

'No, you weren't.'

She sighed, changing the subject. 'So you will help me?' she asked.

He nodded.

'I can't take you far but I can get you across the border – I will have to get back soon though or they will ask questions. I will be a suspect.'

'Oh,' she said, feeling a stab of regret penetrate her grief and fear.

'It's fine. All I mean is that if they do begin to suspect that I had something to do with your disappearance they will begin to look into it – it is better if I am there with some kind of story.'

'Oh,' she repeated, feeling at a bit of a loss. While she'd spent most of the previous evening resenting him for saving her, for making her take the impossible step of leaving Jürgen behind, she now found the idea of being by herself unsettling.

'I will take you across the border, and then I can get you transport to where you need to go. I have some money too.'

'I don't need your money,' she said, frowning.

'Don't be stupid,' he said, a small smile about his lips, while taking a sip of coffee. 'Course you do.'

She looked away; he was right, of course.

'We must go soon – before the next shift begins, then I can take you to Kruså, from there we can arrange the transport. Where is it that your aunt lives – Trine? Is that what you said she was called?'

She nodded, closed her eyes and tried her best to think. 'Trine Anderson,' she agreed. 'She's in Elsinore,' she said.

He whistled. 'That's far. Never mind, we'll get you there.'

*

They crossed the border between Germany and Denmark when it was still dark, under a moonless sky. She'd been walking for a hundred metres when Kalle said, 'You have now been in Denmark for nearly three minutes.'

She looked up in shock. She wasn't sure what she'd been expecting – some kind of barbed wire, a fence, an armed patrol, a ditch or river, but not a small road, leading to another forest. As dawn crested the horizon, they entered the small border town where Kalle led them past rows of terraced houses to the back of a café with a green awning and chipped white paint. He knocked on the back door, down an alleyway. She frowned. 'Are you sure about this – are you just going to ask someone to take me? How can you know they can be trusted?'

'Well,' said Kalle. 'I've known him my whole life.'

She stared at him, but he didn't elaborate. A few seconds later, a tall man opened the door, wearing an apron and a scowl. 'We only open at—' He broke off. He had grey hair, a clean-shaven face, and very blue eyes, so like Kalle's.

'*Hej*, Papa,' said Kalle, and the two embraced. 'I have a favour I need to ask,' he said, as soon as they broke apart.

The man looked from him to Asta then frowned. 'Kalle?' he said.

'This is my father, Johan,' he told Asta, speaking in his accented German.

The man's eyes widened and then the two started to argue in Danish. Asta stepped backwards.

'Kalle, thank you,' she said – even now, even after all he had done, it was hard to thank him, as her gratitude was mixed so deeply into her pain and regret at leaving her brother behind. 'But you got me this far – I can go, I'll be okay.'

The old man's eyes widened and he replied in German. 'Are you mad? They'll catch you and send you back before you can say "border police".'

She gritted her teeth. 'I'll be fine.'

He raised a brow. 'Can you even speak Danish?' he asked.

She didn't say anything. Which wasn't surprising as he'd asked it in Danish.

'Obviously not. Which means they will know you are German and send you right back.'

'Come on,' said Kalle, noticing Asta's stricken face. 'Come inside, his bark is worse than his bite.'

They entered the back of the café, into the kitchen. 'Come, sit,' said his father.

'I can't be long,' said Kalle, and gave a rough overview of what had happened. 'I'd better get back – and retrace my steps.'

As they were speaking Danish, Asta didn't have to relive the moment when that officer killed her brother, but she knew when they had to got to that part by the way his father gasped, and looked at her. How his blue eyes softened.

She looked away.

All too soon, Kalle was leaving.

'You will be all right,' he said. It was a statement rather than a question.

Before she even had chance to tell him all the things she wanted – needed – to say, he was gone, and his father was pulling on his jacket, and fetching his car keys. 'Come, come,' he said, and she followed him back out again to where a small green van was parked on the pavement. He opened the door, removing crates from the floor of the passenger side, and putting them in the back.

She sat down gingerly on the leather seat, as he started the car, and headed onto the road, towards Elsinore.

The silence was uncomfortable, and he hadn't put the radio on. After a while he cleared his throat. 'Kalle said that I should take you as far as Aabenraa; from there you will be able to get a taxi.'

He looked at her, her expression doubtful and frightened. 'I will arrange it, don't worry. I'd drive you myself but it's best if I'm back at the café sometime this morning so that no one will ask too many questions. I can fudge why I was late opening but not why I wasn't there all day. It would be too dangerous for you to stay – in case anyone sees you and the police come asking questions – my customers are regulars, and you aren't exactly forgettable.'

She frowned, then glanced down at herself and nodded. Her hands were covered in mud and scratches. She was wearing boys' trousers and a thick green woollen jumper, both of which had mud stains. Her hair was matted with twigs and knots, and she had several scratches across the one side of her cheek – she looked very like what she was, someone who was on the run.

He nodded. 'And, sorry to say it, but you have a pretty face – people can't help noting that.' He sighed. 'I'm sorry I can't take you all the way.'

She looked at him. 'You mustn't be sorry – it's me that should,' she said.

He sighed. 'There are people that should be sorry, but you're not one of them.'

She looked at him, and despite her grief, it was the first almost smile she made. 'You sound like Kalle, *tak*,' she said. It was the only word she knew in Danish.

After they'd been driving for forty minutes, they reached the pretty harbour town of Aabenraa in Southern Denmark, where he arranged for a taxi and waited with her outside a vegetable market. Asta distantly noticed its appeal, like the way one might catch a glimpse of a postcard, but not peer in for a closer look. The taxi driver was a man they'd found in the telephone book, who arrived ten minutes later, full of apologies. 'I don't usually get calls so early – usually when tourists are coming they arrange some weeks in advance.'

Johan raised a brow. 'I thought a taxi was all about emergencies. Or is that ambulances?' he said with a wink and the man laughed. 'My niece, Sofie,' explained Johan. 'I'm sorry for the rush – her aunt is expecting her, and I've had an emergency at work, so I can't take her. She doesn't speak much Danish,' he said.

The man shrugged. 'My German is pretty bad but I'll give it a go.'

'Don't worry, just get her to her this address in Elsinore,' he said, handing over the fee along with a note where they'd scribbled down an address from the same telephone book that had helped them find the driver – of one of three women named Trine Anderson who lived in Elsinore. If it turned out to be the wrong Trine Anderson, well, Asta would worry about that later.

As Asta got into the taxi, she watched Johan from the window, then waved. She couldn't help the surge of fear that tore through her. She didn't want anyone else to get hurt, not for her.

They drove for several hours, Asta staring out of the window, passing by beautiful towns with pastel-coloured houses and lakes and forests. She was surprised when he came to a stop at a town called Vissenbjerg. 'Comfort break,' he said, nodding his head at a petrol station. 'There's a café there,' he said, pointing to a small building opposite. 'If you need the toilet.'

She nodded, then climbed out, wincing as she landed on swollen, blistered feet. She was still covered in mud.

'You might want to… clean up,' said the taxi driver. 'Change into something if you can. Also, try not to speak German inside, just say, "I fell" – *Jeg gled og faldt* or just *faldt* and "Can I use the restroom?" *Må jeg bruge dit toilet?*'

Asta blinked at him. Did he suspect her secret?

She nodded slowly, then made her way to the café.

At this hour, it was full of customers, some who turned a little to look at her in surprise. She forced a fake laugh, and said in heavily accented Danish, '*Faldt,*' then shook her head as if this was silly, and then enquired, '*Dit toilet?*'

Incomprehensible Danish followed, and she found herself mumbling sorry in German and then wincing at her mistake; the words for right or left bore no similarity to German, but she followed to where a woman with salt-and-pepper hair and a frown was pointing. She nodded, said '*Tak,*' and made her way to what she hoped was the bathroom. If she'd hoped not to appear as a lost German girl, she'd failed miserably.

The small room had been shiplapped with wood and painted white. There was a window over the toilet, with a net curtain overlooking a set of bins outside. There was a simple basin in the corner with a frilly towel over the side. Above the sink was a small round mirror. She locked the door behind her, then went to splash water on her face, staring in shock at her own unrecognisable features. There were streaks of mud and blood which had pooled down her neck and congealed from where that officer had jabbed his knife…

She grabbed some toilet tissue and began to scrub, while trying to do something with her hair. It hung half in and half out of a ponytail, and most of the right side was matted, knotted from where she'd slept and fallen. She did her best to comb it using her fingers, but most of it was in thick knots that would require a comb. She untied the rest, and then bundled it all together, twisting it into a messy chignon at the nape of her neck, which she tied up with the ribbon, smoothing the hair on either side of her face. She still looked like she'd tumbled down a rabbit hole, however.

Her clothes were the worst part. Her trousers and jumper were covered in thick mud but there was not much she could do about that. Whatever small amount of clothing and money she'd possessed had been left somewhere on the forest floor back in Germany. It would only be later when she realised that included among those were the fake papers that Polgo had arranged for them – papers that were meant to help them avoid capture.

She was scrubbing the mud from her nails when she heard the whispers outside the bathroom. She heard a man's voice, which she recognised as the taxi driver. He was speaking to someone, or a group of someones. There was excited chatter, all in Danish. Asta was wiping her hands when she heard a word she recognised, *jøde*, followed by another, *flygtning*, which sounded like *fliehen* – fleeing. Her blood ran cold. She stared back at the door in mute horror.

Had he called someone? The police? He'd seemed to imply before he'd told her to go to the café that he knew her real story – that he suspected that she wasn't Johan's 'niece'. It wasn't hard to work out… a strange half-wild-looking girl in a border town speaking German… an early morning taxi service. It wasn't exactly a masterplan.

Had the taxi driver simply driven her here just so that he could have her arrested? Was there some kind of reward money for this sort of thing?

She closed her eyes, then took several steadying breaths. Then she closed the toilet lid, and scrambled on top, and shimmied her way out of the window, thankful that it was a single-storey building, as she landed silently, yet painfully, on her sore blistered feet.

She had no idea where to go, but she had read a sign that she recognised on the motorway, which was *Elsinore*, followed by *more than two hundred and thirty-six kilometres.*

She'd walk there if she had to.

CHAPTER EIGHTEEN

Lucas Mikkelstrom, the taxi driver, played with his short brown beard as he waited outside the bathroom for another fifteen minutes. Then he knocked softly on the door. 'Girl, are you all right?'

He was worried about her. He hadn't bought her 'uncle's' story; no matter how much the man had tried to pretend, it was clear that something was going on. With it being only 7 a.m. and not too far from the border, well, he could imagine… she looked utterly lost and alone.

It wasn't exactly what her 'uncle' had planned but one look at the girl had made Lucas think maybe his wife, Martina, could help. Woman to woman, that sort of thing. He was beginning to think that was a mistake.

There was no answer.

Martina looked at him, a frown between her eyes. 'Lovey, are you all right?' she called through the bathroom door.

'She can't understand you.'

She nodded, then switched to German. Most people this close to the border could speak it. 'It's okay, you're safe here.'

Again, nothing.

Lucas pinched the skin between his eyes. 'I think she's done a runner.'

Martina blinked. 'What do you mean?'

'There's a window inside there, right?'

Her eyes widened. She knocked again. 'You're safe, lovey, we only want to help. I have some clothes for you.'

Still there was no response.

Lucas sighed, then took a running leap, battering the door with his shoulder. The cheap lock broke apart in seconds, the door banging wide to reveal the empty facility. The only trace of the girl was a streak of mud on the washcloth, and the lace curtain hanging off its wiring as a result of her hasty retreat.

Martina looked stricken. 'Oh, Lucas, we need to find her.'

He leant his head back against the wall. 'She's a *flygtning* – a refugee. I made the mistake of showing her that I knew. I wanted her to see that I was on her side – that I'd help her. I should have just pretended that I bought her story – I spooked her. I doubt she'll ever trust me again.'

'We can't just leave her all alone, stranded in a strange country,' cried Martina, getting on top of the toilet, and peering out the window, as if by some miracle, the poor child would still be there, waiting.

'We can look for her, but my guess is she's long gone – and if she saw me, I don't think she'd follow.'

Martina crossed her arms over her ample bosom, and shot him a dark look.

He tapped a cigarette out of the silver case she'd given him when they first got married, put it between his lips, then raised his hands in defeat. 'I'll go look,' he said.

'Good.'

Asta half-ran, half-walked through small towns with colourful houses, avoiding people as they stared or came forward with concerned looks on their faces. She passed a bakery at midday, and her tummy rumbled bitterly. Every penny Kalle had given her had gone towards the taxi. She avoided everyone. But when she found a small bookshop that sold maps, she pretended to browse, and as soon as she was sure that the owner was occupied elsewhere, she slipped one inside her cardigan.

Heart beating loudly, sure that he would shout and come running after her as soon as she cleared the doorway, she ran as far and as fast as she could. When the rain came pouring down, she took cover in a bus shelter, and traced the journey from where she was to where her aunt Trine lived. Unfortunately, the driver still had the address for one of the Trine Andersons – she'd have to look up her aunt's name again. But she'd do whatever it took to find her and she'd go to all three addresses if necessary.

The journey would take over sixty hours by foot, and one ferry ride. She would commit nine minor thefts – including stealing fruit from a market, a jacket draped over a chair in a café, the tips left behind for several waitresses, and someone's gloves, hat and umbrella that had been left in another café. It would take her six days, where she would sleep most nights bundled beneath her stolen coat or wedged in an empty doorway or in a forest. By the time she finally found herself in Elsinore, she'd spoken to a telephone operator who had given her the address of a Trine Anderson. She stopped by two with no luck, before she moved on to the last name on the list. She lived not in the city itself but in a small fishing village, some ten minutes away by train. It was very late and Asta was cold, and tired, and so she decided to wait inside the barn until morning; she wasn't sure how much further she could go.

CHAPTER NINETEEN

Snekkerston, December 1938

Trine held on to Asta as she howled, her thin shoulders shuddering in her grief. Finally, when the tears stopped coming, she gave her a glass of water, and smoothed back her hair, and settled her into the bed.

'Mutti, I don't know how I will carry on without him,' she said, as Trine pulled the patchwork quilt over her. Bjørn snuggled against her, his golden head resting on her lap.

'You will find a way, my child.'

'But how?' she asked. The request was so simple, yet so desperate. Trine didn't know what to answer, except the truth.

'You will somehow, you just will.'

Trine left the room, and collapsed against a wall, the knuckles of her right hand jammed into her mouth to stop herself from crying out, as the imagined horror of everything that her niece had been put through washed over her. Trine had always been a strong woman, tough, she'd had to be really, with what life had thrown her. When it turned out that she couldn't carry a baby to full term, and she'd miscarried, she'd lovingly made each little box, and buried it. There had been four, and she'd named each and every one. She'd thought she would die along with them, that she wouldn't be able to keep going, but she had. Step by step, moment by moment. Trine knew what so few of the happy mothers she saw in her daily life knew, that if you could survive that – well, you could just about survive anything. But she felt neither strong nor tough now. She didn't feel like the woman who had turned a shotgun on her abusive drunk of a husband and said enough was enough. She felt utterly out of her depth, as she sank onto her haunches and prayed for the first time in years for the strength to help the girl suffering inside that room.

Trine would have to somehow be a mother to a young woman at the hardest time in the girl's life.

Over the course of the next few days, on a diet of Lisbet's soup, Trine's concern and Bjørn's boundless, dogged love and adoration, Asta became more lucid, and yet more withdrawn.

Trine found it difficult to get more than a few sentences out of her, and days after her arrival, she still didn't know the full story of what had happened. Just the small snippets that she had supplied, between coughing fits. Trine didn't push her. Asta was far from well, and was easily tired. The one thing that brought her comfort, however, was Bjørn, and Trine was grateful to him.

Speaking about the dog was a safe topic, and when they did it was, for a brief moment, like the clouds parted, and she saw a glimpse of the little girl that had captured Trine's childless heart from the moment she'd met the twins with their irrepressible grins at age five, eleven years before – before they had any idea what the future held.

'I've never had a dog before,' Asta had said, when she'd been with Trine for a week. 'Papa—' she started, then looked away.

'He wouldn't allow it,' supplied Trine. 'He was always afraid of them, even as a boy.'

Asta was surprised. Papa had always made out that the reason was the size of their apartment, which hadn't always gone down particularly well with Asta, considering that four of their neighbours had dogs. She was also allergic, but that didn't stop her wanting one.

'Perhaps it was just as well,' said Asta, as a large coughing fit overtook her, and she wheezed into a handkerchief. Her thin chest felt battered and sore. She sighed, and lay down, wiped out.

'You know, a friend of mine said that was one of the other "laws" they were looking to change, that we wouldn't be allowed to keep pets?'

'Who?' asked Trine. 'The landlords?'

Asta shook her head. 'The Nazis. They're thinking of forbidding Jews from keeping them.'

Trine blinked. 'I can't believe it.'

Asta was right; by 1941 Jews would be forbidden from keeping dogs, cats and birds.

Asta looked up at her then, and raised a brow. '*That's* what you can't believe?' Just as another cough tore through her chest and she doubled over, fighting for air.

And Trine felt as if she were the child, Asta the adult.

It was during Asta's second week that she ventured out of the bedroom to the kitchen, on her weak, unsteady legs.

'Asta!' Trine cried, seeing her in the doorway. 'You're still very sick, you shouldn't be out of bed!'

Malthe had come to check on her that morning, and said that he was worried; she wasn't recovering as he would have hoped.

He'd patted her on the shoulder, his eyes kind behind a pair of wire-rimmed spectacles. 'She will get better, it will just take time. She is young and healthy, there's no reason to fear.'

But fear Trine did. Especially seeing her looking half-faint and deathly pale in the doorway.

'Please, Aunt Trine,' she wheezed. 'I just have to be anywhere besides that room, just for a little while. While I'm there... I don't sleep, not unless I take the medicine that the doctor gave me... and if I don't sleep, well, then...' She shuddered. 'Then I see him, oh God.'

Trine helped her to take a seat at the kitchen table, her own eyes filling with tears.

Asta blew her cheeks out, determined not to cry. Suddenly, she smiled, and Trine looked at her in surprise.

'I was just thinking that Jürgen would have told me to pull myself together, to stop being such a girl.' She laughed. 'Though, really, he was more the girl,' she said with a watery smile. 'If he got a papercut he'd scream, and the first time he hit his funny bone he started to cry.' She bit her lip, tears leaking down her face. She dashed them away. 'I'm sorry, I shouldn't keep talking about him...'

Trine cupped Asta's face in her roughened hands. 'Oh, darling, no, speak about him – I want to hear, and you cry if you need to cry, scream if you have to—'

'Scream?' she asked, surprised.

'Scream.' Trine nodded.

So Asta did, and Trine joined in. The sound was wild and feral. There was barking, and then Bjørn came rushing to the kitchen.

For a moment, it seemed like Bjørn understood.

The young forest ranger from the Danish-German border, Kalle Blomkvist, who had saved Asta, went over his mental notes. Keep it simple, he reminded himself, don't elaborate.

When they called his name, he waited a moment – be too casual and it could come across as unprofessional, too eager, and that could seem like he was jumpy, had something to hide.

He had one goal – and that was to convince the interviewing panel that he had been nowhere near the red-haired officer Smidt and the girl who had disappeared, seemingly into thin air. The girl they'd spent the past week combing every inch of the forest for.

The door opened and Kalle's eyes widened for a moment. *Jesus*, he thought. *They've assembled an army.*

There were six people seated across a table, each with a serious expression. He reminded himself that he wasn't German, and that he was employed by the Danish border control. Technically he wasn't under their command.

'Take a seat,' said a man with short black hair and a thin moustache. 'As you are aware, a few nights ago, a group of Jewish refugees attempted to cross the border into Denmark.'

Kalle frowned. 'Did they succeed?'

A tall man with piercing blue eyes leaned forward in his seat. 'They didn't get that far. But let's not play games and pretend that they were there for their health – three have been captured: a man by the name of Goran and his wife, Sofie, and an Orthodox Jew named Esther, who all admitted as much… the other three were shot and killed.'

Kalle had to school his face to hide the horror of the man's words. *That is not how they dealt with refugees.*

'What we are interested in is what happened to the two youths that were accompanying the adults, who chose to run off,' continued the tall man.

'Well, I couldn't say.'

'Why is that?'

'Because when the young ones started to run, so did the others. There was an older man and a woman who was nearest me – and when they started to run, I went after them.'

The tall man frowned, then consulted his notes.

Kalle knew that they would have spoken to the other officer, a blond one with a thin moustache called Krill, who would have been best-placed to remember what he'd done as they'd almost run together after everyone started to flee. It was only when Kalle heard a girl's scream that he began to run in the opposite direction. He was sure that Krill was occupied with the old man and woman and hadn't seen, but he couldn't be sure.

'I heard a scream, you see, and I decided to investigate. I saw a young woman, running, and I went after her.'

Kalle made up a lie about deciding to track her but falling in a ditch. 'Knocked myself clean out. I woke up half a day later.'

Thankfully, he had a really large bruise on his forehead from a similar accident that had happened not long after he'd got home from delivering Asta to his father; he'd slipped and tripped, hitting his head on a rock, punch drunk with fatigue.

'And no one saw you – people were combing the forest?'

'Not well enough, obviously.'

One of the other men laughed. 'Well, apparently, you are the best tracker in the forest – pity you couldn't find yourself.'

Kalle offered a weak smile and the other man continued. 'Or the girl.'

Kalle resisted tugging at the unfamiliar and uncomfortable shirt and collar he was wearing; it was stiffer than his usual ranger's uniform, and pressed against his throat.

'Me too – perhaps I could have avoided this headache,' he said, pointing to his scalp.

'Or ours,' said one of the others.

'But no matter. We will rectify that now.'

'Sir?' asked Kalle, confused.

'We need you to work with an artist – get a sketch drawn up that we will begin to circulate in all the border towns.'

'But I didn't see her—'

'Oh, that's fine – there's someone else who will help, against their will obviously. Her twin, I believe – the spitting image of his missing sister.'

Kalle tried to hide his shock. 'I thought – well, I'd heard that he was dead.'

'Almost. Took two bullets. Well, one just grazed his ear, really… but anyway, he's alive. He doesn't want to talk to us, of course, but maybe you can convince him – tell him you'll find her – as you can imagine, he's most distressed.' Then he smiled, as if that amused him.

CHAPTER TWENTY

'You're lucky,' said a male nurse with thin lips, and penchant for cruelty, 'for a filthy little Jew bastard.'

Like most bullies, his taunts weren't particularly clever, or original. And this one was beginning to grate, as it was the third time he'd said it this week.

Jürgen turned his face to the wall. He hadn't said anything, not yet. They wanted to know what had happened to his sister. They wanted to cut a deal, they said…

They could try all they liked; there wasn't a deal to be had that would make him betray his twin.

The thin-lipped nurse bustled over with a glass of water. It was filthy, the edges rimmed in bits of food, and stained with grease. Despite this, Jürgen licked his cracked, parched lips. The bastard was trying to force it out of him any way he could. He wasn't an ordinary nurse – but someone employed by the hospital prison, where Jürgen was being kept until he recovered. For the time being there was at least the pretence of humanity, though it was very thinly veiled.

'But that luck is coming to an end…' said the nurse, his eyes shining. 'Attempted murder – that's what they're charging you with, along with attempting to illegally cross a border – that might be life in prison. But don't worry, I think if you make it they'll send you to a camp. Who knows, you might even get to help build one of the new ones they're talking about… you'll like it there, filth, with all your own kind.'

Jürgen stared at the ceiling. He knew the nurse was waiting for him to grab the water. Jürgen knew he liked it when he did, because he saw the look of satisfaction when Jürgen winced in pain as he tried to sit up, how he gasped, the look of revulsion as his lips touched the dirty glass, yet he couldn't help gulping down the liquid. He wouldn't give him the satisfaction. Not today.

He closed his eyes, though he hated doing that too. Whenever he did, he saw that huge oaf, that ranger carrying Asta away, while she screamed… and screamed.

'I'll just take this… if you aren't thirsty,' said the nurse, with a small greedy smile.

Jürgen gritted his teeth. He opened his eyes, then looked at him through narrow slits. 'Stop.'

The nurse paused, and Jürgen took the glass, a small shudder tearing through him. He tried to block out the nurse's look of triumph.

He swallowed the greasy, dirty water, along with his pride. The latter wouldn't keep him alive, and that was his only priority – to stay alive – so that he could find the bastard that had taken his sister.

CHAPTER TWENTY-ONE

No one told you how exhausting it was to grieve. How all-consuming. How the only escape was sometimes sleep – when for just a moment you were you again. As a young girl, Asta couldn't even fall asleep without the sound of his snoring, who'd once broken down in sobs at the idea of having a wall between them, while they slept in separate beds.

She pressed her face into Bjørn's soft fur as she sobbed. 'I couldn't even face that. How do I learn to live without him?'

As the days passed, it was clear that Asta's condition had worsened, along with her mental health.

Trine called for Malthe, who looked in upon her, and delivered the bad news, a worried look on his face, as Asta fell into a deep sleep, utterly exhausted just from the examination. She was heavily flushed, and suffering from fever.

'It's turned to pneumonia, I am afraid,' he said, setting aside the stethoscope, which he'd used to listen to the girl's lungs.

Trine gasped, feeling her knees buckle slightly. Pneumonia was serious.

Malthe stared at her, his eyes full of sympathy.

'I'd like to take her to the hospital, run some X-rays, and get her started on a relatively new treatment – something we've been doing since the start of the thirties. I don't know if you have heard of it – it is called sulphonamide therapy and has been shown to greatly reduce fatality rates.'

Trine blinked, listening but not listening to his words about this new and important discovery, about bacteria and how it worked, but all she could focus on right then was this illness that took so many lives, which might not be quite as deadly as a result, and she clung on to that small hope.

She couldn't lose Asta – not now after everything the poor child had been through.

Asta spent six weeks in the hospital, being treated by Malthe. Trine visited her every day, before work and after but she was always the same. Tired, weak, and very ill. Worst of all was how little she spoke. She seemed to be suffering from a depression too. Trine brought her books and magazines in German, anything to help lift her out of herself for a while, but they lay untouched.

'She doesn't seem to be improving,' Trine whispered to Malthe, from the doorway. Watching as her niece coughed even as she slept, her brows furrowed.

'It's slow, but I think there's progress. We just have to give her time.'

Finally, Asta was allowed to come home, to continue her recovery. 'I think she's over the worst but it will still be many months before she is well again,' said Malthe.

Trine helped her niece into bed, grateful that she was at least able to care for her again. 'It will be better now that you're here, you'll see,' she said.

Asta gazed at her, not knowing what to say. She felt so lost, so empty. She couldn't imagine ever feeling like herself again. She felt guilty, wishing she could just magically make herself recover, not just physically but mentally too. She hated that she was causing her aunt pain, but every day was like being in a constant nightmare, with a body that wasn't able to do even the smallest things – just getting up to go to the bathroom felt like she had performed a marathon, and sometimes she was so weak that even lifting a hairbrush was a task. Then there was the pressing weight of her depression, that made everything feel dull and dark.

All she wanted to do was sleep. While she slept she could pretend that she wasn't ill, and her dreams took her back to her family, to her twin.

She couldn't face being awake.

'I don't know what to do,' admitted Trine, as spring turned to summer. The days had turned warm, the rapeseed fields were in full bloom, and the countryside was awash with colour and life. It was hard to envision hardship on a day like that, as the impossibly blue sea sparkled in the sunshine, and the boats swayed in the harbour, but across the border in Germany, things were getting even worse, with the news that boats full of Jewish refugees were being returned. It seemed like things were only getting harder for the Jews, and the threat of war seemed inevitable. But her concerns were more for the young, silent girl with haunted, violet eyes that refused to leave her sick room, back home.

She sat at Lisbet's kitchen table, and accepted a second glass of wine from her friend, and rubbed her tired eyes. 'She's so withdrawn. I've tried my best to not push her – I mean, what she's been through at such a young age, well… I can never imagine, but at the same time, it's clear that she is in some deep depression.'

Lisbet nodded, then took a seat opposite her, cutting another sliver of gherkin and putting it on top of some crisp rye bread with cottage cheese.

'You can't push her, you're right,' she said, speaking wisely from her experience of being a schoolteacher for over forty years. 'But what you can do is bring in a catalyst.'

Trine paused, sipping her wine. 'What do you mean?'

'I mean, maybe someone else can try. Like Oliver? You said it yourself when she first arrived, she will need a friend.'

Trine nodded. 'Will he be up for that? I mean, he's a sweet boy… but she is very troubled.'

'He has the patience of a saint. You saw what he did with that mare of yours.'

This was true. Oliver had trained the horse to come on a whistle, to let him ride her without a saddle, and to gallop as if she were a young foal, not an aged mare who had spent most of her life helping to power Trine's ex-husband's smithy before he'd finally joined the new century and went mechanical. To be fair, Uwe hadn't ever mistreated the animal – in fact, he'd treated the horse better than his own wife, but it hadn't been the most pleasant life for either of them…

'I'll put it to Oliver tonight,' promised Lisbet. 'He's been asking after her anyway.'

The first time Oliver came to visit, Asta was wrong-footed. He made himself at home in the wicker armchair by the window, with its view outside of the sea, and no amount of giving him pointed looks that he was intruding in her private space seemed to penetrate.

'What's this?' he asked, going through the stack of books that lay untouched on her bed. They were a mix of non-fiction titles – books on nature and wildlife – and fiction, classic tales that Trine had hand-picked from a second-hand bookshop in Elsinore in order to tempt her niece; so far nothing had worked.

'Books, what else?' she asked.

'Hmmm,' he said, picking up a non-fiction title about the birds of Denmark and turning the pages. 'I prefer animals, myself,' he said, staring at the pictures.

Bjørn chose that moment to leave Asta's side, jump off the bed, then place his large golden head in the boy's lap.

Asta frowned, annoyed at them both. 'Birds are animals.'

'They are?'

'Yes,' she said, wondering what they taught this boy at school; certainly nothing about manners or catching a hint…

'What's your favourite animal?' he asked. 'Mine's a dog, obviously, but I have always been partial to horses too. Also insects, I know it's weird, and girls like you never understand that…'

She glared at him. 'I love insects,' she said.

'Oh good,' he said, which was when she realised maybe she could have got him to go away by lying as he proceeded to speak to her at length about them. Despite herself, she found that she was sitting up a little straighter, and while somewhat irritated, she was more engaged than she had been in months.

After that he came by most days.

Asta hated it when Oliver came over. He was the sort of boy you were meant to like. He was sweet and kind and helpful and Asta absolutely loathed the very sight of him.

He whistled when he entered the cabin, and Bjørn, her beloved furry companion, would betray her with the rapid beat of his ridiculously fluffy tail.

'We are meant to be friends,' she told the dog. 'That means loyalty. Dammit, you're a dog, it's supposed to be hard-wired inside of you.'

'What is supposed to be hard-wired in him?' asked Oliver, in his perfectly acceptable German, a pleasant voice that grated on her every nerve.

She ignored him.

The dog's tail started to thrash wildly in glee. She shot the dog a dirty look, and said, 'A cat would understand.'

Bjørn just looked from her to Oliver, the way that a friend will try to make you see the value in their other friends – a venture that is often somehow doomed to failure.

'You want to go for a walk, Asta? It's a lovely day.'

Asta looked out of the window and frowned. 'It's raining.'

'I know – it's exciting.'

She raised an eyebrow.

'But have you ever watched the rain as it falls into the sea? We could get umbrellas and watch the waves crash?'

She closed her eyes. She was not a nasty person. Or violent, but this boy was testing her. 'No, Oliver, I don't want to go out into the rain or watch the waves crash, sorry… I have in fact just spent the past six months trying to recover from pneumonia as you might recall, considering here I still am, in this house.'

'Oh… I suppose I didn't think of that.' He wasn't down for long. 'Bjørn?' he asked. 'You want to go?'

And the dog leapt out of the bed so fast that Asta shook her head, and shouted, 'Brutus.'

By the first of September, Germany invaded Poland, and just two days later France and Britain declared war.

It was a long autumn, and people were afraid of the future, and as it gave way to winter, it was even worse as the fear and panic grew as nothing much seemed to happen for a while. It was also almost a year since Asta had come to live with Trine.

Oliver's influence had made a big difference. She went outside more often, and was persuaded into going on walks with him and the dog.

Trine was making a stew. She arranged the items on her counter and sighed. Since September's declaration of war there had been major shortages. Despite Denmark and the neighbouring countries of Norway and Sweden declaring themselves neutral, the country had been in a constant state of readiness. Stockpiling had created a problem, as people loaded up on sugar, coffee, soap, toilet tissue and cleaning supplies. Trine had resisted stockpiling herself but she could understand. The only things she had stocked up on were coffee and sugar. She hadn't been proud of herself but she wasn't as bad as the others. A woman in her office had an entire spare room filled with toilet tissue, which Trine thought was exactly the sort of stupid thing that led to unnecessary shortages. All Trine had was a few weeks' extra supply. Later, though, she would regret not being a little more like that woman.

Since the Russians had bombarded Finland three weeks before on 30 November, the idea of any kind of peace was long dismissed. The Danes listened to the news anxiously. There were rumours… wild rumours that Hitler had been taken and put in a padded cell. Across Western Europe, there were many who hoped that was true, considering what they'd allowed to happen with the Soviets and their invasions.

Trine sighed, then cut up the shin for the stew. In two days' time, it would be 1940. She just hoped that the new year would bring about something good.

She looked up when Asta came to sit at the table, and put on her boots.

'Where are you're going?' she asked.

Then she heard it. Oliver's whistle from outside. It was some jaunty tune.

Asta rolled her eyes. 'It's like he lives on another planet.'

Trine grinned, then added one of her three rather precious carrots. There had been a kerfuffle at the grocer's the day before, and that's all she'd got. She stared at them fondly, like orange and purple jewels.

'So you still despise him?' she asked. It had been six months, but Asta still refused to admit that they were friends.

Asta looked up. 'I don't despise him. He just irritates me.'

'So that's why you're going to go walking with him.'

'Well, see, if I don't then he doesn't leave – he'll just stay here all day, and Bjørn will just go to him like he's made of sweets.'

Trine hid a smile. The girl seemed to believe that the dog was hers, forgetting that if anyone was entitled to the dog's loyalty it was Trine. But she didn't mind. She was glad that Asta was feeling something – for so long the girl had been living with an inconsolable grief, followed by a numb apathy; irritation was good. It was the sort of thing that got you out of bed.

'That sounds sensible.'

Asta shrugged. 'We walk – then he leaves, it's better.'

It was.

Trine had to give the boy credit – he knew what he was doing.

Trine and Asta listened to the bells on the radio, bringing in the new year. Asta wasn't the only one with tears in her eyes wondering what it would bring. Famous poets from the Nordic countries read out poems about being stoic. That's all they could be now, standing on a knife-edge wondering what would happen to them.

'In a month, we'd be turning eighteen,' said Asta. 'We had such plans.' She stared out at the lights of the harbour. 'Jürgen wanted to study art – you should have seen his sketches,' she said, her face crumpling for a moment, 'and I was going to study veterinary science.' She looked at Bjørn fondly.

'You still could,' said Trine. 'Here in Denmark, they haven't forbidden it like they did for the Jews in Germany.'

Asta continued to stare unseeing out the window, then shook her head. 'I feel as if that dream belonged to a different girl.'

Trine shrugged. 'For now, maybe,'

Asta nodded. 'Even so, it's time I did something. I think being busy would help. A job, maybe.'

Trine nodded and, ever practical, she went to fetch that day's paper where the new job listings were posted, along with something else. 'I got this for you – I didn't want to rush you – but, well… I think at some point you will need to learn it,' said Trine, handing her niece a book. It was a German to Danish language book. She'd picked it up at the bookshop around the corner from the *Elsinore Gazette*, but had kept it aside, because there was no point in rushing the child until she was ready.

Asta had picked up a few words and phrases – mostly insults – which she'd used on Oliver, to his delight.

Asta held the book in her hands and frowned.

A job would mean that she would *need* to learn Danish; her aunt was right. As she stared at it, she realised it was time that she acknowledged something else too – something until then she hadn't allowed herself to fully realise – this was her life now. Here in Denmark.

Asta took a breath and nodded. 'Today seems like a good day to start.'

CHAPTER TWENTY-TWO

Flensburg, 1940

Jürgen was being transferred. 'Good news,' said one of the officers, coming into his hospital room. The male nurse that had tormented Jürgen since his first day was gloating too.

He had spent the past year battling illness after illness, as his wounds took forever to heal, due in part to the poor treatment he suffered.

'Now that you've recovered you get to go work off your crime, at Dachau – helping to build the sort of weapons that almost killed you. This time, they're going to build better ones so they don't make that mistake again – letting you live.'

The officer threw him a set of clothes – a pair of second-hand trousers, a shirt and a very thin woollen jumper – and told him to get changed.

'How can I?' he asked, lifting a wrist, which had been manacled to the iron bed.

It was a precaution they'd started taking after his second escape attempt. His first had been too early in his recovery, and he'd only got as far as the other side of the room before he was whisked back into bed.

The second time, he'd almost made it out of the building, as he'd managed to steal the nurse's key from his back pocket after he decided to taunt him and they had got into a fist fight. Jürgen had been beaten to within an inch of his life, but all he'd been interested in was getting the key, which he'd clutched in his hand, and later hidden in his mattress until there was a shift change.

That attempt had earned him being handcuffed to the bed and an extra month inside the hospital.

All he could think about was the Dane.

He'd shown up a few weeks after he'd first arrived at hospital. Jürgen's eyes had widened in shock. The man was dressed smarter than when he'd seen him last, in pair of formal trousers and a white shirt, with city shoes. But he had the same beard, the same unruly dark blond hair.

Jürgen would have known that scruffy face and boxer's build anywhere. It was the man who'd carried Asta away, screaming. The ranger.

Before Jürgen could scream at him, demand where he'd taken her, he'd said, 'I realise you have never seen my face before—' Jürgen had opened his mouth to argue, but he'd continued. 'I hear that your sister ran away – and you are looking for her. I would like to help you find her…'

Jürgen had stared. 'I was shot but I saw what happened!'

'That's good – so you can tell us where she is hiding, do you think?'

Jürgen blinked. The man looked from Jürgen to the officer who was taking notes. Was this man trying to tell him something?

'You will help us all by telling us where she is headed – we know that she crossed the border into Denmark illegally, although how she managed it is a miracle; had Blomkvist not been face down in a ditch I dare say it would never have happened.'

'Never,' said Kalle Blomkvist, shooting Jürgen a meaningful look.

Finally, Jürgen understood. Asta was safe. She was in Denmark.

'Did you have some plan – some family or friends or anyone there? Technically, we cannot extradite her yet… until we know where she is.'

Jürgen thought hard; he had to lie so convincingly that it took them in the wrong direction. Then remembered something Esther had said. 'Copenhagen. That's where we were headed. There was a friend of my father's – a doctor, Heinkel. We thought maybe he could help.'

'That's good. Very good. And did this Dr Heinkel know to expect you?'

'No.'

'We will find out, boy.'

Jürgen shrugged. It *was* the truth, if someone named Dr Heinkel actually existed… he would have had no idea because Jürgen had made him up.

'Thank you for your time,' said the Dane. 'I am Kalle – Kalle Blomkvist, by the way. I hope one day you get to see your sister again.'

Jürgen had blinked at him. 'Thank you.'

When the pair left, he heard the officer ask why he'd given his name. 'Oh, I don't know, shouldn't I have?'

'Makes no difference to me. But see, you can't do that – you can't treat them like they're like us, they're animals, and they'll bite you if you let them.'

Jürgen had held back a bitter laugh. He wasn't wrong about that – if he ever got the chance, he would do more than bite.

And now, almost a year later, he was heading to Dachau.

Was it his chance to see his parents again? How big was it? He'd heard rumours from the officers in the corridors that Germany's first concentration and labour camp had become overcrowded. They were building more camps like it to house their undesirables. He knew that his parents would hate it if he went, so he had to stay free. He had to find Asta. If what that Dane, Kalle Blomkvist, was trying to tell him was true, she was alive. And he'd given Jürgen something else – his name; maybe that was how he was meant to find her.

Kalle Blomkvist was worried about the twins. He couldn't help it – ever since he'd saved Asta he'd felt a need to preserve her liberty, and to help her brother, if he could. He had to be careful – too much interest and that would raise questions. He'd had to bide his time over the months as there had been officers crossing the borders with a sketch of the missing girl. But none seemed more invested in catching her than that officer Smidt – the man who had tried to kill her, only to be thrown off course by her twin, who'd hit him over the head with a log, and survived a round of bullets... just to infuriate him further.

Ordinarily, it would likely have blown over – but the twins had cost Officer Smidt a promotion; worse, he had been humiliated, his name something of a joke – bested as he'd been by children. He became obsessed with finding her, even though the Danes had long since given up themselves. And as the months bled into the other, his obsession grew, seeing it as the last attempt to revive his career and restore his reputation. Kalle had heard the rumours, of course. Seen how he'd been ridiculed. He sometimes thought that if Officer Smidt had died in the forest like he was supposed to from the blow Jürgen had given him, things might have been easier all round. Though, to be fair, it would have likely cost Jürgen his life. He would have been executed. Instead he was being sent to a labour camp. Something that Smidt had personally arranged.

Kalle's grandfather had been in the police service, and he'd told him about the obsessive types. Those were the ones you had to watch your back for.

Smidt knew that if he could find the girl – even though the other officers had now relegated her to the realm of lost causes – it would go some way in restoring his poor reputation. Kalle was going to make sure that didn't happen. Just like he was going to make sure that Jürgen didn't wind up in some awful camp or worse, dead.

It was stupid, he knew it. He should just stay out of it. Should keep his head down, and just get on with things. But he couldn't. He couldn't seem to let it go either.

Which was why when he heard they were transferring Jürgen, he began to hatch a plan.

It took a week to realise his scheme. He had to pick a time when the officers were understaffed, when they'd gone to investigate another mass border breach in the forest. He contacted Smidt directly, a day before Jürgen was due to be transferred, telling the officer that he had a new lead on the case. A girl resembling Asta's appearance had been spotted near Copenhagen – but they needed proof it was the girl, or so Kalle claimed.

'I need to be able to speak to him to confirm it,' he said. 'Denmark police insist upon it.'

'Come first thing tomorrow,' Smidt said. 'I'll meet you at the station.'

It was a cold grey morning when Kalle walked through the entrance doors of the station only to find Smidt hovering nearby. As soon as he clamped eyes on Kalle in his ranger uniform, his eyes widened in delight.

'I can't believe it – you think you may have found her?' he said. He ran a hand through his short red hair in shock. 'After all this time? And would the Danish police be willing to hand her over – if it's her?'

'Possibly – yes, if she is indeed a criminal. They are concerned that she is a refugee, you see, considering the rest…'

Smidt frowned. Had Kalle been German this conversation would have been close to traitorous but he needed him and had to cooperate at least.

'But she's not a refugee! She struck an officer – it's a crime, both those twins tried to kill me!'

Kalle tried to keep his face calm. This wasn't true at all – Kalle had seen it from the shadows in the forest himself. The only one who'd tried to kill Smidt was Jürgen but it was in self-defence. If this had been his own country he could have attested to that but here it wouldn't mean anything. Kalle knew that Smidt had pulled a knife on the sister and had fired his weapon upon Jürgen… it was hardly a crime that the Danes would relinquish a refugee for. Still, for now, Smidt did not need to know that.

'Yes, that's what I thought…' he said, nodding his dark blond head, his blue eyes giving nothing away. 'As you can imagine, the only thing we know for sure about this girl is that she is an escaped Jew – she isn't speaking, and we can't turn her over to you until we know it is definitely Asta Schwalbe. However, there is an identifiable mark on the girl's shoulder – a large birthmark – her twin would be the best person to let us know if that matched hers.'

Smidt nodded. Then frowned. 'And he wouldn't lie – to keep her safe?'

Kalle looked at Smidt. He had to give it to him. The man wasn't stupid. It was Smidt after all who had tracked down the van driver, Herman, who had been acting suspiciously, pretending to be taking a delivery across the border, only to drive to the forest. Herman was in prison now – as some of the other escapees had given his name. Smidt had known about Herman, or suspected him at least and he'd eventually traced them all to the forest. Later he'd been fooled by the twins, which galled him so much because he'd been on their trail.

Kalle nodded. 'Yes, that's possible. Hopefully this won't make you uncomfortable, sir, but perhaps we will tell Jürgen that she is going to go to jail but if he helps identify her she will only receive a mild sentence or something… something to help him give her up?'

Smidt's eyes widened and he looked at Kalle in shock.

Kalle pretended to be sheepish. 'Sorry, sir, that's probably beneath you…'

'No, no, that's – well, that's perfect. I think that would work.' He ran a hand through his red hair again and looked up at the tall, burly ranger, with new respect.

'I think then it would make sense not to have anyone else in the room – we wouldn't want anyone reporting what we've said, you know – if it's not strictly the truth,' added Kalle.

'Yes.' Smidt nodded, and soon after they were shown inside Jürgen's room.

Kalle launched into his story, giving Jürgen subtle clues to play along, though he wasn't sure at first if the boy understood.

Eventually, they got to the part about the identifiable mark and Kalle issued a prompt. 'Something that she was born with, perhaps?'

Jürgen frowned, looking up at the two men. He was confused. He'd thought the last time he'd seen the big forest ranger he had been trying to tell him that he could trust him – but now he wasn't sure. He didn't know what to say. Either he said that his twin did have a mark that she didn't, and they left, or he said that she didn't and some poor girl might be deported. So he kept quiet.

Kalle had anticipated this, however.

'I expected this response,' he said to Officer Smidt, as if the boy was a naughty rascal. 'But I have an idea. Can you take the manacles off the boy?'

Smidt frowned. 'What – why?'

'Don't worry – if he tries anything he'll be toast – I just need to check something. Sometimes words aren't really needed,' he said.

Smidt looked confused but he unlocked the boy's handcuffs. Strictly speaking they wouldn't ordinarily have used them but this boy had been proving particularly difficult.

Kalle nodded and came forward quickly. He whispered in the boy's ear, 'Just play along, okay, I'm going to help you.'

Jürgen looked at him like he was mad, just as Kalle cried, 'Yes – a birthmark, just like hers, come look,' and just as Smidt came forward eagerly to see, Kalle slipped a needle from out of his ranger jacket, and shoved it into the man's thin, pale neck. Then he held him, before he hit the floor with a thud.

'What are you—?' cried Jürgen.

'Shhh! Be quiet. Quickly, I've given him a tranquilliser – it can knock out a full-grown moose, so he'll be out for a few hours. Get out of bed – and swap clothes with him. He told me you're a good actor. Well, you'll have to act better than you ever have in your life – today you're him. Help me put him in the bed; hopefully with any luck we'll manage to get out of here before anyone notices the mix-up.'

Somehow, they managed to get out of the room and down the hall without an alarm firing off. Thankfully, on Kalle's suggestion, they'd had an audience alone so there were no officers near the small nurse's station where Jürgen had been kept.

'How long before they notice it's not me, do you think?' asked Jürgen, adjusting his Nazi officer uniform, which itched against his skin. His skin crawled, and he wished he could take it off.

'Stop that,' said Kalle. 'Remember, you're an officer, you're in charge, arrogant even.'

Jürgen took a deep breath, and Kalle watched in amazement as the boy straightened his shoulders and assumed a superior air. He marched alongside Kalle, as if he didn't still have a piece of bullet lodged inside his leg, not deigning to look at the male receptionist as they were buzzed out of the door. It helped that Kalle had rubbed dried ochre into the boy's blond hair. From a distance, he looked a little like Smidt. Kalle kept his palms close to his side, hoping no one would notice the tell-tale stain across them.

CHAPTER TWENTY-THREE

Asta got a job at a second-hand bookshop in the centre of the town. It was a sliver of a shop, where books were piled in thin wooden shelves that snaked around corners to the ceiling.

She was one of only three employees, and to begin with, in the heart of that winter, her job was mainly to make tea and to call for one of the other assistants when a customer arrived. But soon, in her methodical way, Asta was beginning to pick up the language. She didn't have much else to focus on – aside from her constant grief over the loss of Jürgen, and the worry of her parents – so learning Danish was a welcome distraction that she threw herself into heart and soul. She created cards full of nouns, and later verbs, expressions and phrases that she memorised. It would take nearly a year for her to feel proficient in the language, but after three months, her grasp was pretty impressive for someone whose only word had been '*tak*'.

Which is what she'd used to thank Kalle, the man who'd carried her to safety, and saved her life – such a small word, to convey so much.

Almost every day, Oliver came to visit her in the shop, greeting her and Bjørn.

'You know he used to like coming with Trine to work, but I suppose a bookshop is more of a comfortable environment.'

He wasn't wrong. The dog had found several corners in which to rest, and to look as endearing as possible to passers-by. Times were tough with the war in Europe, but customers who popped into the store often found it in their hearts to share a little of their pastries with the dog, who was a perfect actor, pretending with each and every one that this was all such a delightful surprise...

'He's going to get fat if you carry on letting them do that,' he told Asta, watching as an old woman, who'd come past to collect a book of Shelley's poetry, fed the dog the scraps of her morning pastry.

Asta shrugged, then climbed a steel ladder to put back a book that a customer hadn't wanted. 'He'll be the only one in Denmark with a tummy when this war is over,' she said. Her dark blonde hair fell across her face, and she tucked it behind her ears. There was a hole in the rose-coloured cardigan she wore, and her pencil skirt was loose, but she had never looked more beautiful to Oliver than she did at that moment. The overhead lighting shone on her hair, a rare smile darted across her face, and her eyes were alight for just a moment.

As quickly as it had appeared, the expression was gone, as she began to climb down from the shelf. She seemed to have retrieved whatever baggage she had left on the ground and donned it like a cloak.

'You don't have to stop smiling, you know, it's not like it makes you a bad person...'

'Sometimes I think it does.'

'Would he want that – for you never to smile again?'

It was exactly this sort of comment that irritated her about Oliver, though of course he'd become very dear to her over the past year, even if she found that hard to admit out loud. 'Of course he wouldn't – I'm not an idiot. My brother would want me to be happy, but he was no saint either… he'd be furious if I didn't miss him. I hate how people talk about others like that – like that when they're gone they turn into these perfect people who never got cross or jealous…'

To her surprise, Oliver grinned. 'Fair enough. So, tell me about him.'

There was no one in the shop; the other two booksellers were on their lunch break. Asta could either tell Oliver to leave or she could speak about her twin. To her surprise, she chose the latter. Oliver was still there an hour later, when he was due back at college for a lecture. He didn't mind. Some things were worth waiting for.

By March, when Oliver started to fetch her from work, she had to admit to herself that this young man with his sunny smile and jaunty step made life worth living. She had begun to feel something almost like joy pass over her whenever she heard his tuneless whistle as he strolled up the street to the bookshop.

Trine and Lisbet were glad.

'She needs a friend, that much is true,' said Trine.

'But is it more than that?' asked Lisbet. Hope and worry were mixed in her eyes.

Trine shrugged. 'I don't know. They're the same age – almost eighteen.'

Oliver was studying mathematics at college, and the two often shared a train ride into the town, along with the dog.

Asta refused to speak anything but Danish – something Oliver and Trine encouraged.

At the end of the month, they had a low-key celebration for Asta's eighteenth birthday, Trine had made a cake as she'd managed to get some flour and a rather precious egg – and Asta put on a brave face, as she ate it, while Trine, Oliver and Lisbet sang.

It was only later that Trine could hear her crying softly all through the night.

It was Jürgen's birthday too.

Just as Asta was beginning to take a breath, the ground shifted beneath her feet once more. On 9 April 1940, Germany invaded Denmark. The fighting lasted several hours, before word spread from Copenhagen that resistance was futile, the German military was far stronger.

Asta stood outside the shop that afternoon and watched with her colleagues in horror as German soldiers marched triumphantly into the city, passing by the bookshop, victorious.

She would find out later that they had used the same route she had almost a year and a half before.

Oliver clasped her hand tightly, as she shivered, and watched with fear and hatred in her eyes. She paused only long enough for their booted feet to disappear from view to be sick on the road. But no one heard her over the relentless sound of those boots that seemed to march on for eternity.

CHAPTER TWENTY-FOUR

It was called a 'peaceful occupation' as Denmark was allowed to keep their government, while accommodating the will of the Germans. Discovering that she was allowed to continue in her job – as if life was normal – was strange to Asta. Unlike in Germany, there weren't separate rules for people like her. But even so, she was always aware of the threat to liberty maintained by the constant military presence of the Nazis.

'I think – it's mostly something we can live with here,' said Trine, one night during a blackout, as they sat around the kitchen table, Bjørn's head on Asta's lap. 'They aren't ruling as if we are in Germany – with the same restrictions.'

'For now,' said Asta. 'Back home, we also felt like they were putting us through things we could "live with", trust me. They don't do everything all at once, Trine. They turn the water up slowly, it's only later that you realise you've been boiled alive.'

Trine frowned, and stared at her niece, wondering again at how much she had been forced to grow up in such a short space of time.

How could she have survived what she had – only to be put through this now?

There were fears that the Jewish population were headed for the same trouble in Denmark as they had in Germany, and the rest of occupied Europe.

What was worse was the growing sympathy in some quarters for just that.

'It's ludicrous,' said one of the shop assistants, Caj, as Asta was returning a set of books to the shelves. 'Here we are, supposedly neutral, but we have our own socialist party wanting to implement more of the Nazi propaganda. Thankfully the government is resisting.'

Asta nodded. It had made the news the day before; as mounting pressure from the Germans insisted that Denmark deal with their 'Jewish problem', Danish Foreign Minister Erik Scavenius responded to the Germans by saying that 'In Denmark we do not have a Jewish problem.'

For most, these were their friends, neighbours and fellow citizens. Asta had drawn courage from that. But when she left the store later that day, Bjørn at her heels, and she passed two soldiers in the street, her heart leapt into her throat, and it was some time before she could calm down again.

Oliver met her at the corner, saw her white, stricken face, and pulled her towards him. 'You're shaking,' he said, rubbing her arms. 'It's all going to be all right, you'll see.'

She didn't answer, but when he made to pull away, she clung on.

It was the sign he'd been hoping for, so patiently all this time. Asta looked up at him, sometime later, after her shaking had subsided, and felt a stab of guilt. There was a look on his face as if what had happened between them meant something… something she might need to confront later. For now, selfishly, she stayed in his embrace, for now it was the only space she felt safe.

Trine was grateful that she still had her job, but she was even more grateful for the network of people that passed through the newsroom. They couldn't publish every story that came their way anymore but they still listened, and for now, it was like keeping an eye on a boiling pot. An editor she knew, who came to visit her boss, told her about a group of friends of his, and the alliance they were forming. 'For when the shit hits the fan. We might have had to shut down all the land borders but there's one thing the Germans haven't really got a handle on just yet,' he told her.

'What's that?' she'd asked.

'The Øresund.'

It was the strait that connected the town of Elsinore to neighbouring Helsingborg in Sweden.

'Why is that important?' she asked.

'Because it's a way out – if and when we need it,' he said.

Trine had swallowed; it was the use of that 'when' that had made her pause.

Later that day, Trine implored Asta, 'You have to eat.' She watched as her niece picked at her food. Rationing was tough, and some things were harder to get like coffee and sugar, but the Danes were probably doing the best out of everyone in Europe – which wasn't saying all that much, as many were near starvation. Still, considering how badly off some of the other countries were, the idea of laying anything to waste seemed utterly immoral. Asta knew this in every fibre of her being but her anxiety made eating excruciating. Nausea roiled within her but she shoved the piece of bread into her mouth and swallowed the rest of the thin soup that was their dinner.

She sighed deeply and Trine looked at her sharply. 'What is it?' asked Trine.

'Nothing,' lied Asta. 'Just thinking. Oliver will be around later.'

Her aunt's face brightened. 'I'm so glad you and Oliver are together,' said Trine.

Asta looked at the floor. Were they together? He seemed to think so, whenever he took her hand or kissed her cheek. She liked being held by him, enjoyed being in his company. She was grateful for his friendship – she just wished it didn't mean something else to him. Something more.

Then, somehow, another year had passed, with Asta still working at the bookstore, the daily round of soldiers in their streets, coupons, blackouts, war, air raids. By the end of that year, Asta had become almost fluent in Danish. There was never talk again of becoming a veterinarian. Just survival – living through this.

It was a cold December night when Asta heard the knock at the door at just past ten. Her bedroom was the kitchen now. Trine had insisted that she keep sleeping in her room, but it hadn't felt right to Asta, now that she had recovered – and she truly didn't mind. It was close to the wood burner, and the kitchen bench with its piles of blankets was cosy.

She slipped on one of her aunt's old cardigans and padded to the door, switching on the light. Only to blink as a strange man stared back at her. He was tall and broad, with a beard.

She took an involuntary step back.

'I—' he said, looking beyond her into the pitch-black darkness of the house.

'It is you, thank God,' he said. 'I've been to two different houses…'

She blinked. When he stepped forward under the porch light, she felt her knees turn to jelly.

She recognised him – how could she not? Her heart started to thud with a mixture of fear and pain – she would never forget this man for as long as she lived. Kalle Blomkvist. The man who'd carried her away from her brother as he lay dying. The man who'd helped her cross the border.

Even now – after all this time – she had an urge to almost run again.

He could see the fear in her eyes, stark and real. He held up a hand. 'I'm not here for me. There's somebody you need to see.'

Asta felt a scream build in her throat, as Kalle grabbed her hand and pulled her into the freezing cold air.

There was a car parked just around the corner. 'What are you doing?' she said, struggling for breath. Was he turning her in? Should she scream?

'It's okay, Asta,' he said, holding onto her arm tightly so she wouldn't run away, as he dragged her towards the car. It was a black Citroën, the windows dark, but when he opened the passenger door, and she saw an SS soldier, the scream that had been building exploded. Kalle clamped a hand to her mouth, and shook his head. The scream was stifled by the sound of the waves crashing on the sea.

The soldier sat up, very slowly. He was weak and thin, but the smile he offered was anything but feeble. 'Eh, *Küken*, I knew you'd scream the place down.'

CHAPTER TWENTY-FIVE

Asta flung herself at her twin, holding him tightly, as the tears wracked her thin frame. 'You're alive?' she cried, over and over. 'But how?'

'I'll tell you, I promise, but can we get inside – I feel the desperate need to take off this uniform – wearing it was the only way I could get across the border.'

She nodded, finding herself laughing and crying.

Then somehow, between herself and Kalle, they managed to get him inside. He was finding it hard to walk, his leg dragging behind him. Asta called for Trine, who came to the kitchen, eyes wild with her shotgun in hand, and her dressing gown only half on.

'What are you doing in my house?' she hissed.

Bjørn was barking like a wild thing, and Asta raised her hands, wiping her tears. 'Trine – it's Jürgen – he's alive!'

It took some time for Trine to lower the shotgun, to look past the brown uniform in her home, to say, 'Jürgen?'

To be fair, he didn't look like the young boy she used to know. He was a man. Asta saw it too; the young boy in her heart, the other side of herself, looked almost like a stranger now.

Jürgen was easily tired, but he insisted on telling their story.

'After Kalle saved you, he was called in for questioning by the German border police,' said Jürgen.

Asta looked up suddenly at the big man, who had taken a seat on what was essentially her bed. He nodded.

'There were a lot of questions about that day, you see – I'm one of the better-known trackers – so it seemed odd that I could have let a girl slip past.'

Asta blinked. She hadn't even stopped to think of what danger he must have been in from helping her.

'I'm sorry.'

'It's fine, I'm a quick thinker… but the real surprise was that during the interview they told me that Jürgen had survived – as well as the officer he hit, the red-haired one, Officer Smidt.'

Asta put her head in her hands. For so long she had pictured Jürgen's body dead in a forest, so this was like a dream. She couldn't be sure that she wasn't just sleeping.

She wiped away the tears from her eyes. 'I've had this dream before,' she said. 'I don't know what I'll do if I wake up.'

Jürgen shook his head. 'It's no dream, *Küken*. In fact, a lot of it was a nightmare – until now.'

They took it in turns throughout the long night to tell her everything that had happened over the past two years.

'I was going to be transferred to Dachau for attempted murder. The officer I almost killed, Smidt, well… let's just say he was making it his mission to see that I paid for our escape. No one could find you, but they were circulating an image of you… taken from my sketchbook,' he said, touching his pocket. 'But thankfully no one had really seen anything – well, that, and the fact that I told them we were headed for Copenhagen, so I think they spent most of their time there.'

'I helped with that – spreading a rumour that you were seen near there,' said Kalle.

Asta blew out her cheeks. This whole time, her portrait had been with the border police – at any moment she could have been deported back to Germany, probably straight to the concentration camps where they were sending all their Jews. They had been putting pressure on Denmark to do the same.

Kalle looked at her. 'When I found out Jürgen was alive, well, I sent a note – but it was to the wrong address. I remembered that you said your aunt lived here, but there were three people with her name in the telephone book. My father let me know that the first name of the three on the list was where he'd told the taxi driver to take you – as we hadn't heard anything we thought it must have been the right address and we went there first today. No one was home, so we then checked the other, which wasn't far, before we came here …'

He looked sad as he realised. 'It never got to you.'

She stared at him, shook her head. 'No.'

Trine slammed her hand down on the table. They all stared at her in shock. 'Two years – two years we could have known you were alive; did the other Trine not think – not open that letter and read it – and figure perhaps there was another woman with a name like hers – someone she could have forwarded it on to?'

She touched the shotgun, like she was thinking of paying the other Trine Andersons in the phonebook a visit, to demand an explanation.

Despite herself Asta grinned. She caught Jürgen's eye, and it was like they were nine again, giggling over something silly they'd done.

It was past four in the morning when they finished their tale, finally getting to the part where Kalle had snuck Jürgen out of the hospital, dressed as an officer. Telling them how they'd lived on the run. The terror they'd felt when Denmark was invaded, how they were stuck.

'It was terrifying – we were nearing the border, when suddenly we heard the soldiers. We'd missed them by a few hours as they stormed across – they took the roads and the route through the forest. But thankfully we had been moving so slowly that we were behind them when it happened, as I was still so sick—'

'They didn't treat him very well at the hospital.' Kalle nodded, a shadow falling across his blue eyes.

Jürgen nodded too. Then he gave Asta a small smile. 'I had this male nurse, named Hauser, who just despised me. I didn't make it easy for him, a bit like Udo…'

Asta shook her head, remembering the boy in Jürgen's grammar school who had made his life hard when the Nazis first came to power, and how difficult her brother had found it to keep his cool.

'I didn't starve, but…'

'Just about,' said Kalle, picking up the story of how they were stuck just a few miles from the border. 'There were so many crossing through the same area we felt sure we were done for,' said Jürgen, beginning to cough. His body shook as it seized him for some time.

Asta rushed to get him some water.

'We waited a few days, hiding in the forest in a cabin,' he said. Kalle and Asta's eyes met, and she looked away; his gaze seemed to bore inside her soul.

'Then when Jürgen was feeling a bit stronger, we took a very winding route across the border. We just had to bide our time because I wouldn't have been able to go home – our descriptions were with the police.'

Jürgen nodded. 'We hid in Kalle's uncle's farmhouse, just outside Klimvert, for several months – in a loft room, out of sight. They were really kind to us. But when soldiers came sniffing around, we had to make another plan.'

From there they described staying with other friends and acquaintances, working in small fishing towns, trying to make ends meet – staying away as much as possible from the cities which were flooded with officers – all of whom had Kalle and Jürgen's likenesses – until finally at long last they had made it here.

'But you're safe now, that's what matters,' said Trine. 'And no one will come sniffing around here – we're a bit forgotten about, thank heavens.'

Asta nodded, clasping on to Jürgen's hand, unsure if she would ever let him go again.

'Unfortunately, the officer we tranquillised – to steal his uniform and escape – was Officer Smidt, the one I tried to kill,' said Jürgen.

'It was the only way I could think of getting Jürgen out of that place,' said Kalle. 'I had to use Smidt's obsession about finding you to get him to break the rules…' And he explained about the imaginary birthmark and how they were going to 'trick' Jürgen into giving up his sister. 'The trouble is I couldn't kill him – I mean, he deserved it, but if we were caught we'd have been executed.'

'Of course you couldn't,' cried Trine.

'But it means that we left him alive – and, well, if he hated us before,' said Jürgen, '*Küken*, he despises us now. Thankfully he hasn't found us yet.'

'And they won't,' said Asta, clasping her brother's hand.

Jürgen looked at her. 'I'm just so happy to see you again.'

Tears coursed down her face, and she nodded back. 'Me too, you have no idea.'

She looked up at Kalle; there was so much she wanted to say to him, so much she needed to say but would there ever be words enough? 'Thank you.'

He reached out and squeezed the top of her arm, and nodded.

Asta's head was buzzing with everything that had happened. All that had changed.

The threat of this officer, Smidt – who was no doubt looking for them – was something she couldn't worry about for now.

Jürgen was here.

He was safe.

It was the most beautiful, most wonderful thing in the world.

She got up, after barely an hour's sleep, and slipped outside the room. Jürgen was still sleeping, curled up in the furs of the kitchen bench. Kalle, however, was nowhere to be seen. She found him sitting outside on the porch, a blanket around his shoulders, and a mug of steaming coffee in his large hands.

'Hope you don't mind, I put the kettle on.'

She stared at him, then came to sit next to him. 'Kalle, you could carry this house off on your back and I wouldn't mind.'

He smiled, then looked down, embarrassed.

She was staring at him, so he turned to her with a small smile, his blue eyes vivid even in this low light. He was, perhaps, one of the most physically attractive people she'd ever met, but it was clear that he wasn't overly aware of it.

'Why did you do it?' she whispered.

He looked up at her. 'Do what?'

Asta blinked at him. 'All of this – saving me – saving Jürgen – risking everything…'

Kalle sighed, and took a sip of his coffee. Then he shrugged. 'Honestly, it was like something in me snapped.' She looked confused, and he tried to explain. 'I just couldn't do it.'

'Do what?'

'Just stand back and watch. Watch as they came back and took you away… maybe worse.' A muscle clenched in his jaw.

He looked away, and there was an expression of deep shame across his face. 'A few months before I met you, there was a couple who tried to cross – but got caught. He wound up dead with a bullet in his back, and the girl… well, I think she wished she had died.'

Asta frowned, and he ran a hand through his hair, and closed his eyes.

'Two of the officers – including Smidt – captured her. You couldn't miss Smidt with that hair. I saw it all from the top of a ridge. I was making my way down, when I heard her start to scream. I saw them tear her clothes off and begin to take turns.'

Asta gasped.

There were tears in his eyes. 'I was frozen where I was. There were two of them, and they were armed, but I didn't do anything. By the time I had decided to act it was too late – they'd already shot her in the head – after they were finished with her.'

Asta blinked back tears.

'For a long time, I used to see her in my sleep,' Kalle said quietly.

Asta gingerly touched his arm. 'There was nothing you could have done for her.'

'I don't know. Something would have been better than nothing – and, well, when I saw him there with you – I just… couldn't.'

Asta bit her lip, tried to stop herself from crying. 'Thank you.'

He placed a hand on top of hers, and it was warm; when he moved it away, she had to stop herself from reaching for it again.

CHAPTER TWENTY-SIX

Being on the run for so long had taken its toll on Jürgen's body, not to mention the knock-on effects of the gunshot wound that it turned out had never properly healed. He was running a fever, his lips were parched and he was dehydrated. Asta stared at him with her heart in her mouth. She couldn't lose him after everything that had happened.

Malthe was called for in the morning, and he examined him with a frown between his eyes. 'They've left part of the bullet inside; I think it would be best if we took you straight to the hospital.'

Jürgen didn't want to go. The last time he'd been in a hospital he had faced an impossible choice – be put to death or recover enough to go to a labour camp.

'It's different here, son, no one will discriminate against you – besides, the doctors and staff are all Danish. There are no officers to worry about, you won't get treated like… well, worse than an animal.'

Which was all true. They settled him into a hospital room as they waited for his surgery. Asta marvelled at the sheet delight of being able to spend a day with her brother, even in such circumstances. Like her, he was in good spirits despite everything they'd been through – they were together again, at last.

Asta didn't go into work that day, but stayed by Jürgen's side, marvelling at the changes that had happened to her twin. 'Your face is thinner,' she said. 'Less boyish.'

He nodded, grinning. 'You too.'

He showed her his sketchbook, and they spoke more of all that had happened. 'It was stupid, probably, to draw what I saw – I've tried to keep it vague, but I just needed something to do – something to keep me sane.'

Asta nodded, she knew what he meant, and explained about the fervour with which she'd thrown herself into learning Danish, her job at the bookstore.

When she caught the train home that night, she found Oliver waiting on the platform, and they walked back to Trine's cabin. He held onto her hand, his face radiating happiness for her. When they got back to the house, Kalle was waiting on the front porch, Bjørn on his lap. His blue eyes lit up when they saw her, and he stood up quickly. Their eyes met, and no one said anything for a moment.

Asta felt something inside her pull towards him, and she squirmed out of Oliver's cloying embrace. She looked up at Oliver, with a smile plastered on her face, which faltered for a second as she caught the look in the boy's eyes. He hadn't missed the spark that had darted between Kalle and her.

'Come and meet Kalle,' she said.

He forced a smile, and said, 'Of course,' reaching out for the dog, who leapt into his embrace, first.

After Oliver made his excuses, Asta watched as Kalle prepared to leave – and something in her stirred, a kind of wild feeling she hadn't felt before. Practical Asta with her notecards and her methodical ways didn't like to feel out of control, ever, or to display that sort of emotion but Kalle was making it hard.

'You can't go,' she said, as he put on his jacket.

He turned to look at her in surprise, and something seemed to pass between them again. His blue eyes held on to hers for longer than was necessary, and then he looked away.

'I should – I've stayed longer than I should have already,' he admitted, running a hand through his short, dark blond before he pulled on a thick green woollen cap that only made his eyes stand out more. 'I – just, well, I just wanted to find out what the doctors said.'

Asta nodded. 'Well, sit down have a coffee, then I'll tell you everything.'

He nodded, and followed her back. She looked from him to the boiling kettle, and her hands shook slightly as she filled two mugs with cheap coupon coffee. Then she told him exactly what the doctor had said. 'He's going to be okay, but they just want to remove that bullet, and run some tests.'

'That's good,' he said, as she handed him the mug. Then he said, 'Your aunt's not home.' His gaze held her own. It made her stomach flip.

'No, she works late some nights – with the paper.' She shook her head. 'And there's the Resistance – she thinks I don't know but, I mean, it's not the biggest town. Still, everyone keeps everyone's secrets here,' she said with a smile.

He took a sip of coffee, then looked away.

'You seem different from—' he started, then broke off.

'Different?'

'Nothing, I mean, of course you're different, it was a silly thing to say.'

She shrugged. She'd been younger. Frightened out of her wits.

'You're the same, though,' she said.

He could still remember how terrified she was of him, how she'd wanted to be anywhere but near him. He could imagine how he had made her feel.

He stood up. 'I should go – thanks for the coffee.'

Something in Asta tensed. If he went now – that was it. She'd probably never see him again. This stranger, with his rough, wild manner, his deep blue eyes, who had risked everything for them. Something in her broke through, like a wild shoot through frozen earth.

'No.'

He stared at her in surprise.

'Please… you can't leave us… you can't leave me.'

He stared at her as her cheeks flamed.

'Why? You'll be safe – trust me, Smidt doesn't know where you live. As far as he's concerned you were heading for Copenhagen. Besides, if he's after anyone it's me. Trust me—'

She set her mug down again, and said it again. 'No.'

'You'll be fine,' he repeated.

Asta swallowed, then looked at the floor. This wasn't easy. She felt a momentary pang of sympathy for Oliver. Then she shook her head, and said it as clearly as she could. 'I want you to stay.' And then like a runaway train, she added, 'With me.'

*

Asta's heart beat wildly in her chest. She couldn't believe what she had just done. She, who had waited exactly nine months before allowing Oliver to put his hands on her. She, who hadn't permitted him more than the briefest acquaintance with her body, after all his patient waiting and kindness, had just begged a virtual stranger – a man she'd met exactly twice in her life – to be with her.

He hadn't made a move, hadn't got up off the kitchen bench, and she'd set down her coffee mug. Then turned to look at him. She was shocked at the look on his face. It was wild and raw and she blinked, wondering if she'd made a mistake, but before she could try to say something else, he was at her side, his hands in her hair, his lips finding hers.

Trine agreed that Kalle was safest staying with them.

'You've helped save my niece and nephew,' she'd told him later that night. 'This is the least I can do – besides, I don't think Jürgen would thank me if I kicked out his friend after he'd risked everything to bring him to his family. If that officer knows where you live, he'll know where your family is – it's better to stay somewhere he won't think of looking.'

The barn became the obvious choice, and in the morning when Asta and Trine went to the hospital to check on Jürgen, and then on to work, he set about making it into something liveable for himself and Jürgen, when he was recovered.

Asta found him sitting in the barn, next to Millie the horse, when she got home later that day. He was brushing the mare, and there was fresh straw and water for her. Asta had brought blankets, and a spare rolled-up mattress.

She smiled as she saw him, though she couldn't help the flood of nerves that overcame her. Shortly after their kiss the night before, Trine had come home. They'd heard her footsteps on the drive, and had broken apart, breathing heavily. Thankfully, Trine hadn't noticed. It was she who suggested the barn, though, so perhaps Asta's aunt had guessed more than she let on.

He'd managed to create a fire in an old drum, and the barn was if not toasty, at least not freezing. She nodded at the now clean stall next to Millie's, the blankets still in her arms, like a safety net. 'I'm sorry it's so rustic.'

He shook his head. 'After the places your brother and I stayed over the past few months – this is luxurious.'

She nodded. There was still so much to know, so much to ask about their escape.

He regarded her gravely. 'So, they did the surgery?'

'Yes. The bullet's been taken out – he should recover fully, so Malthe says. They're just going to keep him for another week to be sure.'

'I'll go visit him tomorrow.'

She nodded, and there was an awkward silence.

'Asta?' he said.

'Yes?' Her heart started to thud.

'You know' – he looked down as he brushed the mare – 'you don't owe me anything.'

She frowned, confused, then glared up at him, throwing the blankets onto the swept floor.

'Thanks,' she said thinly, and turned to leave.

He caught up with her fast, but she was too angry to even look at him. 'Just leave me.'

But he wouldn't. 'I just mean—' he said.

She twisted up to look at him. 'I know what you mean…' Then she wrenched her arm from his.

He closed his eyes, and listened to her stomp away.

Dinner was tense. Trine pretended not to notice as she told them all that she'd heard, news about the Resistance. 'They're not backing down,' she said. 'I don't think they expected that.'

Asta nodded, but she wasn't listening.

After dinner, Oliver stopped over, and Asta wished that she'd made her excuses and stayed in the hospital with Jürgen instead.

When Oliver suggested that they go for a walk, she agreed, not inviting Kalle along, and the two went for Bjørn's usual evening stroll, though all too soon, she regretted that too, as Oliver kept trying to hold her hand, to hold and kiss her.

'I'm sorry,' she lied. 'I'm just so distracted – everything with Jürgen – the shock, excitement.'

He'd nodded, his face concerned, but full of understanding. 'Of course.'

There was a long pause and then he asked. 'And that man, Kalle? Will he be staying for a while?'

Asta frowned. 'I don't know. Maybe.'

It was sometime after one, when the kitchen door crept open, and Asta sat up from her nest at the kitchen bench.

There was Kalle, just inches from her. She blinked in surprise.

'I'm sorry,' he said. Then he touched her face, gently. 'I just – I've thought about you for a long time—' He broke off. He blew out a breath of warm air that tickled her neck. 'I just – I didn't expect you to feel the same, that's all I meant.'

Her heart started beating faster. She nodded. Then looked down. 'I've thought of you too.'

When he kissed her that time, it was softer, gentler, and then more demanding. She'd never wanted anything more than she did right then.

By the time Jürgen came home from hospital it was clear to Asta that she was in trouble.

She'd been slipping out every night to see Kalle, and they spent the night in each other's arms. Where everything the two had been through, all the stress and constant fear, all the grief and pain, falling for each other was like stumbling across a river, in a desert, and they drowned in each other, getting lost in the magic of being young, and in love.

CHAPTER TWENTY-SEVEN

Asta worried about telling Oliver and hurting him, and she put it off for far too long.

'I don't mind that the two of you have fallen for each other. I mean – after everything that boy did to save Jürgen – to save you – trust me – I can understand it,' said Trine one night, catching her arm, just before she was about to head to the barn to sit by the fire drum with Jürgen and Kalle.

The pair had beds either side of Millie's stall now, and Asta had become like a thief in the night, sneaking into Kalle's whenever she was sure that Jürgen was asleep.

'But Oliver is a kind boy – and in his own way he saved you too. He deserves better than this.'

Tears slipped down Asta's cheeks, and she didn't bother denying it. 'I know.'

She made up her mind to tell him the next day, but as fate would have it, Oliver saw her with Kalle before she got the chance. It was early in the morning, just after the bells had rung for the new year, when Oliver had thought to come past for a new year's kiss, and found her, standing outside against the harbour lights, being kissed by somebody else.

*

When Asta hadn't seen him for several days, and he refused to see her, she figured that her secret had come out somehow. It was like a blow to the chest. She didn't feel for Oliver the way he did about her, but she cared for him deeply. Every word that Trine had said was true. Oliver was her best friend, and it killed her that she had hurt him. In typical Oliver style, he hadn't told anyone what had happened – loyal to the end. But Asta guessed when Lisbet asked one day when she'd come around to Trine's with a box of pastries and to see how Jürgen was getting on – and she mentioned the night that Oliver had come past to start his new year on the right note, and Asta realised what must have happened.

With Jürgen's skills as an artist, he was soon given a job at the *Elsinore Gazette*, and began working alongside Trine. Kalle had found a job at the Øresund harbour, where they didn't ask too many questions about his background, and thankfully hadn't run a police check – or they might have discovered that he was wanted for assaulting a German officer, and suspected of transporting refugees illegally across the border. If caught, he could spend years in prison or be sent to a concentration camp himself.

Asta found that for the first time in years, she was actually happy. She spent her days in the bookstore, where despite the occupation there was a constant demand for new reading material, and she got to know her regular customers and befriend the rest of the staff. Her evenings spent talking to Jürgen, Trine and Kalle were filled with laughter, fun and, late at night, love.

Things with Oliver hadn't returned to normal, but she missed him, as did Bjørn. Asta didn't stop trying to see him, and eventually she got lucky one lunchtime. It was Bjørn who spotted him first; his happy bark made her look up in surprise.

Then she saw Oliver walking outside the store, and managed to run after him.

'Oliver!' she cried. He stopped in his tracks, and turned slowly. The look that passed across his face made her wince. It was naked with pain.

'I – I'm so sorry, Ollie.'

He didn't say anything and tears filled her eyes.

'I never meant for that to happen, I hope you know that.'

He didn't respond and her heart ached as she stared at his beloved face.

'I do love you.'

He closed his eyes, and sighed. 'Just not the way I love you, though.'

'No.' There was no use in denying it.

Then he frowned. 'I don't get it. We're – well, we would be perfect together. That man – Kalle, he's—'

She nodded. He was rough, and a bit wild. Oliver wasn't wrong. 'I think that when it happens you just can't help it. Kalle—' she said, and he winced at the name. 'We've been through something together.'

'And we haven't!' he cried.

Asta dashed away a tear. He was right, of course he was. He had been her best friend, patiently coaxing her out of herself when she thought she'd lost her twin. For a long time, he'd been the only reason she got out of bed in the morning. She loved him, but as a friend, and unfortunately it was the deep pull of her attraction for Kalle that had made her truly see that.

'It's because he brought Jürgen back, isn't it? Who could compete with that? I mean, look at you – it's like you're all put back together again. If I could have found Jürgen myself and brought him to you, you know I would have done.'

Asta blinked. 'I know that, of course I do, Ollie. Of course I will always be grateful to Kalle for that. Just like I am to you for being my friend when I needed one more than anything in this world. But it wasn't just that – it's – I can't help it – I just—'

'You're attracted to him – that—' He didn't finish, and Asta's heart broke just a little more; even now, even after he'd been so hurt, Oliver had such control, couldn't call Kalle the names he probably deserved.

'Yes,' she said simply. Not knowing if it was crueller to tell the truth or to lie. Only knowing that he must not think there was something he could have done, some way he could have tried harder – it wasn't like that.

'But I didn't choose him over you – I hope you can understand that.'

He looked hurt and confused. 'Of course you did.'

'I will never not want you in my life, Oliver, as my friend.'

Oliver took a deep breath. 'I – I don't know if I can… if I ever will be able to.'

And she watched him walk away with tears coursing down her cheeks.

A few weeks later, Asta had something else to worry about. A wave of nausea spread over her; it was the third time in a week that she'd felt like this. She pushed back the plate of food that been placed before her, excused herself from the table, and rushed to the sink to bring it up.

Trine looked at her in surprise. Then she shook her head. 'Oh, Asta,' she said.

Asta ran the tap and gulped down water. 'I'm sorry – I know it's wasteful – I couldn't help it. It happens sometimes when I'm anxious, you know that.'

Trine stared at her, then put her rye bread back on her plate. 'But you are not anxious.'

'Only a little,' she admitted.

To be honest, over the past few months, since Jürgen had arrived with Kalle, she hadn't felt much anxiety. Even though they were living through the occupation – they were together, and things were better, better than they had been in years.

'Oh, Asta, child,' she said. 'You're about to get a whole lot more anxious very soon.'

Asta frowned, then her eyes widened. She hadn't studied university level veterinary science not to get there pretty quickly. She gasped. She looked up at her aunt, who nodded. 'Pregnant.'

CHAPTER TWENTY-EIGHT

When the first snowdrops appeared, Asta and Kalle married in a civil ceremony. She wore a dress that Trine made her from two of her old frocks, and a slip of satin from Lisbet. Asta had been touched by the women's generosity. Lisbet tried her best not to let the fact that she had broken her son's heart mar her friendship or affection for the girl.

'Probably if she hadn't gone through hell I could just comfortably despise her in peace,' she told Trine, as the two had sat making the dress a week before the ceremony – it was a surprise gift, in a time of making do and mending.

'She did make it hard, I'm sorry,' said Trine.

Lisbet had sighed. 'Well, he'll find someone someday.'

'You know she loves him, right?'

Lisbet nodded. 'She just loves that scrubby bear-man more.'

And for some reason this made the two of them howl with laughter.

The ceremony was a simple affair, but one full of love. There wasn't champagne or luxuries. The cake was a kind of odd blend of ingredients made with powdered egg, that somehow tasted delicious, despite all the laws of science.

It would have tasted delicious no matter what to Asta and Kalle and to Jürgen and Trine, who had learned to grab with both hands the small, special moments when they occurred, as you could never be sure when or if they would happen again.

As spring turned to summer, and Asta's belly swelled, Jürgen moved into the kitchen to give the two newlyweds privacy, and Trine thought rather seriously of finding a new residence for the mare, Millie, so that the pair could have a proper home.

The one thing giving them all hope for the future in the late summer of 1943 was that most people began to feel that Germany was losing the war. More and more Danes began to join Resistance movements, showing the Germans that they were no longer afraid and many didn't recognise their authority. It was all starting to seem as if things might finally turn around, but then on 29 August, the day that Asta went into labour, Germany proclaimed martial law, imposing stricter, tighter measures.

CHAPTER TWENTY-NINE

Things changed overnight. More and more soldiers were deployed into Denmark, to take matters in hand – to put an end to the Resistance.

One of those soldiers was Franz Smidt. Who had been left at the hospital – his uniform stolen, tied and bound and left half naked on Jürgen's dirty hospital bed. Betrayed by the ranger and border patrol officer Kalle Blomkvist and the boy who had tried to kill him – the boy whose sister had escaped his clutches and made a mockery of him and ruined his chances of promotion. He'd felt a sense of shame in being bested by the children before but this was even worse – for a proud man like Smidt, this was utter humiliation, and this time he wanted more than justice – he wanted revenge. He wanted each one of their heads.

He'd tracked down Blomkvist's home – not hard once Denmark was under occupation, and then he'd begun to put the story together – to realise just how far back Blomkvist had gone against them. He'd been to Copenhagen several times with his drawing of the girl and a photograph they had on file of the boy and Kalle Blomkvist. But nothing had turned up. Then, despite his obsession, he'd been deployed elsewhere.

It was at a chance meeting in a café in Vissenbjerg, two hours away from the border, that he showed a picture of the girl who resembled so much the brother that he was now looking for. For a tidy sum, one of the café regulars – a man with a handlebar moustache and bulging grey eyes – told the remarkable tale of a young girl who had fled through a bathroom window, a few years before.

'I was there the day it happened. Saw this girl covered in mud, hair like she'd fallen down a ravine, come into the café… couldn't speak Danish, asked for the toilet with a heavy accent and seemed confused, and said sorry in German. Then one of the waitresses, Martina, stood speaking to her husband – he's a taxi driver, apparently, he picked her up and was meant to be taking her somewhere… only she ran away, didn't she?'

Smidt paid for his coffee, then gave the man another bill. 'Do you know where the driver was supposed to take her?'

'Elsinore.'

'Are you sure?'

The moustachioed man nodded. 'Heard him and the wife speaking as he ran into the street to look for her – he didn't see me. He said he was called just after dawn and paid a small fortune to take her there. Then she ran away. I'm not likely to forget something like that.'

He nodded. 'No,' he said, then smiled.

It took a word here and there to be asked to be stationed in Elsinore.

'Why do you want to go there?' said his commanding officer, signing it off. It wasn't a big city, after all.

'There's someone I'd like to find.'

The officer had smiled like he understood, and Smidt deflected it, because he understood nothing.

CHAPTER THIRTY

Asta gave birth to a daughter on 30 August, on a morning that followed a bloody battle between Danes and Germans. Jonna arrived, red and screaming, tiny fists balled into the air, and despite all the fear, she captured her parents' heart from the start.

Arrests were made of prominent Jews and citizens who were vocal against the Nazi party. The rumours that Jews were going to be rounded up and sent off to concentration camps, like they had in the rest of Europe, spread like wildfire. Many Jews began to flee their homes, hiding out in their friends' houses and barns, but when nothing appeared to happen in the weeks that followed, some returned.

Asta and Jürgen knew that time wasn't on their side. They'd been through this once before. It hadn't helped to wait then and they were sure it wouldn't help now either.

Lisbet offered them their own barn to hide and wait.

It turned out – for the moment at least – to be a blessing, as while walking outside with Jonna, wrapped inside a blanket, Jürgen saw an officer with red hair in the distance. It was Smidt.

He ducked quickly back inside Lisbet's barn.

'Smidt is here,' he told them when he returned, handing over his niece to his twin.

'No!' cried Asta, her heart jack-hammering inside her chest. 'Did he see you?'

Jürgen shook his head. 'No – he was looking the other way, thank God. He was holding a piece of paper that had all of our sketches on it – he must have worked with an artist. Maybe someone told them we were staying with Trine …'

Kalle's blue eyes were wide. 'Hopefully, he doesn't know about the Sørensens, well, not yet.'

'For now,' said Asta. 'How long before someone tells him who Trine's friends are?'

Lisbet shook her head. 'No one here will betray you.'

Asta looked at her askance. 'How else would he have known to look here – someone must have recognised us.'

Lisbet frowned. 'If someone identified them and said they were staying with you – then it's possible someone knows you are with us. It might not be safe here anymore.'

They all looked at her in horror.

Kalle was the one who said what they were all thinking. 'It's too dangerous – as soon as he's gone, we need to find somewhere else to stay.'

Trine's editor, Henk Garsman, had a solution. It was a friend of a friend. 'He's a fellow editor, named Børge Rønne. Well, they've formed a group – they're going to get people out via the Øresund, across the strait to Helsingborg, Sweden. Its code name is the Elsinore Sewing Club.' The network initially comprised four friends that included a police officer, a bookbinder, a news editor and a police clerk. The club grew over time, but the four remained the core drivers of the group.

In the coming years, official reports would vary concerning how many the club would transport across the strait with some putting the number at 700 and others closer to 1,500. But 143 trips were made from 1943 to 1945. The club was part of a network of resistance operations that helped save hundreds of lives, and ensured the survival of almost all Denmark's Jews. Unfortunately, as the war progressed several members of the group were captured and sent to concentration camps themselves – the very places they tried to ensure those they helped escape – though many would survive and were able to tell their stories long afterwards.

But for the time being, arrangements were made to get Trine, Asta, Jürgen and Kalle – who still faced criminal charges – to safety.

By the time Smidt had greased enough palms and figured out who Trine's friends were, they had all moved into a small house in Elsinore that belonged to a friend of one of the members of the Elsinore Sewing Club.

They dared not leave until it was safe for them to get across the Øresund. 'At the moment,' said Henk, Trine's boss, on a visit to see them, 'this Smidt is making things difficult. One of the members of the Sewing Club is a police officer who has been trying to lead Smidt away, as his presence is a bit too close for comfort. Hopefully they can get him stationed in one of the bigger cities – which will give us the time we need. Right now, if we take you across it could compromise the whole network.'

Asta and Trine stared up at him. 'Thank you, Henk,' said Trine.

He shrugged. 'I always knew the paper would have to do without you someday, Anderson, I just never thought it would be like this.'

'Me neither,' she admitted.

'Well, you're safe for now – we'll get you food and whatever you need, so just lie low till we send word, all right?'

They nodded, and thanked him again.

*

In September, a few weeks after the uprising, several Danish Jews broke into the Jewish community's office to steal a list of the names and addresses – which meant that they now had a list of most of the Jews in Denmark.

News broke and spread among politicians that the Jews were going to be captured on the night of Rosh Hashanah – the Jewish new year in October. It turned out to be a good thing as the rabbis were able to warn the citizens in time.

Shortly afterwards, Henk came by the house. Asta was rocking the baby, who wouldn't stop crying, to her chest, and Jürgen was pacing the floor. Kalle and Trine were sitting on the kitchen bench.

'It's time, Smidt has been deployed to Copenhagen – with the news that they've finally got the go-ahead to get rid of the Jews, they need more officers there. It's the chance we need – you'll be taken tomorrow morning.'

They stared at him in shock and surprise. Then Trine rushed to embrace him. He patted her back awkwardly, and left.

Early on the morning of their departure, Asta received a note from Oliver, which had been slipped beneath the door of their safe house in Elsinore, just after dawn. It was simple, but imploring, asking her to meet him one last time at the bookshop where she used to work. The note was full of pain, and longing, and it stabbed her heart. It mentioned how hurt she'd made him, how much he still wanted to be friends, how worried he was for her.

'I have to go – I have to at least say goodbye,' she told Kalle and Jürgen, when they found her with it, not long afterwards.

'I'll come with you.'

'No, Kalle – I mean, after everything…'

'I'll wait outside or keep to the shadows, but there's no way I'm letting you go through that door without me.'

She stared at him, and felt a rush of love, then held out her hand for his, and he squeezed it. But she told Trine and Jürgen there was no point in them coming too.

'Worst-case scenario – we will get on the next boat.'

'That's not the worst-case scenario,' cried Jürgen. 'It's dangerous, Asta, we need to stick to the plan! If he really wants to say goodbye he can come here or visit you in Sweden.'

'No, he can't, if he gets caught he'll get sent to prison – you know the cost of helping us. This is my only chance. You don't understand – before everything that happened, when I thought I'd lost you, he was my only friend, he made me carry on living.'

She could never just leave, never just forget him.

'It's fine,' said Kalle, 'I'll keep them safe.'

Asta nodded.

Trine held on to baby Jonna. 'It's okay, Oliver won't keep her long, and he wouldn't ask her to meet him if it wasn't important. Besides, the worst of the danger has passed now that Smidt has moved on.'

They nodded. That was true.

When Asta and Kalle got to the bookstore, she frowned. It was dark and empty. Usually by this time in the morning, the lights were on, and there were already a few customers inside.

Oliver's note had said to meet in the busy street to avoid being noticed, but as she walked inside she shared a puzzled look with Kalle.

'Oliver?' she called.

Perhaps he had convinced one of the booksellers to switch off the lights to make it look like no one was there. They were all old friends.

'Oliver?' she whispered.

There was the sound of footsteps, coming from the back, and she breathed a little easier. Kalle closed the door behind him.

It was their first mistake.

CHAPTER THIRTY-ONE

There was a sound like a muffled scream, and by the time Asta had turned the corner, the blood drained from her face, and she stopped in her tracks.

Oliver was bound, and strapped to a chair. In front of him was a small table, along with a pen and a piece of paper. His face was bloody, and one eye was swollen shut.

'Oliver!' she cried, as Kalle was slammed into her back.

There was the sound of a pistol being cocked, and she turned and swallowed to find Officer Smidt standing there with a pistol pointed at them.

'I told you they would come,' he said to Oliver, who shook his head, tears leaking down his face.

Smidt had put tape across Oliver's face, but now he pulled it back violently. Oliver stared at Asta with tear-filled eyes.

'Why did you come?' he asked.

'Because you told me to.'

He hung his head. 'I thought you'd see through it – that you'd know I'd never ask you to do – something so stupid. I thought you'd read what I said about being friends and understand.'

Tears spilled down her cheeks. She understood now but it was too late.

'All these tears,' said Smidt, looking at Asta and then at Kalle.

Then he looked at Oliver, and patted his shoulder. 'They just cause you suffering, these animals.' Then he sighed. 'It's like a bad dog, you know, best to put them down.'

And he fired, first one, then the second shot.

Oliver watched in horror as Asta fell to the ground. It felt like he was falling too. He stared in shock as he forgot to breathe. There was the sound of screaming. It was some time before he realised it was him.

He watched through tear-filled eyes as Kalle dove after Smidt, but by then he'd already been shot. He kept coming, as shot after shot was fired, till Smidt managed at last to topple him to the ground. He was a big man, and even in his dying breath, he fought hard wrestling the gun out of Smidt's grip. Oliver fell over in his chair, struggling against his bonds, managing to wiggle his arm just enough to reach for the pistol that had slid out of Smidt's reach, which Kalle had then kicked towards him. Oliver grabbed hold of the pistol, and fired. It hit Smidt in the side of his head, he was dead before he even hit the ground.

CHAPTER THIRTY-TWO

By the time Oliver managed to get himself free, Trine and Jürgen were inside the shop. The sound of Jürgen's crying would haunt Oliver to his dying day.

Somehow, Trine managed to get him away from Oliver, to protect him. One of the members of the Elsinore Sewing Club, Thormod, the police officer, was soon on the scene too.

'There's nothing you can do for them now – but go – get to Sweden. Kiær, the skipper, is waiting, he'll take you. If this gets out – well, it'll be the death penalty for sure, and you don't want to be anywhere near this, trust me.'

'But—' cried Trine, as Jürgen sank to his knees, cradling his twin in his arms. Trine comforted the baby as she cried, as if she knew what had happened – how her whole world had crumbled in the space of minutes.

Jürgen and Trine made the trip across the Øresund, Asta's child in his arms. Everything had changed in the space of a few hours. He turned from a boy into a man in that moment, on the short boat ride over, as the waves crashed around them and the salt spray stung his face. His blue eyes turned hard, and he pulled the child closer to his chest. By the time he had set foot on Swedish soil, he vowed to be the child's father, to be everything she needed.

Someone was speaking German, and he turned away. He stared down at Jonna; her eyes were open, her face was calm. She had no knowledge of anything that had happened, all the pain that they had faced to get her here. He set his jaw; he would make sure, somehow, that it stayed that way. It was the least he could do.

CHAPTER THIRTY-THREE

Northern Sweden, 1995

The snow was settling outside the forest, and the air was quiet and still. Inside the cabin, Ingrid held her beloved *morfar* in her arms, as the last of his story came pouring out.

'Oh, Morfar, why didn't you tell us – why didn't you tell Mum? She had a right to know.'

'I know… I don't know why I never said anything,' he sighed, standing up, putting another log on the fire, his old hands shaking.

'It was just so much – so much pain, so much suffering. After Trine died when Jonna was five, I figured it was simpler to just keep it to myself. To be Swedish and to live a different kind of life. I put it in a box, and I just…'

'Refused to open it?'

He nodded.

'I wasn't alone. It's what we did then, you know. No one liked to speak about such things.'

Ingrid nodded. She could believe that. Nowadays, there was talk therapy and medication, and recognised names for things like post-traumatic stress disorder.

She couldn't imagine keeping all of that to herself.

*

In the days that followed, Jonna came to visit, and at last, Morfar shared his story with her as well. Ingrid left them to speak privately, walking in the forest with Narfi, but every time she came back, they were still talking. He showed them his old sketchbooks, and with tears running down his cheeks, he told them about Asta, and Kalle. There was a drawing of him, done not long after they had escaped. Jonna touched it with shaking fingers. 'He was handsome,' she said.

Jürgen nodded. 'Yes, and kind – he was such a good man, your father,' he said, tears coursing down his worn cheeks. 'I should have told you all of this so long ago.'

Jonna held the old man in her arms, and rocked him. 'He was my father, yes, but so were you – the best one in the world. The best father and grandfather in the world.'

Ingrid nodded and came to embrace him as well. They sat like that for a long time, as the fire in the wood burner burned low.

A few days later, Jürgen showed them the last piece he'd been keeping to himself for all these years.

'There's something else,' he said.

Ingrid's eyes widened, and he shuffled over to the window, where there had always been two small metal tins with locks.

She frowned.

He rubbed his eyes. 'It's them,' he said.

'Them?' she asked.

'Asta and Kalle.'

'Morfar?' she cried. She'd seen those tins on his windowsill her whole life… but never, not once imagined this.

'I couldn't scatter their ashes.' Tears splashed down the old man's face. 'Oliver brought them over, a few months afterwards when we sent word that we were safe. I kept them with me,

I couldn't bear to part with them, not after everything that happened. Aside from you two, this was all I had left; I couldn't just let them go. See – it was years later, of course, after Trine died, when I finally learnt what happened to my parents.' He paused then said, 'Auschwitz.'

A simple word, for so much pain and terror.

ONE YEAR LATER

Hamburg

Ingrid and Jonna walked arm in arm along the canal. The sun was beginning to set, and a pair of children ran away along the path, their laughter a chorus in the chilled spring air. There was a sound of a horn being blasted from a ferry transporting its passengers across the way.

Ingrid stared as it went past, looking at the window where no mascot was displayed, no stuffed gorilla named Frederick that a pair of twins with their irrepressible grins and their lust for life used to dress up every day to give the commuters a laugh.

Ingrid paused, and stared at the sketchbook in her hands, and her hands shook as she touched the picture of Asta. They both felt like they knew her now, after spending so many nights by his side, hearing all the stories he'd kept from them for so long. It was like a dam wall had burst.

Jonna came to stay with Ingrid; her father insisted. It was precious time, this, and she was grateful for it. In the year that followed, the three of them spent hours every day just speaking. He was still confused a lot but he wasn't as angry or as sour – it was like a weight had come off him. This seemed even more cruel when they discovered that he'd been keeping another secret from them – a slow-growing cancer that finally caught up with him one morning when the last of the snow had melted.

Outside her window, Ingrid saw a bear make his way through the forest; she was surprised to see one so close to the village. It was later that they found Morfar, in his bed, having achieved peace at last. She would always think that perhaps he'd sent that bear for her.

'You ready?' asked Ingrid, wiping a tear from her own eyes.

'Ready,' Jonna replied, a wobble in her lips, as they scattered three sets of ashes, which mingled into the water of the canal, their lives bound together in death, as they had become so in life.

Above their heads was the flapping of wings, and a flight of swallows returned to their nest. Ingrid caught her breath as she remembered what he'd told her once about how a swallow will always find its way home if it can find its nest.

A LETTER FROM LILY

Thank you so much for reading *The German Girl* – I hope you enjoyed reading it as much as I enjoyed writing it.

If you did enjoy it, and want to keep up to date with all my latest releases, just sign up at the following link. Your email address will never be shared and you can unsubscribe at any time.

www.bookouture.com/lily-graham

If you did love *The German Girl*, I would be very grateful if you could write a review. I'd love to hear what you think, and it makes such a difference helping new readers to discover one of my books for the first time.

It means a lot to hear from my readers – you can also get in touch on my Facebook page, through Twitter, or my website.

Warm wishes,
Lily

LilyRoseGrahamAuthor

@lilygrahambooks

www.lilygraham.net

AUTHOR NOTE

Asta and Trine's story was inspired by the remarkable true story of the Elsinore Sewing Club, a code name given to a group of people who helped save the lives of around 700 to 1,400 (reports vary) Danish Jews by helping them flee occupied Denmark and certain death or transportation to Nazi concentration camps by creating a network that transported them safety across the narrow strait, the Øresund, to neutral Sweden.

The group was initially formed of four friends – Erling Kiær, Thormod Larsen, Børge Rønne, and Ove Bruhn – and during this difficult period many more would join. One of the members, Kiær, was a skipper, and Bruhn was a police clerk. The Danish attitude towards the Jews was that they were considered friends, neighbours and citizens – and while to a large part the Elsinore Sewing Club helped to inspire this story, it is the real bravery and integrity of the Danish and Swedish people who have done so as well – it is estimated that Denmark helped to save over 7,000 Jews. While in reality the members of the group used aliases and carried out their operations in secret, I wanted to highlight their names in my story – please forgive this inaccuracy.

I also was inspired by Peter Prager's story and his interview with the USC Shoah Foundation. Peter describes his childhood growing up in Berlin, including the school years as the Nazis came into power – one memorable and chilling event being the day that a biology teacher told him that Jewish heads were 'inferior'. Listening to Prager's story, that moment in particular made me wish that he had back then a mother like the twins', who would have assured him at the time of what nonsense and prejudice that was. Thankfully he came to the same conclusion shortly afterwards himself. Prager survived by using the Kindertransport and went on to live in England for the rest of his life.

ACKNOWLEDGEMENTS

Writing a novel is always hard but this one almost didn't happen; there were just so many times I genuinely considering hanging up the towel. The fact that it is a novel at all is thanks to my incredibly kind and patient editor, Lydia Vassar-Smith, who has encouraged me every step of the way while I battled crippling self-doubt. I think as readers we see an author's name on the cover, and think that's where it stops and starts – but it really doesn't. Editors should have their name in lights, truly. All this to say: thank you, Lydia, you are, as ever, the best and I'm sorry for the headaches, thank you for the patient coaxing and hand-holding, for moving the schedules and for never making me feel like I should actually give up and become a dog-walker (this was a persistent fantasy for the past year, grin).

My deepest thanks to the team at Bookouture for their incredible support, for the beautiful covers, incredible patience, kindness and just being so lovely to work with.

Thank you, as ever, to my husband, Rui, who is always there offering support and encouragement.

To Fudge, my snore monster bulldog, you have definitely helped keep me sane.

Last and especially not least, thank you so much to the readers and bloggers who have reached out to me over the years, thank you so much for your support and kindness for my writing; it means the world.

Printed in Great Britain
by Amazon

84987026R00149